Look Twice

BY THE SAME AUTHOR

Poetry
Fairground Music
The Tree that Walked
Cannibals and Missionaries
Epistles to Several Persons
The Mountain in the Sea
Lies and Secrets
The Illusionists
Waiting for the Music
The Beautiful Inventions
Selected Poems 1954–82
Partingtime Hall (*with James Fenton*)
The Grey among the Green
The Mechanical Body

Fiction
Flying to Nowhere
The Adventures of Speedfall
Tell It Me Again
The Burning Boys

Criticism
A Reader's Guide to W. H. Auden
The Sonnet

For Children
Herod Do Your Worst
Squeaking Crust
The Spider Monkey Uncle King
The Last Bid
The Extraordinary Wool Mill and other stories
Come Aboard and Sail Away

As Editor
The Dramatic Works of John Gay
The Chatto Book of Love Poetry

LOOK TWICE

An Entertainment

John Fuller

Chatto & Windus
LONDON

Published in 1991 by
Chatto & Windus Limited
20 Vauxhall Bridge Road
London SW1V 2SA

A CIP catalogue record for this book is available from the British Library

ISBN 0 7011 3761 4

Photoset by Rowland Phototypesetting Limited
Bury St Edmunds, Suffolk

Printed and bound in Great Britain by
Mackays of Chatham PLC, Chatham, Kent

Contents

I

Departures and Arrivals

'SO YOU ARE returning to Paris already, Mr Gromowski?' asked the stationmaster, holding a pencil in front of his chest in both hands; it was a kind of bow, though without any inclination of his body.

The thin man in the straw hat flicked his reddish sidewhiskers ruminatively. He looked round with a little laugh.

'Oh dear, yes,' he said. 'I'm afraid so.'

'Not the same opportunities here, I suppose,' continued the stationmaster, 'to someone of your fame and fortune.'

'No, no,' returned Rudolf Gromowski, Illusionist Extraordinary, billed as having played before the Crowned Heads of Europe (that is to say, having once appeared with Lily Langtry in a Command Performance, he made her disappear before the eyes of King Edward of England, who was so busy eating a quince ice-cream that he barely noticed). 'It is not that.'

'The political situation, of course,' said the stationmaster, looking about the milling concourse. 'Not that I blame you. It's complete chaos.'

'Politics have nothing to do with it,' said Rudolf. 'I am leaving Gomsza for purely private reasons.'

'Of course,' said the stationmaster, with a wink. He raised his pencil in the air to summon a porter.

'Take Mr Gromowski's bags to Platform One, and see him on to the Paris Express.'

The man wiped his nose on his sleeve and began to load Rudolf's bags on to his trolley.

'I had some crates delivered to the station this morning,' said Rudolf.

'Full of white rabbits, I dare say,' said the stationmaster. 'The porter will take you to the Left Luggage Office. Bon voyage, Mr Gromowski. I hope you will come back when things have returned to normal. I shall look forward to seeing you at the Aquarium, or perhaps even at the Circus this winter? You are very lucky to have a ticket, by the way. This may be the last serious train to leave for the West for some time.'

Gomsza Station was indeed full of people who did not have tickets. There were angry and frightened queues at the booking-office. People moved from one window to another, seeking the more crowded ones in the hope of greater success. The platform-ticket machines were empty. There were police in the entrance hall and strolling in pairs throughout the concourse. Groups of people were shouting at each other. At the entrance to the platforms an important-looking man with an attaché case was standing close to the ticket-inspector, talking into his face. The inspector was wearily and without emotion shaking his head, but was backed up against the framework of his booth, the hand holding his punch raised above his shoulder in yielding impotence.

The Left Luggage Office was at the end of the platform. Beyond it, the glazed ironwork canopy abruptly terminated in scrolls and flourishes. Against the continuing wall, instead of the notices, posters and vending machines of the station proper was a row of pear trees growing in espaliers. It was a warm August evening. The pears were plumpening, the sunlight dancing on the silvery leaves in sharp contrast to the subdued light beneath the canopy and the black shade of the Luggage Office.

The official who was dealing with the luggage wasn't cool, however. He had trouble in dealing with the passengers' enquiries in order, and when he reached to the crowded shelves for cases and parcels there were twin maps of the country under his armpits.

The older man ahead of Rudolf in the queue seemed familiar to him. He was a big man, with strong shoulders and hands, and a heavy sad face like a dog's. He turned round to look at Rudolf. Yes, they did know each other. Their eyebrows and the corners of their mouths moved apart in the act of greeting as if symmetrically connected by invisible elastic.

'Rudolf Gromowski?'

'Grosiewski! Radim Grosiewski!'

'Well, well. I don't suppose I ever thought we'd meet again. It must be, what, ten or eleven years?'

'Easily.'

'You were the most celebrated entertainer in Gomsza. I was proud to paint your portrait.'

'No, no,' laughed Rudolf. When he was embarrassed he had the habit of making repeated upward strokes of his sidewhiskers with the nail of his forefinger. 'The admiration was mutual, I assure you.'

'What happened to the portrait?' asked Radim.

'I imagine,' said Rudolf, with agonised emphasis, 'I imagine it's still hanging in the Club, if they don't feel that I've disgraced them.' He giggled, and stared at Radim's shoes.

'I remember the sittings very well,' said Radim slowly. 'You were famous for making things disappear. I wanted to make you disappear in turn. Did I ever tell you?'

'Me disappear?' said Rudolf. 'Good Lord! How?'

'From the portrait,' said Radim. 'It was an idea I had. It fitted in with my thinking at the time. I can't really explain.'

'You mean I wouldn't have been in the painting at all,' exclaimed Rudolf. 'What a clever idea, eh? Save you a lot of trouble.'

Radim shook his head.

'No,' he said. 'I can't explain.'

'Well, never mind,' said Rudolf brightly. 'I'm still here.'

'We're all still here, aren't we? But not for long.'

'I hope not. If they can get a move on with my crates. Have you got much stuff?'

'A basket,' said Radim.

'A basket?' repeated Rudolf, thinking of eggs or apples.

'A basket,' said Radim.

Radim's basket was enormous, as high as his chest and about

five feet square, with wicker handles on each side. It took three men to lift it into the fourgon. Rudolf's crates were neat affairs of tacked plywood, aluminium corners and stencilled ownership and directions.

'Careful, careful!' said Rudolf, as the men tossed them inside.

'Why, that one was quite light,' said Radim in astonishment.

'Yes', said Rudolf. 'It's just a box.'

'I can see it's a box.'

'I mean, it's a box inside a box.'

'Remarkable.'

'What's in yours?' asked Rudolf.

Radim looked at him keenly.

'Me?' he said. 'I've got the whole world in here.'

'The whole world?' asked Rudolf. 'How extraordinary.'

Radim turned and shrugged.

'It's either the whole world or it's nothing,' he said.

It turned out when they contacted the Wagons-Lits conductor that they were to have adjoining berths.

'What an extraordinary coincidence!' said Rudolf. 'But I say, did you notice? It's a German train.'

The conductor had been wearing the uniform of the Internationale Eisenbahn Schlafwagen Gesellschaft. He was a stout man with cropped hair and a black moustache.

'You'd expect it to be French. I was sure it was to be French: St Petersburg – Vilna – Gomsza – Berlin – Cologne – Paris. Look, it's spelled "Köln". I hate the Germans. There's no culture until one reaches Paris.'

On the platform the sense of dramatic confusion was sharpened. Passengers clustered round the waterseller as if he were dispensing a sacrament, and his waxed paper cups littered the platform. A lady with one curl unpinned and hanging ludicrously down in front of her eye was leaning out of a carriage window insistently shouting 'Florian!' through the crowds. A party of priests, checking luggage over and over again, appeared to have lost something. A man dressed in black in a wheelchair was being lifted into a carriage; for some reason, his face was entirely covered by a cloth.

The locomotive was a patient black monster with great glass eyes through which a young engineer peered, one after the other, rubbing them from inside with a chamois leather. Valves emitted steam like nostrils. The driver, surrounded by a group of would-be passengers, appeared to have some tickets, which he was thumbing greasily from the pocket of his waistcoat like a hand at cards.

'Look at that,' said Rudolf.

'How much do you think he's charging?' asked Radim.

'He could charge what he likes, couldn't he?'

'In marks?'

'Of course. He doesn't expect the trains to be running across the frontier once the Government collapses.'

Their carriage was at the rear, next to the fourgon.

'The train seems to be very full,' said Rudolf. 'I'm sure they're letting too many people on.'

The IESG conductor's air of iron control was illusory, born of a stubborn desire to find a place for everything when there was none.

'He would make an excellent philologist,' said Rudolf, watching him lick his pencil before writing random numbers on a sheaf of vouchers which the party of priests thrust at him as he passed by, crossing off numbers in his book that could hardly have corresponded, since they appeared to have been crossed off already. His face wore an intently immobile expression of inflexible solemnity indicating that he was completely at sea.

'Or a bureaucrat,' said Radim.

'He *is* a bureaucrat,' replied Rudolf. 'I think our country is entirely surrounded by them. Which would you rather have, a Prussian bureaucrat or a Russian bureaucrat?'

Radim pondered.

'It's a nice question,' continued Rudolf. 'Bureaucracy is only a kind of machine, a human machine, and machines break down. When the machine breaks down, the Prussian bureaucrat turns to brutality and the Russian bureaucrat to drink.'

'I take no interest in politics,' said Radim.

'Oh, that isn't politics,' said Rudolf. 'It's human nature. Though I don't deny that we Gomszans can be credited with the invention of anarchism not so much as a response to oppression and partition, but as a response to bureaucracy. We have always been Europe's Romantics.'

'I'm not interested in anarchism either,' said Radim. 'I'm only interested in painting.'

They were waiting to be shown to their compartment.

'Good Lord!' exclaimed Rudolf, pointing down the platform. 'Look at the driver now!'

The train driver appeared to be putting the tickets in his mouth.

'Is he eating them?' asked Radim.

'Destroying the evidence,' said Rudolf, tartly. 'But surely he managed to sell them all?'

'I'd have thought so,' said Radim. 'There are plenty of people still trying to get on the train.'

'Including us,' said Rudolf impatiently.

But they were not tickets. They were slices of bierwurst.

There was some trouble in the carriage, which was dim, with the blinds drawn. A nervous young man with a wispy moustache and an expensive white linen suit seemed to be objecting to their entering the compartment.

Not a muscle of the conductor's face moved, but a trickle of perspiration that had erupted in secret beneath his cap was now openly exploring his jaw like a fast slug.

'I'm sorry, sir,' he said. 'The kleine schlafzimmer only is exclusive. In the compartment itself there are other reservations.'

The young man ran his long fingers in a gesture of exasperation through his mop of frizzy hair.

'There were express instructions,' he said. 'There are important reasons. Weren't you told?'

'I'm sorry, sir,' repeated the conductor without apology. 'The train is very full. You'll understand the circumstances. We're not running to the usual schedule.'

'I should think not,' muttered Rudolf to Radim. 'Where did they find this carriage? I've never seen anything like it.'

'I believe you,' said Radim. 'You're more used to this sort of travel than I am.'

The carriage was indeed unusual, being one of half-a-dozen

originally built in 1877. It had been bought from Russian State Railways in 1893 and reconstructed by Wagons-Lits-St Petersburg. It had a small number of berths for its size, only twelve, arranged as three pairs of communicating apartments, each pair with toilet attached. The furnishings were sumptuous: rose silk with blue hangings and gold buttons on green plush, all in Louis XVI style. Mouldings concealed every screw and nut. The toilet had a WC with running water and was panelled in sycamore. The inner apartment that the conductor had referred to as the 'schlafzimmer' was indeed already partly set up as a bedroom, and the strange man in black whom they had seen being lifted into the train earlier was lying on a berth, his wheelchair beside it.

'And what about my maid, then?' asked the distraught young man.

The conductor grunted unhelpfully. He had other things to think about. For him that was the end of the matter. He left.

The young man made a sound that was half a sigh and half a snort of impatience, and disappeared into the inner apartment, closing the door behind him. After a moment the maid entered, carrying a small valise. She hid her face from Rudolf and Radim, and almost immediately knocked gently on the communicating door, then went into the inner apartment.

'Well!' exclaimed Rudolf. 'We've got some strange travelling companions, haven't we?'

'They could be worse,' said Radim.

'Of course, of course,' said Rudolf. 'I didn't mean that. I meant really strange.' He pulled up the blinds. 'There, that's better. We can see what we're doing now.'

Radim put his feet up on the opposite seat, and rubbed his eyes.

'I wish the train would start,' he said.

'Why?' asked Rudolf. 'I always rather like this moment when one is settled, and other people still to find their seats. Or even to find each other.'

The woman with the unpinned hair was on the platform now, still calling: 'Florian! Florian!' Rudolf looked at her from the window benignly.

'Who do you think Florian is?' he mused. 'I guess he's a little boy in a sailor suit who ran off to buy an ice-cream.'

'I don't care who Florian is,' said Radim. 'I wish the train would start. Then nothing can happen. We shall have priority. It's in the nature of a railway line: we can't be overtaken by the anarchists.'

Rudolf turned from the window and flung his straw hat into the luggage rack.

'We might be cut off by the anarchists,' he said with a smile. 'Riding down from the mountains.'

'From the mountains?' said Radim. 'Are you making fun of me?'

'Not at all,' said Rudolf.

Radim looked at him sharply, but Rudolf had turned back to the window and was whistling slightly between his teeth.

'Really strange,' he repeated. 'I don't know if you saw that fellow in there lying down? Black clothes? Black gloves? A black veil over his face?'

'Not properly,' said Radim.

'And the boy,' continued Rudolf. 'There's something odd about him, isn't there? Why did he have the blinds down? I couldn't get a good look at him.'

'It's the evening sun,' said Radim. 'It's very strong. The old fellow is ill.'

'I thought when I first saw him that he was in mourning.'

'He seems pretty much a corpse himself.'

'We shall soon know about it if he is,' said Rudolf. 'Oh, look, they're loading ice into the dining-car. That'll be useful.'

'I don't see why we can't all fit in here,' said Radim.

'There's the maid,' said Rudolf. 'There are usually bunks in the fourgon for servants, but the fourgon seemed pretty full of material possessions to me. Everyone's bringing with them whatever they can.'

'I don't see what a young man like that is doing with a maid anyway,' said Radim. 'Doesn't he have a valet?'

'Yes, how odd,' agreed Rudolf. 'And if the old fellow is in mourning, why is the young man in white linen?'

At that moment the connecting door opened and the maid came out with the empty valise. The boy appeared at the door to hand her another one, then disappeared again. The maid went out and down the corridor.

'Aha!' said Rudolf. 'Did you see that? The mystery solved. A black arm-band.'

But the mystery seemed far from solved. What was it about the cut of his suit that couldn't be blamed on the waywardness of white linen? For linen was stiff and malleable at once; it hung flatly, stretched into folds like a curtain; the weight of a single rose made the lapel droop; it asserted its weave against the struggling contours of the body; its only virtue was its coolness. But the suit of this young gentleman! It was tight in the trouser, yet hung off the shoulders. The jacket rode the hips, yet hid the wrists. It made every error that a two-sosti seamstress learns to avoid.

Radim joined Rudolf at the window and peered at the throng.

'I expect the passage to Hell would be something like this,' he said gloomily.

'But my dear fellow,' said Rudolf, 'one has no inclination to *go* to such a place. There would be no clamour on the banks of the Styx.'

'That would be part of the hellishness: the compulsion but not the desire,' replied Radim. 'The anxiety about the ticket, the scramble for a place.'

'No, no,' said Rudolf. 'I conceive of Hell as the precise opposite of clamour. Hell is the absence of desire. Hell would be, quite simply, the having no desire to *be* anywhere.'

'And yet one is always somewhere, surely?' said Radim.

Rudolf smiled.

'Not in Hell,' he said.

'That's a contradiction,' objected Radim. 'If one is nowhere, one cannot be in Hell.'

'I always feel like that on a train journey in any case,' said Rudolf. 'In the present circumstances, getting somewhere is the exact counterpart to getting away from the predicament of travel.'

'Another paradox,' said Radim sadly.

'Every departure is an arrival,' said Rudolf. 'The Arch-Duke is dead. Long live the Arch-Duke!'

'I'm glad the Arch-Duke isn't in fact dead,' said Radim. 'He's the only stable factor in the administration of this country.'

'You're right there,' agreed Rudolf. 'Powerless, but stable. So stable that I do believe the Tsar might trust him with real power if the Tsar were not himself in such extremely hot water. As it is, the real power is there for the taking. What we have is virtually a revolution. The reins of the government held out, on offer to anyone who will take them. And what happens? Everyone leaves! Did you know that the Gomsza police have issued more than forty thousand passports for foreign travel?'

'And most of them on this train,' said Radim. 'I've never taken much of an interest in politics.'

'You are a true citizen of Gomsza,' said Rudolf.

The train was getting ready to leave. Doors were being slammed with a regularity that indicated the hand of porter rather than passenger. The urn of the waterseller, a great brass sphere decorated at the rim with a pendant design like the lace of a matron's bosom, was being lifted up from the platform where he had been plying his trade. The corridors were thickening with third-class travellers who could not find a seat to match their ticket. There were no doubt some who did not even have tickets, risking not only a confrontation with the conductor, but immediate arrest by the police, who patrolled the corridors like beaters at a shoot.

A whistle was blown.

'Not long now,' said Radim.

'You will be glad to see that Florian is found,' said Rudolf, nodding in the direction of the dishevelled woman who was just climbing back into their carriage carrying a small and equally dishevelled dog.

'Not much,' said Radim.

At this eleventh hour, a trap drew up just beyond the station railings with a great flurry, the horse rearing with terrified eyes, its mouth foaming, the bit tugging back its lips. It was like a horse in a Géricault tempest. The driver leapt out and began to manhandle a quantity of pigskin luggage on to the platform, tossing it over the railings, climbing over the railings, helping his passenger over the railings. The railings might have been knee-high matchwood. They were nothing in opposition to this great exploit.

The passenger was a small, dark gentleman, accustomed to security, self-possession and routine. He was clearly trying hard not to show his anxiety. He approached the train in a kind of lurching saunter, pretending to consult his watch, his eye flashing out in panic at the parade of slamming carriage doors. He pushed irritably amongst the ticketless crowd.

A guard, observing the pair enter the station by these unorthodox means, came forward officiously.

'Stand back, sir, if you please,' he said, holding out his arm. 'The train is leaving the platform.'

'But we must get on it!'

'I'm so sorry, sir,' said the guard condescendingly. 'But you would have to have a ticket.' Clearly he was dealing with a lunatic, a desperado.

'Of course I have tickets,' said the dark gentleman. 'See: here they are. Show me which carriage, please.'

The whistle sounded for the second time. A golden sosti or two changed hands. The lunatic was redeemed.

'There's no time for that, sir,' said the guard, lifting a bag. 'Get on anywhere. Here.'

He opened the door of the nearest carriage, the one that Rudolf and Radim were staring out of, absorbed in this drama.

'I know that man,' said Rudolf, rushing into the corridor. 'He'll never do it. The train is moving.'

Indeed, far ahead there was a great noise like the expiring panting of a giant; pistons slid back cleanly to their unbelievable length and minor sighs of steam enveloped the platform. The train inched forward.

'Here,' said Rudolf at the door of the carriage, grabbing a case. 'Let me help you.'

'Oh thanks,' said the dark man. They chain-loaded all the cases. The man who had driven the trap, who seemed to be a servant, hung back defiantly. The dark man was on the train.

'What on earth are you doing, Marek?' he said. 'You must come with me.'

'No, sir,' said Marek. 'My mind is made up. I'm not going to leave Annelinde.'

'Annelinde?' exclaimed the dark man. 'You must be mad. The girl has given you ulcers.'

Marek looked up at him with a smile of resignation. He shrugged, and one large tear rolled out of his eye and travelled down his dirty cheek.

'I know, sir, I know,' he said. 'But I'm very attached to her.'

The train was pulling away from the platform. Between master and servant there was a momentary rehearsal of gestures of trust and regret, loyalty and fear, like God reaching to Adam. But which was God and which was Adam? There was the ghost of the anguish of the relay runner, the wild hope of the child at the Christmas party, fingers reaching for fingers.

'Here's your ticket, Marek! Change your mind!'

Marek shook his head with a fond smile, the tears now striping his dusty cheeks like the make-up of a circus clown.

The ticket fell to the platform. The last view they had was of the crowd of frustrated passengers falling on the scrap of pasteboard, tearing it, in their greed, into worthless fragments.

The dark man turned from the window, the door shut behind him, the train gathering speed.

'Well,' he said, with a short laugh. 'That's that.'

'You are right to take it in that spirit,' said Rudolf. He was very excited by all that had happened and was attacking both his cheeks at once with his fingers as though disposing of a cloud of gnats. 'It's like the last chapter of a novel, full of significant finalities. Never mind, never mind. Like a true hero you have treated it all as a beginning not an ending. Another paradox for my friend here.' He indicated Radim, who nodded at the newcomer in silent greeting.

'I know you, don't I?' asked the dark man.

'You do, you do,' exclaimed Rudolf. 'Allow me nonetheless to introduce myself: Gromowski. Rudolf Gromowski. And this is the painter, Radim Grosiewski.'

'Of course,' said the dark man. 'You are the man who makes things disappear. Everything, that is, except reality.' He laughed, and gave a short bow. 'I reported your debut at the Aquarium years ago for the *Gomsza Inquisitor*. A very great privilege. My name is Romuald Grochow.'

They all shook hands and returned to the compartment.

2

The Argument about Marek and Annelinde

THE YOUNG MAN in white linen looked in disbelief at what were now three invaders of his compartment; sat on one side looking at the three sitting in a small row on the other side; then burst into peals of laughter.

He had drawn down the blind on his side of the compartment once again, and sat therefore in shadow. The train had now built up speed. The lateness of the hour and the flatness of the country produced a fierce magical glare that flickered intermittently through the carriage window, filtered, even directed, by the clumps of trees and occasional farm buildings that stood within a certain distance of the track, acting like the shutter of a camera.

'I saw your little drama,' he said. 'And here you are! I wonder how many more passengers will find their way to this compartment?'

Romuald Grochow inclined his head briefly in a steely acknowledgement of this remark, and immediately left, turning in the corridor in the direction of the head of the train.

'Oh, look,' said Rudolf, in a torture of embarrassment. 'We shall all have to fadge together, don't you know? Grochow is a distinguished journalist. He's probably on an assignment.'

The young man laughed again.

'An assignment to get out of the country as fast as he can, you mean.'

'Now that's being too hard,' said Rudolf. 'We all have our reasons.'

'Oh yes, certainly,' said the young man. 'And since we all seem to be sharing this compartment, perhaps we should also share our reasons.'

'That's going too far,' said Radim. 'There's an established etiquette for travellers, you know.'

The young man raised his eyebrows.

'Oh, is there?' he said. 'I wonder what that might consist of? Might it have anything to do with consideration for others?'

Radim did not reply.

After a moment, Romuald returned. His ticket was in his hand. He was apologetic.

'The train is absolutely full,' he said. 'They're bedding down in the corridors in the third-class carriages and there are eight or nine to a compartment. I think we are lucky in here. The waterseller, who's an evil-looking fellow if ever I saw one, seems well on the way to becoming a millionaire. The conductor has disappeared.'

'He'll be in the dining-car,' said Rudolf. 'Didn't you notice among the sulphurous fumes from its chimney the challenging odour of roasting veal? And didn't you notice the conductor's shape? He's just the man to lose regularly at cards with the kitchen staff for the opportunity to eat the first few slices. Just to make sure that it's of the right quality, of course.'

'The dining-car seemed to be full already, I'm sorry to say,' observed Romuald. 'There was even a woman who appeared to be about to suckle her child. I didn't wait to see.'

'You weren't gone very long,' said Radim. 'Did you get to the front of the train?'

'Well, no, I didn't, as a matter of fact,' said Romuald. 'I had another look at this ticket, and strange to say it seems that I should be here after all.'

The young man shrieked with laughter again.

'I knew it all along!' he cried. 'Did you plan it? Are you a gang of some kind? You all appear to know each other. This compartment is meant to be private!'

And with this, the young man burst into tears.

'Oh Lord,' said Rudolf. 'We're being very insensitive, you know. I expect you wanted some solitude for your grief.'

'No, no,' the young man said. 'I'm quite all right.'

And in a moment he had lighted a cigar and was blowing careful plumes of smoke into the air. Really, it was hard to tell if he was laughing or weeping.

'You will have to be my three musketeers,' he said.

The trio exchanged glances. Was the young man perhaps hysterical? Bereavement could affect people in strange ways. It was hard to see him clearly, sitting in the shadow of the blind, and now enveloped in smoke that he did not seem particularly to enjoy.

And what in turn did the young man see? Three men as unlike as could be: one thin agitated whiskery young man who did most of the talking; one small dark wiry man, the latest comer; and one melancholy clumsy giant who said rather little.

The more concerned the three men were, the more conspiratorial, the more apologetic, the more amused the young man became. To an extent the fraught nerves of departure had been pacified now that the journey was under way, and the regular motion of the carriage lulled them all into an acceptance of things as they were.

Rudolf leaned forward, as much to fathom the expression on the young man's face as to make himself better heard.

'Please don't think us too inquisitive,' he said. 'But may we enquire into your sad circumstances? The cause of your mourning, and of your journey?'

'You ask a great deal,' was the reply.

'Forgive me,' smiled Rudolf sympathetically. He put his finger to his lips discreetly. Just at that moment Romuald was rubbing his eyes with fatigue. The young man could not help laughing again.

'Now you look like the three monkeys: See-no-evil, Hear-no-evil and Speak-no-evil!' he exclaimed.

Only Rudolf smiled in return, and uncertainly at that.

'I say,' he said. 'Do you really feel all right?'

'Yes, I'm all right,' said the young man. 'I'm really quite glad that you're here, after all.'

'Oh, that's all right then,' exclaimed Rudolf. 'You know, there's a sort of camaraderie in travel. We're all uprooted from our ordinary lives. We need to stick together, you know. I am Rudolf Gromowski, by the way. Stage illusionist.'

'How do you do?'

'And this is Radim Grosiewski, the painter.'

'How do you do?'

'And our newest arrival, Romuald Grochow. Political editor on the *Gomsza Inquisitor*, am I right? Yes.'

'How do you do?'

They all shook hands as solemnly as if they had been signing a Treaty of Partition. They looked enquiringly at the young man. After a moment's hesitation, he said:

'My name is Józef Pyramur. I'm travelling to Dresden with my father.'

'We are delighted to make your acquaintance,' said Rudolf. 'I believe that we are all travelling as far as Paris, is that not so?' The others nodded. 'For our various equally mysterious purposes.'

'There's nothing mysterious about my purposes,' said Radim. 'Why does everyone presume that you have to be some kind of political refugee to be travelling on this train?'

'Because it is full of them,' said Romuald. 'That's why.'

'But I'm going to Paris for purely professional reasons,' said Radim.

'That may be so,' said Romuald. 'But it would be inconvenient, wouldn't it, to be still about when General Minski takes the city?'

'Aren't you being alarmist?' asked Rudolf. 'I thought that the Arch-Duke's Hussars had that old devil pretty well cornered.'

'Cornered?' exclaimed Romuald. 'He's crossed the Livula at Varnow and barely an hour ago I could hear the sound of his cannon at Lamosz.'

'Where's that?' asked Józef Pyramur sharply.

'It's a small village about fifteen miles north-west of Gomsza,' said Romuald.

'A freak wind,' said Radim. 'We've heard nothing here.'

'You must have heard the explosion at the Post Office last night,' said Romuald. 'Or do all you artists live in ivory towers?'

Radim shook his head.

'Minski is an opportunist,' continued Romuald. 'He's likely to exploit whatever situation he finds when he gets here. Suppose the anarchists really do gain control in the next few days? The police can't deal with the strikes. Even a butcher like Korn can't simply go on shooting pickets for ever. For every picket that falls there are two to take his place.'

'I can't quite credit it,' said Rudolf. 'Why doesn't Korn call in the Cossacks. We all know he's in the Tsar's pocket.'

'He daren't do that,' said Romuald. 'He'd like to, but he doesn't quite dare. The First Army wouldn't stand for it. The First Army's loyalty is one hundred per cent for the Arch-Duke. There'd be the worst kind of civil war.'

'The Second Army is preoccupied with General Minski, I believe,' said Józef.

'It makes no difference, since Minski would be ready to take on the Tsar himself. Don't forget that Minski has respectable nationalist credentials.'

'There would be a bloodbath,' said Rudolf.

'I don't know what there would be,' said Romuald. 'After all, the Tsar has a lot on his hands at the moment, including the Japanese in Manchuria. What odds would you give that he can keep his empire intact for the next five, ten, fifteen years?'

'You mean that Gomszan independence in some form is really on the cards?' asked Rudolf.

'Absolutely,' said Romuald.

'And what would happen to the Arch-Duke?' asked Józef.

'My own view is that the Arch-Duke is essential to the stable survival of Gomsza,' said Romuald.

Józef smiled.

'I'm glad to hear you say so,' he said. 'Is it not thought that he might be in danger?'

'From Minski?' said Romuald. 'It's true that the Arch-Duke should have appeased Minski years ago. There was a time when he would have been quite happy with the administration of the Northern Provinces.'

'What,' said Rudolf, 'and lived off beetroot and holly beer for the rest of his life? Surely not. Minski wants his civilised pleasures like the rest of us.'

'Don't forget that Minski is a man of the people,' said Józef. 'You'll never catch Minski at the opera.'

'Nor me either,' said Romuald. 'But I don't think you meant danger from General Minski, did you? Just what other danger did you have in mind? Are you suggesting that Korn is planning a putsch?'

There was a silence. Józef Pyramur did not seem eager to answer this question. But almost straightaway he said, as if conscious of changing the subject, and changing it, moreover, to the one topic from which in common delicacy he could not be diverted:

'My mother was an opera singer. My father and I are travelling to Dresden to take possession of her body.'

'Ah,' said Rudolf. 'We had, of course, taken note that you are in mourning. Please accept our condolences.'

'Thank you,' said Józef.

'You see,' said Rudolf. 'It bears out what I was saying. All the circumstances of travel are special, and some are not so readily ascertainable as yours. These circumstances have unseen complications, reasons that are confused, degrading, tragic, absurd, heroic. And the same applies to reasons for not travelling. Like our friend's young man, what was his name . . . Marek? He threw away his ticket for an ideal love.'

'You can know nothing about ideal love and its sacrifices,' said Józef fiercely.

Rudolf gave a short wild laugh of protest, flicked one side-whisker so hard that he might have been trying to flick it off his face, and was stung into silence.

It was Radim who spoke.

'There are many things which may destroy love, and there are many things which may destroy ideals,' he said gently, 'but they are rarely the same.'

'Sometimes they are the same,' said Romuald, feelingly. 'We are defeated by our very selves and the stupid compromises that we have to make.'

'Yes,' said Radim. 'But it is still possible to see clearly and to choose. Your servant Marek seemed to be able to avoid compromise. A whole future in your protection and service, and escape from turmoil, for the sake of his true love. I find that touching, don't you?'

'Not if you'd ever met Annelinde,' said Romuald. 'She's a shallow tease of the first water.'

'Ah,' said Radim. 'Women can indeed be so shallow that they spread themselves everywhere.'

'I see it as a failing in Marek,' said Romuald. 'A failure of nerve. A failure to perceive his best interests.'

'He had to clutch at her for safety, did he?' asked Radim. 'Still, he was decisive. It was done with his eyes open. It had a nobility. We felt like applauding.'

'You are all wrong, gentlemen,' broke in Józef. 'I do not think it a failing in Marek to adore his Annelinde. Love is, like religious conviction, a state of being (one cannot even call it a state of mind) quite beyond criticism. Even the acts it makes us perform are forgiven in advance and often generally admired. But nor do I think it necessary that these acts should be heroic; sometimes they are the better for being sacrificial.'

'But Marek sacrificed his position and his safety to be with his sweetheart,' said Radim. 'She was waiting for him. Let us hope that *she* will be faithful.'

'Let us hope that indeed,' said Józef. 'But, you know, this "being with", what is it? It is often nothing more than the prelude to biology. True love can withstand absence. It can even withstand possession by another.'

One by one the trio had been rebuked, and fell silent. It seemed only natural that whatever was to break this silence, should be a fresh beginning. The young man in white linen had taken the initiative, and the trio were as attentive as the lulling rhythm of the wheels would allow. Thus Józef Pyramur began his story. His voice was soft, precise, tuneful. The slightest aside or qualification had all the modulated deliberation of spoken dialogue in a romantic operetta.

3

The Odiousness of the One-handed Lover

THE DAY MY childhood ended (said Józef) was also for me the day on which I was most deliriously happy.

It's strange, isn't it, how extremes of excitement and disillusionment often arrive together, perhaps after weeks or months of absolutely unexceptional living? I do believe that the most powerful gods are the gods of chance, who do nothing but exert themselves continually to prove that there is little that is regular or predictable that is of importance to human beings. I'm not talking about scientific laws, naturally, which you might think useful and reliable. Those are lesser gods, mere subalterns to a capricious Fate. My mother showed me a poem to this effect by an English poet called Hearty: there was a recognisable ring to its resignation. I suspect that he had been reading some of our Gomszan poets.

My father is Cyprian Pyramur, the cellist. He has had a distinguished career, I would say, though never as a soloist. After many years with the Philharmonia he was appointed the principal cellist in the Arch-Duke's private orchestra. He is by nature a solitary man, shy, meditative. He is entirely devoted to his music, performing at Court when required and playing in a quartet with friends for his own amusement. For a long time when he was a young man he thought that he would never marry, both because it might interfere with his wholehearted pursuit of his art, and because he never believed that he would have the courage to propose to a girl. He did not even know any girls.

Then one day he met a young Austrian singer called Hilda Schmeck in the Plac Teatralny. I remember how he used to love to tell me this story about his first sight of my mother. Parents often do, don't they? Perhaps it is their way of enforcing on children some sense of their destiny, although in practice it usually strikes the child as maudlin sentimentality. To me it seemed mythological, and I cherish its memory.

She caught his eye as he was seated at a café drinking a glass of chocolate and toying with a custard pudding that he knew he should not have ordered. Did she catch his eye, or did he catch hers? Knowing her, I should suspect the latter. A solitary man seated in the square in the middle of the day eating a custard pudding! Everyone else was at work. But how was she to know that he was a music teacher, free between his morning at the Conservatoire and that later afternoon hour when his individual pupils would be at home and ready for their weekly suffering? As for her, she was in the chorus in some routine *zigeuneroper*, and had taken a break between rehearsals to get some air. She was naturally dressed in peasant skirts, shawl, earrings, bare feet, and so on, ready to go back on stage and glower from behind a campfire or whatever was required of her.

My father thought she really was a beggar, and gave her twenty-five copecks, which later she used to wear round her neck in memory of his first kindness to her. She was very young. Younger than I am now. And sensationally attractive. She had practically run away from home to pursue her career, and I suppose my father was the first man she had met who seemed likely to be able to help her to get on without exploiting her. She always used to say that if he had known she was not a gypsy at all but the youngest daughter of a respectable inspector of taxes living in the Hauptgasse, he would never have dared to speak to her at all. They were married within a month, and of course her career came to very little once I was on the way.

She sang a good deal at home, I remember, and her lieder evenings were as familiar to me as my father's quartet evenings.

Indeed, to the extent that my knowledge of my parents depended entirely on this domestic evidence, their musical achievements seemed equal to me. It was not so, and I'm sure that my father had no intention of allowing her an independent professional life as a singer. It would be the equivalent of sending her out of the house in bare feet again.

What can a son say about the quality of love between his parents? It is at once the most familiar thing, the daily condition of which he alone is the privileged witness, and at the same time a profound and occluded mystery. There was a physical well-being in the relationship, and a sense of humour, that protected me throughout my childhood.

But then my childhood came to an end.

Oh, I had put away my toys, but I had my childish illusions still. One of them was the illusion of the absolute and permanent mutual fidelity of my mother and father. Another involved the magical lure of the stage. That was my passion at the age of twelve, acquired no doubt from my mother and her memories of singing in the chorus in opera houses all over Europe in her youth. I wanted to know from her just what each was like, how large its chandeliers, how resourceful its stage machinery. I made models out of cardboard and chocolate papers and produced Humperdinck by candlelight.

Perhaps encouraged by my questioning, and stirred by the memories it produced, my mother once again took up the question of singing professionally. My father did not object to her taking further lessons, but somehow he made it plain that a return to the concert-platform, let alone the stage, was not to be countenanced. It was as though any success which might attend Hilda Schmeck would have to be subtracted from whatever was due to come the way of Cyprian Pyramur.

My father isn't an arrogant man. I suppose that he wanted to make sure that I was sufficiently well looked after. And perhaps he was being over-protective of a wife who was still young and beautiful. Perhaps he feared her freedom.

He was absolutely devoted to her.

But I think he was already tormented by her restlessness. For one thing she was physically active. She insisted, for example, that we made as frequent visits as possible to my grandparents who lived in Bregenz on the Bodensee. The effort of travel was quite enough for my father in itself, since he can't bear his routine to be interrupted and trains make him sick, but on top of that she would propose an extra week or two in the Vorarlberg, collecting alpine flowers in the highest passes, or, if it was winter, skiing. He would do it, of course, but he was not at ease. I sometimes think that the only exercise my father takes is when the cello is between his legs. Then he shakes his head fiercely, as if to shake off the drops of perspiration that gather there, and his fingers move on the strings as invisibly as a dragonfly moves, pausing for beautiful moments, tense and splayed, in the course of their hectic flight. His ordinary physical existence lacks conviction. He is a bear. And on these holiday walks, plodding breathlessly behind with the accumulated handicap of too many custard puddings, he had to suffer the sight of extravagant attentions and compliments paid to his wife by unattached young men who presumed that he was her father. She was, as so many women are, even more attractive in her late 'twenties than she had been in her late 'teens.

She had lost that downy cushiony look that young girls have, and wore her gypsy hair in sober coils that gave her face an even leaner gravity. Can a son be properly appreciative of his mother's appearance? One's first dozen years are, I'm told, the longest of one's life, but it is not so long a period that all memory of the first physical intimacy with the mother is lost. When she sang high notes (and even more when she sang very deep notes) her bosom seemed to draw to itself the sensuous energy of all physical objects within the range of sound and to become charged brimful with their attendant splendours. Her throat and breasts seemed to absorb the whole world and to give it back transformed. And for myself I was content to bathe in their vibrations as I knew I had once drawn from them a more tangible sustenance.

What had seemed in her girlhood saucy and adventurous, became defiant and eccentric. When she invited friends for tennis she insisted on playing in trousers, something unheard-of in Gomsza at that time. But I think her friends (and more particularly my father's friends, though there were fewer of those) were not so much shocked by the trousers, shocking as the trousers were, as by the fact that my mother clearly played to win. My father decided, wisely I think, that he should provide some sort of safety-valve for this potentially explosive furnace of will. The notion was absolutely correct, but the occasion proved to be disastrous. I should say that the occasion, too, was perfect, except that it contained one essentially unforeseen and disastrous element: Kleinblut. It was my father's greatest mistake.

It was just at that time that the Arch-Duke was putting the finishing touches to the private theatre in the Palace grounds. You remember the speculation, even the criticism that it aroused? Few people at the time quite realised how economical the project was, for the existing Winter Gardens were already very extensive. There were not only the enormous glass-houses, with ironwork designed by Davrinski, that could have accommodated giraffes, but also the original eighteenth-century boiler rooms and gardeners' lodgings, not to mention the artificial ice-rink, believed to be the first in the world, upon which Pushkin had once cut a figure of eight while drinking a glass of champagne. All these were ingeniously retained in the final design.

Nor is it, contrary to popular rumour, a particularly large theatre. This stands to reason, as it was always envisaged that performers and stage management, far from being outnumbered by the audience by something like sixty to one, would in fact outnumber the audience by something like the same proportion, since the Arch-Duke intended that only his closest family and occasional guests should be entertained at the Winter Gardens by a form of dramatic entertainment obtainable nowhere else: Total Theatre.

And who was the most energetic apostle of Total Theatre? Who was it, moreover, who had so ingratiated himself with the Arch-Duke that his own private enthusiasms could be instantly translated into reality by ducal command? And who therefore was it who not only initiated the experimental theatre in the Winter Gardens, but inevitably became its first director? Volo Kleinblut.

Kleinblut was using this opportunity in Gomsza to realise an absurd naturalism on the stage. Everything had to be realer than real. For example, for *Aida* he had to import tons of sand and heap it on the stage, and hire a regiment of hussars for the conquering Egyptian army. Most productions make do with a few spear-carriers rushing behind the scenes to come round again as quickly as they can. Kleinblut even had an elephant. Needless to say, productions like these went way over the budget and most theatres wouldn't hire him any more. It wasn't too bad with something like Chekhov, except that he made all the actors live on the set, and real food was cooked and served on stage at the performances, which the health authorities said was unhygienic. The trouble was that he was only interested in opera, and that cost money the way he wanted to do it. It cost money anyway. He reckoned that once he'd won the Arch-Duke over into building him a special theatre, with an orchestra pit for two hundred players, then money for productions would keep on flowing. That proved not to be quite the case.

Kleinblut had a distinguishing feature unique amongst conductors. He had lost his left hand.

He didn't wear a false hand with a glove as many people would do. He just left the scarred stump peeping out from his cuff, unexpectedly sharp-looking, and quite shamelessly naked. It meant that he had to conduct all his scores from memory, because he couldn't turn the pages. However, he was able to be much more emphatic in his directions to the orchestra, and he used the stump to electrifying effect. At particular climaxes practically the whole sleeve would fall away from the upheld abbreviated wrist, which would quiver all the more expressively for requiring you to imagine the gesticulations of its missing fingers.

The accident interrupted an unusually promising career as a concert pianist. As a student in Vienna he had won so many prizes so easily that they had to invent new prizes to give him. He had received the blessing of Liszt, and was said to be able to play pieces by that old thunderer that even Liszt himself found too difficult for performance.

There was a mystery about the accident. Few people believed that it could have been self-inflicted, yet when the topic came up nearly everybody admitted that they had heard some such rumour.

He had been splitting wood on his brother's country estate and had been attacked by a jackal; or he had cut it off himself in a strange fit of anger, or inattention, or drunkenness; or the brother had cut it off in jealousy; or had been asked by Kleinblut to cut it off. The last suggestion was the most sensational, the most privileged, the one made in tones of hushed awe. And it was, despite its improbability, the one that most convincingly lodged in your mind, for Kleinblut's elder brother was a former military surgeon who had distinguished himself with successful amputations in the Franco-Prussian War, and had retired to manage his estates. The only reason that could be given for such a course of action was the consequence of a bizarre wager: "I can play better with one hand than any other pianist with two hands" or even "I can myself play better with one hand than two."

The evident falsity of such a proposition didn't in itself devalue the theory, since everyone knew Kleinblut to be a strange genius, impelled by mania and grandiose delusions. He immediately commissioned works from all the leading composers written for the right hand only, and many of those were, though of course technically most exacting, works of great resourcefulness and inspiration. You may wonder why we never hear them now, played by ordinary double-handed pianists, works like Brahms's magisterial *Symphonic Variations on a theme by Gluck*, and D'Indy's *Rhenish Fantasy*, a work of prodigious simplicity. Kleinblut eventually destroyed them all. It was his privilege, written into the commissioning contract, and the composers could do nothing about it.

He destroyed them in a fit of pique, because he discovered, too late, that he had lost the wrong hand. He found it easy enough to play the scores, but was irritated by the fact that it was his little finger that was primarily required to commandeer the melodic area of the keyboard, the stronger fingers being reserved for arpeggio descents into the lower octaves. He could never quite give the music the sort of convincing articulation that would have come naturally if the reverse had been the case. If it had been the right hand that had gone, then works written for the left hand only would have had the thumb and little finger the right way round.

The solution to this technical misfortune might have been to have ordered an inverted piano, with bass notes on the right-hand side of the keyboard and the treble notes on the left. But this would have been an imaginative leap foreign to Kleinblut's stubborn aggressive genius. His achievements belonged to onslaught rather than subterfuge. If his piano career lay in ruins, he would become an impresario.

The extravagant literalism of his stage realisations was an example of such onslaught. It was not so much a question of interpretation as of battering the text into submission, as he had battered the most recalcitrant chords of Brahms, Alkan or Busoni, until what in most pianists' hands sounded like disintegrating scaffolding would hang luminously above his ebony and ivory machine like a cobweb at dawn, pearled with effortless harmonies. It was, he claimed, only through gaps in technique that an audience's faith would ever be able to leak. If the technique were perfect and complete, then the illusion would be perfect.

Transferring this belief to the musical stage involved a full exploitation of theatrical machinery and a faithfulness of representation that went far beyond the demands or expectations of any of his predecessors. In his *Magic Flute* there was a snake worked by electricity that cost half of his total budget, and the stage was thick with droppings from real birds for Papageno to catch; finches, bluebirds, tits, all trained to fly only in the beams of blue light that controlled them from the wings. If anyone dared to ask him why he could not rely on symbolic representation, he would explode with anger. That was a language for children, in his opinion. If an opera called for birds, there had to be birds. When he conducted the St Matthew Passion the management insisted on a team of trained nurses in the auditorium because so many susceptible music-lovers fainted at the sight of the blood.

Needless to say, I was much excited by Kleinblut's arrival in Gomsza. I suppose I would not have known about it, had it not been for my father's employment at Court, for the public, knowing that they would have no opportunity to see the performances, pretended to take no interest. The newspapers treated it all as a mystery, and it was nothing therefore that I could presume to boast about to my schoolfellows.

My interest was quickened also as a consequence of my father's great mistake. Our little family was drawn into the fatal activities at the Winter Gardens as an innocent sailing vessel, risking a short-cut through treacherous seas in search of calmer waters, finds itself sucked into a vortex of disaster.

My father decided, as a way of giving my mother a chance of doing the very thing that she so craved to do, to let her join the chorus at the Winter Gardens for that very first season. The opera was *The Magic Flute.* So much of the Arch-Duke's money had been spent on the electric snake and the bird-trainer, not to mention the theatre itself, into which at the last moment all kinds of unforeseen and costly machinery had to be installed, that economies were suddenly and decisively called for. One such economy was to recruit the chorus from the Gomsza Operatic Society. Auditions were held, and my father not only encouraged my mother to apply, but influenced the chorus-master to give her preferential treatment. I don't know how necessary this was, for my mother's voice, naturally rich and strong, showed to advantage after her recent training, and it turned out that her teacher had already mentioned her to the chorus-master, who was a close friend of his. Indeed, it is quite possible that even without my father's connivance she would have become involved with the performance. Afterwards she always said that she felt it was fated.

They were so impressed with her that she was given the part of one of the three attendants on the Queen of the Night, which had not yet been cast, and she soon came to the notice of Kleinblut.

Like many convinced and powerful men, Kleinblut bestowed his favours like a sultan. For some reason no woman worthy of his attention could ever bring herself either to refuse it or resent its being given to others. The chosen felt too privileged to be rivals. It was like being elected to a secret society.

What did Kleinblut whisper to his favourites behind the scenes? Was it: "I can make you a star?" Or was it a more personal offer?

The closest I came to discovering was on the happy day when my father at last said he would take me into the Winter Gardens one afternoon to watch a rehearsal. I had been pestering him for weeks, sensing somehow that it was he that I had to pester. My mother was in a dream, and I think she had almost forgotten my existence. My father's musical world, his own life at Court, was like a kind of labyrinth into which she had wandered and become lost. At the heart of the labyrinth was the Winter Gardens, and its monster, Kleinblut. The labyrinth, whatever its delights and dangers, still somehow belonged to my father, and it was to him that I had to apply.

I was so excited. The transition from my model theatre, with its flimsy struts and cut-outs, to the real back-stage world of the Winter Gardens seemed as natural as my promotion from one class to another at the Lyceum. I had not realised the sheer amount of heavy work necessary to achieve the most routine theatrical effects: springs were activated that were so strong that it needed three men to set them; ropes were unwound, tugged at and re-tethered; men ran in little black gutta-percha shoes across cat-walks sixty feet up. I might have been a spectator at the launching of a magnificent schooner two hundred years ago, I thought, as the backcloths of indiscriminate cloudscapes and haunted forests billowed down from the darkness like mainsails, and the wings echoed with the acknowledgement of hushed commands.

A small boy lost in wonder becomes virtually invisible provided that he actually keeps out of harm's way, and if any of the hands bothered to ask me what I was up to I had only to say: "My name is Józef Pyramur" for them to nod and let me pass. I even saw the Arch-Duke himself when he came to enquire about the progress of the opera, and immediately felt an envy and admiration for a man who could so calmly and authoritatively command all these endeavours purely for his own pleasure.

The afternoon seemed endless, absorbed in its own unfolding, a series of events all the more fascinating for being only imperfectly understood. The controlled disorder of rehearsal and the magic of the opera itself went to my head. Crouched and hidden in a corner between pieces of scenery, I felt the dizzy freedom of being quite ignored. No one would call on me to perform a task or deliver an opinion.

I almost became used to the oddities of back-stage behaviour: a magician eating a sandwich; men in rouged lips and tights; women in states of undress previously unimaginable simply walking about, adjusting pins, even bending over. Men and women touched each other casually, without apparent interest, in tokens of intimacy never seen publicly in drawing-rooms.

Then this world of delight collapsed, and my mother was in a moment taken from me. I could see, as no one else could possibly see since I happened to have a privileged view of the hidden corner it took place in, an act of such bizarre outrage that I could hardly believe it. I saw a woman's back, clasped by a man's hand. The back was criss-crossed by a lattice-work of strings supporting a blue silk costume which was no doubt full at the front, but which left the back virtually bare except for the strings. The hand was playing up and down the spine in what I immediately took to be a grotesque parody of a cellist's finger-stopping. I don't know how I knew that it was my mother's back, but I immediately knew that it was. Then of course the cellist's hand belonged to my father, I reasoned. But this could not be so, for at that moment the whole orchestra was being taken through the overture by the young assistant conductor while Kleinblut and the singers rested. My father was playing the music that accompanied this charade.

As the silk strings were slowly unpicked, the man's other hand came round as though to grasp the waist. But it was not a hand.

I suppose I kept looking out of curiosity, a human motive that can conquer every moral scruple. I also told myself that at any moment my mother would make her objection quite clear and throw to the winds any remaining deference due to a man who was, after all, her employer, and on whom therefore the outcome of her great musical opportunity depended. If for a moment politeness or delicacy delayed her firm rejection of these advances, it would not be long, surely, before this hideous approach met its firm rebuff. And would it not soon be observed by others? How far could it go?

In the next few minutes all these questions were answered, and I became the unwilling guardian both of a personal emotional secret and a general physiological revelation. Each shocked me, insofar as I could contemplate them separately; together they amounted to a complex event in which shame, hatred, disbelief, excitement and a dozen other emotions fought for supremacy in my thudding head.

I managed somehow to keep the secret, but I did not have to keep it for long. When *The Magic Flute* was over, Kleinblut went to Dresden, whose opera house had outbid the Arch-Duke for his services. Such outbidding was not difficult, to be frank, for the Arch-Duke's necessary economies virtually ruled out any further productions that season. Kleinblut was to pronounce Gomsza a "backwater".

And my mother went to Dresden with him.

This was the collapse of our family, and now I knew what it was that could destroy families. I didn't yet know that this was also what could create them. Nor did I know that it was foolish of me to mistake circumstance for essence and begin to hate the theatre that I had so loved, even turn in revulsion from the exalted delicacy of Mozart as though that icy sensuousness had knowingly consigned to the abstraction of beautiful sound a similar dirty little secret. I thought my father was a broken man, and I prepared to endure our tragedy.

But if you remember, I began by saying that love can withstand absence. It can withstand possession by another. It is true. My father still lived for the Hilda Schmeck of his imagination. He wrote to her every week, to addresses from which he knew she had long moved on. He kept cuttings of her operatic successes.

I wanted to go and kill Kleinblut. I refused to go to the theatre. I could not even bear to hear my father play his cello. I was difficult at school.

My father was endlessly patient with me, and said that we could never understand the feelings of others. When I said that I wanted to take a broken beer glass and smash it down on Kleinblut's head, screwing it in as one might cut out rounds of raw pastry, he shook his head sadly as though he were disappointed in me. I think he really believed that my mother had long nursed a secret unhappiness whose fault was entirely his. I wanted to make him read that poem by Hearty, to show him that this needn't be so, that it was simply that the dice had allotted to him rather than someone else the latest buffet of Fate. Then I reflected that he was probably happier the way he was, loving an absent woman as a kind of expiation. I let him alone. I reckoned that if a bankrupt wanted to try to balance the books as a way of keeping his self-possession, then it would be a cruelty to tell him that it wasn't necessary.

That was what I felt then, over five years ago. Now I think that he was being purely noble. After all, I now see that my mother could hardly have been so taken with Kleinblut that she could accept being only one of five or six women (not always the same) that he kept in tow. There would have come a time when she had grown used to her resumed career and what few glories it could really offer her, and would have thought about returning to us. My father was keeping alight a welcoming and forgiving flame. He didn't ever reflect that Kleinblut may have hypnotised her. Then he had the stroke that put him in his wheelchair.

When she died, that monster had moved almost permanently into his natural habitat, the operas of Wagner. How his singers suffered! His Rhine Daughters caught bronchitis from swimming in tanks of real water which mirrors reflected through ninety degrees to an angle which enabled the audience to inspect their nudity. He personally coached his Sieglinde in the art of convincingly conceiving Siegfried. His Brunnhilde was severely kicked by Grane, a carthorse who had been given injections to make him behave heroically. Some of these roles had been taken by my mother.

Kleinblut the literalist was in his element. As Bayreuth was more and more taken over by symbolists and lighting experts, he felt it was incumbent upon him to pursue Wagner's prescriptions beyond the letter. He invented machines which produced different *kinds* of smoke, distinguishing for example between the smoke from Alberich's forge and the smoke from burning Valhalla. The audience were also made to feel intense heat and cold, and were sprayed at the appropriate moment with all the natural aromas of the forest.

It was not only the audience who suffered this realism. The singers, too, could not escape with token props. His Siegfried, covered in badly-healed scratches from a real and only half-tame bear, had then to wield a sword that had been borrowed from the Dresden Historical Museum and weighed fourteen kilos.

My poor mother was actually killed during a performance of *Rheingold*. She was singing the part of Freia, who in the last scene of the opera is ransomed from the giants by the offer of the gold as a substitute payment to them for building Valhalla. They insist on having as much of the gold as will entirely cover her. Kleinblut of course arranged that the stuff lugged around on stage should be heavy enough to look convincing (it was some sort of lead alloy sprayed with gold paint) and so she was covered with great ton weights of the stuff. When the giants complain that they can still see Freia through a chink in the gold, Wotan is forced to yield up the famous Ring as well. It's the only bit he has left, and besides, Erda has just warned him that the Ring is laden with doom.

When I heard the story I couldn't help reflecting on the ironical symbolism of it all. Wotan, the one-eyed philandering god, represented Kleinblut himself. My mother was Freia, who can only be liberated by the yielding up of a circlet of gold (which of course represented her violated marriage). "*Zu mir, Freia!*" sings Wotan. "*Du bist befreit!*" And he throws the Ring on to the tottering pile.

But instead of effecting her rescue, it brought the whole lot down and crushed her to death.

4

The Puzzle of the Hidden Key

'SO YOU SEE,' said Józef Pyramur in conclusion, 'for my father, love was an absolute. There was no question of changed circumstances affecting the quality of his devotion.'

'A most touching story,' said Rudolf.

'Extraordinary,' said Radim.

Romuald was silent for a moment. His dark eyebrows were forced together in an apparent concentration of sympathy for the bereaved father and son, but his lower lip thrust his mouth into a rueful smile equally compounded of fellow-feeling and suppressed criticism.

The sun had set and the light was going fast. The train was now speeding through flat empty country, vast fields of stubble with the occasional square of tobacco or maize. The infrequent roads that linked the farms were hedgeless and empty, thin dry tracks of communication.

'Forgive me,' said Romuald. 'But I have good reasons for being interested in how a man should behave in such circumstances. Here you are, travelling to Dresden with the most melancholy of objectives. Did he not think of going earlier, to admonish her, to bring her back?'

'He respected her freedom,' said Józef.

'I do see that,' said Romuald. 'And perhaps in truth he was happier without her, with only the idea of her.'

'Ah yes,' said Rudolf. 'We all live with these illusions, don't we? And perhaps he felt in his heart unworthy of her?'

'He can build her a suitable monument,' said Radim.

Józef Pyramur spoke softly in the darkening carriage.

'You are all wrong,' he said. 'Without her he was nothing, and all he felt in his heart was that he had become the nothing that he was a dozen years before. She had failed him, but she had not ceased to exist. Or rather, it was impossible that she should suddenly cease to have ever existed. That is her only monument.'

'A family grave?' queried Radim. 'Somewhere for lilies, a focussing of thoughts?'

'Alas,' said Józef. 'Even that is doubtful. I said that my father and I were travelling to Dresden to take possession of the body. I doubt very much if we shall be able to bring it back. We shall have to see what the situation is at the frontier. I can't think that the trains will be entering a country in revolution.'

At that moment the lights came on in the compartment.

'Aha!' exclaimed Rudolf. 'The electricity! Inestimable and invisible commodity!'

'I've often wondered how they create it on trains,' said Radim. 'Can they store it? Or do they somehow make it?'

'I believe,' said Rudolf, 'that when it was first introduced into the railway system, trains ran with a separate carriage full of batteries. There may be batteries under the floor, but I rather think that there will be axle-driven dynamos.'

'A marvellous invention,' said Radim.

'Electricity has the unusual property of making things appear,' said Rudolf. 'Most human activities have the opposite effect.'

What appeared to greatest effect in the suddenly illuminated compartment were the faces of its occupants, each now freshly defined for the benefit of the others. Only Józef seemed to find the light less than welcome. He involuntarily raised his hand as if to shield himself from it. His face was flushed from the telling of his story, a glow of enthusiasm that covered all his cheek, jaw and throat right down to his collar, a soft sharp-lapelled affair that seemed rather too large for his smooth neck. After a moment he leapt up and opened the door to the schlafzimmer.

The maid appeared in the doorway, and there were words between them. Rudolf, Radim and Romuald couldn't hear what was said, but the impression was given that Józef was arguing while not wanting to be seen to argue. Extraordinary to be arguing with your maid! They were sure that for some reason Józef was being denied access to his father. They pretended not to try to listen.

Romuald was still meditating on Józef's story, and suddenly cried out:

'We all miss our opportunities!'

They stared at him. A tear was glistening in the corner of one eye. It seemed that what he had heard about Hilda Schmeck stirred in him the memory of some similar experience of his own.

'You!' he said to Józef. 'You were more jealous than your father. Why didn't *you* go to Dresden to persuade your mother to return?'

The maid had shut the communicating door in Józef Pyramur's face as soon as his attention was distracted. He was forced to return to his seat and ponder Romuald's question.

He looked puzzled.

'I was only twelve years old,' he said.

'But you had the right feelings,' said Romuald. 'And you would have had the resolution to see it through. If you had been my age you would have done it. Wouldn't you?'

'I don't know,' said Józef helplessly.

'You would, you would,' said Romuald. 'But I'm a coward, a worm, a faithless worm.'

He brought out a handkerchief and fiercely blotted his eyes. The others looked about them questioningly. It was Radim who spoke first.

'Tell us,' he said. 'Tell us all about it.'

'It's not an edifying story,' said Romuald.

'Never mind,' Radim insisted. 'It will make you feel better. And when you have finished we can go and investigate the dining car.'

'It will be soon done,' said Romuald. 'It is a short and sorry tale, and it begins only a few hours ago.'

So Romuald Grochow began his story. His voice was scornful, edgy, impulsive. And he acted out the dialogue in his story with a strong sense of drama, making expressive shapes with his small brown hands as he did so.

Professor Casimir was toasting himself in front of a freshly-lit fire in the iron stove that stood in the ancient fireplace of his farmhouse at Lamosz (said Romuald) and seemed disinclined to stir himself. He beamed and twinkled, like an uncle with a birthday present.

"I could just as easily shoot you now," he said, laying his gun on the small table in front of him.

I could not take my eyes off the gun. It was outrageous, gross, fascinating, like some obscene display. The room was transformed by it. It was a large comfortable room with worn flagstones and an old dresser, serving as living-room, kitchen and goodness knows what else. The Professor worked in one corner of it at his *Commentary on Ambrosius*, surrounded by worm-eaten volumes and loose papers. In another corner was apparatus for making wine: jars, carboys and flagons, many of them with a strange interrogative twist of glass in their corks, in which a bead of air suspended in liquid rose and fell, like the breath of a patient in extremity. If anyone was that patient it was myself, but I defied such a thought.

The gun was, of course, simply an object like any other. Perhaps if it had been lying on the table when I had arrived I wouldn't have given it a second thought, but would have presumed it to be a commonplace part of the Professor's curious country life-style, an aristocratic whim of his, akin to his fussiness, his pedantry, his gastronomic tastes, his ability even at his age to attract women. More specifically, of course, his ability to have attracted Vera, and (it was a perpetual horror to contemplate) to have induced her to marry him.

On our long walks, whenever she could find some pretext to get away from him, perhaps for a trip into Gomsza to the hairdresser's, or to look after her sister's baby for the afternoon, I would tackle her on this subject. It was an endless source of irritation.

"Rom, Rom," she would cry, her head on my shoulder, butting it repeatedly, like a little girl deprived of ice-cream. "You don't understand. You will never understand." And she would grasp the lapels of my collar and half reach up, half pull me down for a kiss of chaste affection, a motionless attachment of the lips, firm, sacred, businesslike, something between a vow and the sealing of the wax on a letter.

But I did know. Who could not know? It was an old story, not dissimilar to Kleinblut's effect on your mother. She had been dazzled by this genial scholar, celebrated throughout the country for his animadversions on the secular heresies of this age of change, celebrated for his resonant oratory, celebrated for having the ear of the Archbishop as well as the ear of the Chief of Police. Hers was indistinguishable from the fluttering of a dozen provincial hearts after his public lectures at the Institute, and what had she been when he condescended to notice *her* among all the others? Assistant to a discredited surgeon, his dogged receptionist? Little more than a clerk?

It was his style, I knew, that had seduced her. The tone of his critical articles, *de haut en bas* leavened with merriment, in which his political conservatism felt no need to ingratiate itself. The elegance of his town house in Gomsza, the last man to keep a horse and pair, the first to instal one of the new telephone machines that eventually drove him into the country. The style of personal address, the inevitable politeness, the trimmed moustache. Oh, how that little heart fluttered to be noticed!

It was disgusting. He could have been her grandfather.

His sense of style derived from his practice of the art of the appropriate. He felt it was appropriate in an age of moral turpitude and impending revolution to promulgate theocratic views and to cement the social bonds of Catholic orthodoxy. He felt it was appropriate on retirement from the Institute to sell the Gomsza town house, with its cinnamon stucco and baroque verandahs, and move to his fifteenth-century farmhouse in the country. He felt it was appropriate, on doing so, to take a young wife with him, someone who would take care of him in every way, someone who would, as he might have put it, "see him through".

He also felt it appropriate, if he were to challenge his wife's lover with a gun, to do it with something as traditional as a duelling pistol. The thing lay on the table with its great scrolled silver handle like a miniature romantic blunderbuss.

"Yes," repeated Professor Casimir. "I could easily shoot you now, and I would have no difficulty in proving to the police that it was a crime of passion. After all, Romuald, I found the letters. That was careless of you."

He chuckled.

"Perhaps I could say that I surprised you in the act of breaking in to retrieve the letters, afraid that Vera had tired of you and was ready to tell me everything. I think that would merit a complete acquittal, don't you? Especially as I know that the Chief of Police would be pleased to have you out of the way."

I was irritated. I knew this manner of his, like a cat toying with a bird before eating it. Hadn't I attended his logic classes years before at the Institute? Didn't I know how he loved bewildering and demoralising the dimmer students?

"You're wasting your time, Casimir," I said briefly, as I walked across the room to the door at the rear, through which were the stairs that ascended to the upper storey. "I've come to take Vera away, and you know that it's against all your principles to use violence. You can't stop me now."

"Quite right, dear boy," said Casimir, stoking the fire, which now twinkled as merrily as the old man himself. "Though perhaps principles are more troublesome to drag around with you than you at your age suspect, fragile and cumbersome baggage, easy to ditch in a crisis. Before you go upstairs perhaps you'd like to explain to me your own view of our current crisis. You always were one of my brightest pupils, and your views, even in the atrocious *Inquisitor*, are always interesting. You would not have remained my friend if they weren't."

"A satellite, Casimir, not a friend," I replied. "You have no friends. Everyone is afraid of you. They cultivate your favour. They trade flattery for influence. But your influence has gone now, hasn't it? It began to fade long ago, but now it has gone for ever. What you choose to call the "crisis" will change all that. The arguing is over, the people are on the streets, and now General Minski's Third Army will call the tune."

Casimir roared with laughter.

"A tune, you call it?" He gestured to the window. "Listen to those guns. It's the most tuneless sound in the world. It doesn't even sound very dangerous, does it? It sounds more like eggs breaking on the rim of a mixing bowl."

"Those guns are real enough," I said. "And they're not so far away either. I heard this afternoon that they've already crossed the Livula. The bridges couldn't be held."

"Of course, of course, dear boy," replied Casimir. "And it will not be long, will it, before they reach the railway line? And once they have reached the railway line there will be little hope of your escaping to the West. Your purpose, your urgency, your best clothes, oh yes, everything about you tells me of your plans. Although I was, in fact, fully apprised of them by Vera."

"You're a liar, Casimir,' I said angrily. "Vera wouldn't betray me."

"Who said anything about betrayal?" purred Casimir. "You are the only betrayer. You have entered my house as a friend, at my invitation, and now you enter it as my rival, as my enemy. You expected me to be making my weekly visit to the Institute Library at Gomsza. You were so confident that you did not even look to see if the carriage had gone from the stable. What effrontery!"

I turned impatiently to go through the door, to climb the stairs and to claim my love. To rescue Vera at this critical hour, to save her from the stale shackles of this sterile and perverted marriage and the chaos threatened by the advancing battalions of General Minski, was my only thought.

"Wait a moment, Romuald," said Casimir. "Wait before you rush upstairs to your expected joy, your criminal assignation. Why do you think I am not at the library? Why do you think I am here, ready for you? She has told me everything. Not without a little persuasion, I may say."

"You monster!" I exclaimed.

"No, no, Romuald," said Casimir. "You must know me better than that. We are still a civilised nation. The hordes have not reached us yet."

"Minski would know what to do with the likes of you," I said. "It is time for a change."

"I see," said Casimir. "But I think the Arch-Duke is a sufficient guarantee of continuity, don't you? I think you once did. I suppose I always did think of you as a parlour socialist despite your greed and ambition, but I confess that I never imagined that I would hear you giving a covert welcome to General Minski. I'm afraid that to the Goths and Vandals every patrician presents the same superbly shaven cheek. It is too late, I think, to muster peasant credentials now."

It was hot in the room. I felt a tricklet of perspiration crossing my ribs and arriving at the already damp constriction of my waist.

"However," continued Casimir, "for the philosopher there is always time. The discipline of thought takes one out of time as the discipline of chastity takes one out of the world."

"You talk of chastity!" I laughed bitterly. "Your marriage is the talk of Gomsza. Your name has become a by-word for lewdness. It's a scandal."

"I'm afraid that you and I will never understand one another, Romuald. And you will never make a philosopher. You are too impatient. You are one of those of whom Ambrose said: 'Marry, and weep.' You will never be in touch with the higher things of life."

"I've listened to enough of this," I said. "Marek is outside with the trap. The last train leaves in an hour, and I intend to take Vera with me. We love each other, that is all, and I could no more leave her to a loveless life with an old pedant than I could leave her to the doubtful mercy of General Minski. There is every reason to go, and you cannot stop us now."

"Ah, well," murmured Casimir. "There you are wrong, Romuald. I can, of course, stop you."

"I don't believe you ever meant to use that ridiculous antique," I said, indicating the gun. "You've admitted as much. And after all, you're a reasonable human being. There is no point in preventing us from leaving."

Was it my imagination, or was the idiotic crump of General

Minski's artillery getting louder? I had no time to waste in arguing with the Professor. I bounded up the stairs to Vera's room, the little room with the eaves and the bunches of cherries on the wallpaper, where only last week we had breathed promises to each other while Professor Casimir humped the dusty tomes of theology to his carrel in the Gomsza Institute Library.

"Vera, Vera," I whispered through the door. "It's me, Romuald."

"Oh, Rom," I heard her tear-choked voice reply. "What are you *talking* about down there? Isn't it time? Mustn't we go?"

"Of course, my sweetest," I said. "But open the door quickly."

"I can't," said Vera. "He locked it and took away the key. Rom, I didn't know what to do. I thought he was being so reasonable. I packed all my things, and he just smiled. Then when your trap came up the path he locked me in. It was so sudden! I had no time to think. I tried to warn you. I waved my handkerchief from the window, but Marek had already driven the trap round to the front door."

"Damn," I said. "So that was what he meant." I looked at the door, but it was one of the original doors, a work of solid loving craftsmanship, carved round its panels with the little friezes of geese and bullfinches so typical of the district. I could no more have broken it down than I could have burst through the floorboards into the room below, where no doubt the Professor still sat, laughing at me.

"Can you get out of the window, Vera darling?" I asked urgently.

"No, no, of course not," she replied. "Don't you remember? It's a tiny casement, and only the top pane opens. Besides, there'd be no way of getting down."

"What can we do?" I said despairingly.

"The key, the key!" said Vera. "Get the key from him! There were only a few minutes between his locking the door and your arrival. I could hear you talking. He must have the key."

"Vera, he has a gun," I said.

"That silly old pistol?" said Vera. Her voice sounded impatient. "It isn't even loaded."

Professor Casimir was seated just as I had left him. He spoke as though I had not left the room.

"You were often wrong as a student, Romuald. Although you were so clever, nonetheless you were too impatient of success. You were never really prepared to use the faculties you possessed. You did not trust time as a true philosopher does."

"We none of us have much time left, Casimir," I said. "Give me the key."

Casimir shrugged.

"I do not have the key, dear boy," he replied. And as if to prove it, he stood up and silently pulled out both his pockets with a comic grimace, like a scene from the kino.

"Where is it, then?" I asked. "Quickly. You've got to tell me."

"No, no," he said calmly. "I don't have to. That's what you haven't understood."

I took a step towards him, but he shook his head and smiled.

"You would have to get it from me by force," he said. "But I know you too well. You could no more use force than I could. Yes, yes, I've read your editorials. Very impressive. A very advanced position. You appear to be perfectly committed, in theory of course, to whatever means are necessary to achieve the perfect life. A theoretical revolution!" He tittered theatrically, putting his hand to his mouth. "You do not see what a charade it is, as much of a charade as that gun, which of course I introduced to you just now precisely in order to make the point I am making. You and I are both incapable of violence. That is why, when General Minski arrives and if the Arch-Duke doesn't put him in his place, we shall both be in equal peril. Yet it is you, Romuald, the armchair anarchist, who is proposing to flee the country. I wonder why? Is it because you have nothing of the philosopher in you?"

I groaned, and sank into a chair. It was true that I could not bring myself to harm Professor Casimir. It was not that I thought of myself as a coward, but there was something in his bearing, in his age and authority, in his role as a husband I had wronged, however odious, however senile, that forbade my laying a hand on him.

"But Romuald," he said, with a sudden inflection of kindliness and concern, "you mustn't think that I do not have your interests at heart. I do, I do! I have always enjoyed your visits, your eager talk, your cautious reliance on King's Side Openings. Your character has always fascinated me, with its contradictions of prose and passion. I shall give you a chance."

I began to curse him, but he raised his hand and quieted me as though I were simply objecting to a favour or compliment.

"No, no," he said. "Really, I mean it. Let us try an experiment. A philosophical experiment. Or is it a moral one? The key is in this room. I give you my word on it. I have had no time to hide it elsewhere, as I expect Vera has told you. If you find it, I cannot prevent you from leaving. You can spend the rest of your life on the boulevards of Paris drinking absinthe and proclaiming loudly what you would have done in the revolution if you had stayed. And Vera can keep a little *bijouterie* on the Rue Jacob. It would be a fate you both deserve, and would probably enjoy, as the petit-bourgeois always tolerate the licensed comforts of hell. I am too old to contemplate such a hopeless existence. But if you do not find the key . . ."

He paused, and smiled regretfully, lighting his pipe with a spill from the grate, puffing smoke into the air like a visible manifestation of his troubled thoughts.

"If you do not find the key, Romuald," he went on, "there is the rub. Then we will find out what your 'love' really amounts to. If you cannot lay your hands on that little toothed prong of iron and brass, what will you do? Will you stay here with us, and await the arrival of Minski's troops? Will you stick by her, and suffer all the deprivations of what is sure to be at the very least a troubled and chaotic period for our country? Or will you leap into your trap and instruct Marek to drive like a devil for the station while there is still time?"

My heart sank. I think I already knew, even as I feverishly dashed from corner to corner of the room opening microscope cases and overturning tobacco jars, that I would not find the key. He, of course, did nothing to assist or impede me, but kept watchfully still, like a host at a parlour game. I became more and more flushed and distraught, the sweat openly beading my brow and darkening my shirt. I ripped his books from the shelves. I spilled canisters of sugar. I uncorked his flagons of wine and turned them upside down over the flagstones, so that they glugged and gulped like cisterns until the whole floor was awash with sweet sickly veils of parsnip, plum and elderflower.

I looked everywhere, confounded and enraged by his tolerant amusement, and by my own failure.

There was a knock, and Marek stood at the front door in agitation.

"We ought to go, sir, if we're to catch that train. If you come now I think we could just do it."

He looked at me with that loyal, pained expression of his. I knew *he* would be happy enough if I saved my skin. Beyond him, at the end of the track that led to the Casimir house, was the road that led to freedom. Already, struggling along it with small handcarts filled with pathetic belongings, pans, bolsters, chairs, a side of bacon, a canary in a green cage, were the first refugees from the eastern provinces, fleeing from the rumour of outrages perpetrated by Minski's troops. My own portable property, conveniently laundered in the form of negotiable bonds and currency, was stowed tidily between layers of personal linen in my cases in the back of the trap. Marek repeated:

"Come on, sir!"

The scene behind him was like a leaf from a mediaeval triptych, the Expulsion from Eden, perhaps, or the Judgment of the Damned. In the foreground the torment; and behind, the daily life that the damned souls have abandoned or been abruptly torn from. In this case, it was the harvest, half-gathered. Stooks were loosely propped, whole fields abandoned by the sickle, like books half-read and put aside. When nations make war, it is the bread that suffers.

I knew I had looked everywhere. But I knew I had not looked everywhere, because I had not found it.

Casimir raised one eyebrow at me.

"You see?" he said. "You have no time. And that is because you are not a philosopher. A philosopher has all the time in the world. And the world itself, with all its futile pleasures, is something that he scorns. You think you are in love with my wife, but when it comes to the point you are ready to save your own skin. As for me, I have none of these specious ideals. As a philosopher, I could sit before this fire and . . . what shall I say, have time enough to conceive of a new kind of fuel to replace coal, conceive of it, that is to say, before I have used up the precious resources that we have plundered from Nature."

At this I lost my temper.

"Casimir," I exploded. "You are talking utter rubbish! You are a complete sadist, a madman. I have no more time for you, or any of your kind."

I had made my decision, and I was furious with myself for making it. Not so much for abandoning Vera, because I argued to myself that she must have been a fool to agree to marry Casimir in the first place. No, it was because I was so obviously taking the way out that he expected me to take. I was conforming to his expectations, confirming his prejudices. It was too humiliating. He had issued a challenge, like the Queen's Gambit, which he always used to win, and I had yet again failed to meet it. I felt that this failing was in some sense a key to my life, and that it was a challenge I was going to fail again and again.

I left him smiling serenely and poking his fire. I leaped into the trap, and Marek whipped the horse into a furious gallop.

"Damn you, Casimir!" I shouted. There was a face at Vera's window, a pale smudge like the mere ghost of a hope. The sun was getting low over the little copses, and over the abandoned harvests, of the country that I was forsaking. There were new countries, and there were new loves. Marek and I would see the world, like Don Giovanni and Leporello. But as I thought of Vera I remembered her little hands and her chill lips, and I was overcome with regret.

And as I sat back in the trap, hurtling for the station which I now had very little hope of reaching in time, mopping my forehead and wondering why I was so hot, wondering what it was exactly that I had lost and wondering what I had to hope for, suddenly I knew why Professor Casimir had lit a fire in August, and why, even if I had guessed where the key was, I would hardly have been able to retrieve it and use it. And at that moment, though I tried to tell myself that it didn't matter one jot, I knew what sort of a fool I was.

5

The Unveiling of Józef Pyramur

ROMUALD SEEMED THE better for having told his story, but he sat back with a slight air of defiance, and folded his arms.

'Ah, yes,' said Rudolf, ruminatively. 'Oh dear. Yes. Well.'

He gave a short laugh, and Romuald glared at him.

'There *is* something challenging about keys, isn't there?' said Rudolf. 'I mean, they do always disappear. It's in the nature of them to disappear. Or rather, they're always around, but never the right ones. I've got a whole drawer full of them and I've no idea what they're for. Perhaps if I knew, it would change my life.'

'I really don't need you to poke fun at me,' said Romuald.

'Nothing further from my mind, old fellow,' said Rudolf. 'But one thing puzzled me in your story, and it wasn't the whereabouts of the key. You seemed moved by the account by our young friend here gave of his mother's operatic escapade, and asked if she couldn't have been rescued, brought back to the fold, or something like that?'

'Yes,' said Romuald.

'You talked of fatally-missed opportunities, I think?' went on Rudolf, twisting his hair in his fingers.

'I did,' said Romuald.

'But there's an enormous flaw in the analogy,' said Rudolf. 'If I may say so.'

'Oh yes?' said Romuald.

'It's simply that in your case it is *you* who is the adulterer, that's all,' said Rudolf. 'I intend no moral criticism, naturally. But we did listen to your narrative with the strong expectation of illuminating parallels.'

'The parallel,' said Romuald savagely, 'is the weakness of inaction. And the weakness of insufficient desire. We all deserve to lose what we cannot make a sufficient effort to retain.'

'So when you said some time ago that Marek's sticking by Annelinde was a failure of nerve,' argued Rudolf, 'you were talking through your hat?'

'Almost certainly,' said Romuald. 'Oh yes, I'm a complete buffoon, aren't I? Well, you needn't have anything to do with me. I'm not only a buffoon, I'm a liar.'

'You made it all up?' asked Józef.

'No, no,' said Romuald. 'But when I said that my seat was in this carriage I was not telling the truth. There aren't two more seats in here anyway.'

'Of course,' said Radim. 'The other ticket! It wouldn't have been a servant's berth in the fourgon. It wasn't Marek's ticket. It was Vera's.'

'Yes,' said Romuald.

'You didn't intend Marek to come with you in the first place,' said Józef. 'How did you expect him to make up his mind in twenty minutes?'

'I thought he'd be loyal to *me*,' said Romuald. 'Then I couldn't face pushing my way through half the train to find my real place. I thought I'd be happier here with all of you.'

'My dear fellow!' exclaimed Rudolf. 'Of course. And so are we. Absolutely delighted. Aren't we?'

The others agreed.

'Kick me out, if you like,' muttered Romuald.

'Absolutely not,' insisted Rudolf.

Radim, who had been very silent, suddenly said:

'Didn't you even *try* to break down the door?'

'Not a chance,' said Romuald. 'I suppose if it had been you it would have broken up like a cigar box at the first touch of your shoulder.'

Indeed, Radim's jacket seemed swollen with muscle, shoulder, chest, arm. He might have been concealing a skinned animal beneath it, slung around his neck.

'Casimir's test was designed for me,' said Romuald. 'It ought to have been easy for me, as perhaps the door would have been easy for you.'

'What about dinner, gentlemen?' suggested Rudolf.

It was quite dark outside now, and there were so few lights from the scattered farms that for much of the time they might have been in a tunnel. It was not absolutely late, but it was perhaps late for the dining car. They were all hungry.

'Will your father join us?' asked Rudolf.

'Oh no,' said Józef nervously. 'He'll want to stay in the compartment. I'll tell Maddalejna to ring for a tray.'

He knocked on the door between the compartments, calling gently: 'Maddalejna, Maddalejna.' After what seemed a defiantly lengthy pause, the door opened a crack and he went into the schlafzimmer.

'There really is something strange about that set-up,' whispered Rudolf to the others. 'That maid seems to be keeping Józef Pyramur away from his father.'

'Perhaps she's a nurse,' said Radim.

'Maybe,' said Rudolf. 'But she doesn't look like one. I'm sure she's a maid. She's a personal maid, too, which doesn't make sense. If she's Hilda Schmeck's maid, why should the Pyramurs keep her on for five years?'

'Perhaps she's been in the family all her life,' said Romuald. 'Does it matter? I expect the old man needs a lot of looking after.'

'How paralysed do you think he is?' asked Radim.

'I only caught a glimpse of him twice,' said Rudolf. 'He seemed to me to be completely immobile.'

'What I don't understand,' said Radim, 'is if he is so disabled, why didn't Józef Pyramur go to Dresden to collect his mother's body himself? Why all this trouble, with the wheelchair and everything?'

'Yes,' said Rudolf. 'And why be still so dressed up? It doesn't look natural anyway, the gloves, the hat, and a veil, of all things. It's the most extreme form of public display you can imagine. It's the garb of the professional mourner, the sort of chap you'd hire to walk behind a hearse.'

'Ssh,' said Radim. 'He's coming back.'

Together the four of them made their way up the train to the dining car. The corridors were difficult to negotiate. Two little boys were playing cards, a sailor had slung a hammock, and just outside the dining car (as if deeming the situation appropriate) an old man had lit a small stove and was frying onions.

'My God,' exclaimed Rudolf, fanning away the smoke as they passed. 'If the train has got into this state here, what will it be like in the third-class carriages by now?'

'Did you see that sailor?' asked Radim. 'Do you think he is a deserter? Surely all the armed forces are on active service during the emergency?'

'I doubt it,' said Romuald. 'That would be too efficient. Perhaps he is being posted to the Western frontier for special duties.'

'I've never understood what the Gomszan Navy actually does,' said Rudolf. 'We have no coast to defend.'

'No,' said Romuald. 'But there are different kinds of navies. The Gomszan Navy isn't a maritime force, naturally. It's a fluvial navy. Very useful in the seventeenth century, if you remember your schoolroom history. The Turks had the nasty habit of sneaking down the Livula on rafts. The Turks were everywhere. They got as far as Vienna, but they never reached Gomsza. Thanks to the Navy.'

'They haven't played much part in trying to keep General Minski away, presumably,' said Rudolf.

'They've no defences against modern artillery,' said Romuald. 'In fact there's no military power in the navy at all, but they're terribly good at communications. Always been at the forefront of communications. So hard to move upstream, you see. That's why sailors are useful at frontiers.'

They had some difficulty in finding a table. As Romuald had said earlier, the dining car seemed to be full of people who were not actually eating. The waiter, a grey-faced old man with a pronounced stoop, had given up all pretence of control or efficiency. He greeted them with an undisguised lack of enthusiasm.

'The veal has gone,' he said, flicking at the tablecloth with his napkin. He made it sound like an expected departure, voluntary, and not at all regrettable. He began opening a bottle of mineral water for them.

'Ah,' said Rudolf. 'I knew it. The wagons-lits conductor. Remember the train driver, Radim? I'll bet that there isn't any bierwurst left either.'

'I don't want bierwurst,' said Radim. 'There ought to be some caviare on this train. And salmon.'

'No caviare,' said the waiter. 'No salmon.'

'But you've come from St Petersburg,' objected Radim. 'The train should be bursting with caviare.'

'It's all been eaten,' said the waiter. 'There's tripe soup.'

'Oh,' said Rudolf. There was a pause.

'Four soups?' enquired the waiter.

'Isn't there anything else?' asked Romuald.

'Sausages,' said the waiter.

They all looked at each other in perplexity.

'Four sausages,' said the waiter, writing it down. 'Vodka?'

'Of course we want vodka,' said Romuald. 'But look here . . .'

But the waiter was already shuffling away and did not hear him.

'It's no use, I'm afraid,' said Rudolf. 'When in Rome, you know. There may have been caviare as far as Vilna. Here in Gomsza it is tripe soup. No doubt once we have reached the frontier there will be bierwurst again. And after Cologne, snails. That's how it is with these long-distance trains. They have to stock up as they go. I was once on the Orient Express, dining perfectly agreeably off oysters and champagne. After Ruse we jolted in four-wheeled carriages and the meals became picnics of unchewable fowls and bizarre Turkish pastries. At one time there were incredible delays at the gauge-breaks, too: you had to change bogies, because the whole system was different, Russian birch-logs as compared with Prussian coal.'

'And who do those coal-fields belong to, anyway?' put in Romuald. 'They were originally part of the Gomszan Empire.'

'Ah,' said Józef. 'You are a federalist, I see.'

'And why not?' said Romuald. 'A free federation of Slav peoples is the only hope of restoring our self-respect and full national identity.'

'I think you are confusing a nation with an empire,' said Rudolf. 'There are enough empires already.'

Romuald exploded.

'Are you seriously suggesting that the current boundaries should be respected in perpetuity?' he asked. 'You are as bad as someone like Casimir. He totally misunderstood the whole federalist idea.'

'Well, I don't know about Casimir,' said Rudolf. 'But if he feels that federalists are proposing to sell Gomsza's birthright to foreigners, then I don't disagree. Incorporation is a better policy. That would integrate the border areas at some future date into a unitary Gomszan state.'

'Unrealistic,' said Romuald. 'If you want to fight the Russians on their own terms, a multi-national federation in Eastern Europe is the only solution.'

'It would be the end of Gomsza,' said Rudolf.

'It would be the end of the Duchy of Gomsza perhaps,' said Romuald.

'Ah,' said Józef. 'Now you're contradicting yourself. You spoke up earlier for the Arch-Duke. No wonder Casimir seems to have thought you no better than a Bolshevik.'

'There would still be room for the Arch-Duke in a federation,' said Romuald.

'An Arch-Duke without a Duchy!' exclaimed Rudolf. 'Now there's a thought. I could perhaps construct some comic illusion around that. Now you see it. Now you don't.'

'The Duchy is an illusion anyway,' said Romuald angrily. Several people turned round. 'What is the Duchy but an asset of the Tsar? The Russians don't have so much time for us, but that's because we are like a rich man's toy: the wrapping paper is still loosely around us, and they have other things to play with.'

'Bravo!' cried Rudolf. 'Since the waiter has kindly brought us our vodka, I suggest that we drink to that sentiment. It is one on which I am sure we are all agreed. No Gomszan has any wish to be a plaything of the Tsar.'

He filled their glasses.

'To freedom!' he said, lifting his own. The others followed suit.

The glasses had to be tossed back in one gulp. Józef seemed uncertain about this, attempting to sip his, but Rudolf would have none of it. He laughingly manipulated Józef's elbow.

'Come on, drink up, young fellow,' he said. 'Don't tell me you don't drink vodka!'

'Not,' mumbled Józef, 'very often.'

'Well, we can make up for it now,' said Rudolf.

'Yes,' said Radim, filling the glasses. 'We need many toasts. To make us happier than we are.'

'Only the continued prosperity of whatever or whoever we drink to can do that,' said Rudolf. 'Gentlemen, I give you the Arch-Duke and his ministers. May they survive the present troubles.'

'The Arch-Duke!' they all murmured.

Four glasses were upended, four faces tilted to support them, four throats opened and swallowed, and four empty glasses were returned with satisfied little thumps to the tablecloth.

The water-seller was passing through the dining car at this moment, in the vain hope, it seemed, of selling his wares in the first-class section of the train. His trolley with its great brass urn bumped awkwardly into every table, and the passengers looked up in irritation. His gaze wandered interrogatively around the car, but the diners not only had their own free water, but were so plentifully supplied with stronger liquids that they did not have much need of it in any case.

The waiter returned with the soup, four shallow bowls in which the liquid revolved to the rhythm of the train. Rudolf looked at his without much enthusiasm.

'They say we shall be held up at the frontier, gentlemen,' said the waiter, placing a basket of bread rolls on the table. 'Not worth retiring until all the formalities have been completed. They'll have everyone on parade tonight, all right.'

'Oh Lord,' said Rudolf. 'You'd better bring us some more vodka, then.'

'Of course, sir,' said the waiter. He looked at Józef and raised his eyebrows. 'Gentlemen of the theatre, are you? I like a good play myself.'

'Well, I am, as a matter of fact,' began Rudolf, but the old waiter had already turned away and was moving up the car. 'What a curious fellow!' He laughed.

'Not so curious,' said Romuald, nodding at Józef. They all looked at the young man. 'Or at least not as curious as our young friend here.'

Józef blushed, looking perplexed but cornered.

'My goodness,' said Rudolf. 'So that's it!'

Romuald reached over to the young man's upper lip.

'Excuse me, Master Pyramur,' he said. 'But your manhood is slipping.'

And he peeled off Józef's moustache.

'What do you make of that, Rudolf,' said Romuald.

'Gum arabic,' said Rudolf, with authority.

The young man had been behaving so strangely for much of the time that they rather expected him to burst into tears again. But despite his embarrassment he put down his soup spoon and ran his hand through his mop of hair from forehead to nape as though to clear the air or to prepare for an address, and simply gave them an enormous open smile. It was a smile of shared deceit, confession, pleasure, appeal. It was the greatest grin of complicity that any of them had ever seen.

They looked at each other and smiled too. Of course. Now that they knew it, they felt that they had always known it. Józef Pyramur was a woman.

All this lasted only a few seconds. She quickly retrieved the moustache from Romuald's stupefied fingers and managed to fix it back again.

'I *mustn't* be seen,' she said emphatically. 'Did anyone see? Did they?'

Rudolf, who was sitting next to her, glanced down the dining car.

'I really don't think so,' he said. 'But that old waiter was as sharp as a button. He spotted it straight away. It must have been the vodka. Alcohol's a great enemy of gum arabic, you know. I don't expect you'll be able to keep it there for long.'

'Damn,' she said. 'I really don't want to be found out.'

'We've found you out,' said Romuald.

She gave them all another wonderful smile.

'I know,' she said. 'But you're my friends now. You're going to have to protect me, aren't you? My three musketeers.'

They were stupefied, but Rudolf spoke for them all when he said valiantly:

'Of course we will. Yes, indeed. Without question.'

'Excellent,' she said. 'You see, I've got to rely on someone. Or else Kleinblut is going to find me. Kleinblut or my father.'

'Kleinblut?' said Rudolf. 'You mean there really is someone called Kleinblut? That part of your story was true?'

'Well,' she said doubtfully. 'I don't know about "true". Not very much of it was true at all. But yes, there is someone called Kleinblut. And my father is called Cyprian Pyramur.'

She moved the mustard pot in line with the salt cellar as if to identify these two. Her hand hovered over the pepper.

'Hadn't you better tell us who you are,' prompted Romuald. 'And what all this disguise and secrecy is about?'

'Yes,' she said in a prompt and dutiful manner, thinking hard.

She put her hand on the pepper pot and moved it in front of her, as far from the mustard and salt as was possible.

'Let's eat our soup first, shall we?' she said. 'I'm just as hungry as I was before, even for Gomszan country fare.'

She took up her spoon, but the others seemed transfixed.

'Soup all right, gentlemen?' asked the waiter, bringing their second bottle of vodka. He looked pointedly at their untouched bowls.

'Perfect,' she said gruffly, dipping the spoon. 'By the way, waiter.'

He was about to shuffle away again, but turned back.

'Yes, sir?' he said.

'We are actors, as you so correctly surmised,' she said. 'But I do hope that you'll say nothing about it. We don't want any fuss. Trophy-hunters and so on.'

'Of course, sir,' said the waiter. 'I quite understand.'

'What's your name?' she asked.

'My name, sir?' The waiter was surprised to be asked. 'It's Tadeusz, sir.'

'Thank you very much, Tadeusz,' she said, slipping him a coin.

'Why, thank *you*, sir,' he said. 'Most kind.'

And he shuffled away at last.

They ate their soup.

'Well,' said Romuald. 'And what is *your* name, then?'

'My name is Hilda Pyramur,' she said, with sparkling eyes, leaning towards him, but glancing also at Rudolf and at Radim to include them in her confidence. 'And in two days' time I expect to be Hilda Schmeck. I'd better tell you all about myself.'

6

The Damaging of the Dazzling Genius

THE STORY I told you earlier (said Hilda) was a fabrication. I had to have a cover for my disguise as Józef, of course, and I needed your sympathy and confidence. I still do, more than ever, for I am being pursued by two of the most evil men in Gomsza. You'll be bound to think me melodramatic to say such a thing, but it's true, and one of them is my own father.

I didn't make everything up. How could I? My father is indeed Cyprian Pyramur, principal cellist of the Arch-Duke's private orchestra. And there is a man called Kleinblut who has just the maimed left hand that I have described. You would scarcely believe how much between them they have made my life a misery.

My father is very far from the timid complaisant creature I made him out to be. He is a ruthless opportunist, an exploiter of the innocent, a disciplinarian, a sadist. He would do anything to secure his position at Court, to augment his fortune, to advance his interests.

I was raised in the country, where my mother had been given a small estate as a dowry. My father brought nothing to the marriage except his musical skills and some gambling debts. He was a charming rogue who must have swept my mother off her feet. My grandparents indulged her, hence the estate. If they had ever once had thoughts of forbidding the marriage I never heard of it. To my father they were always cool and distant, though impeccably correct, even generous, in their dealings. For my mother's sake they lent him large sums of money which I am sure were never returned. She was an only child, and above all they wanted her to be happy.

The estate was not intended to be anything more than a summer resort, a kind of plaything with old oak woods, some thistly pasture and a toy orchard. They expected that my mother and father would live in the city when he needed to pursue his musical career. The musical career was not neglected, but neither was the opportunity to make some money out of the estate, for my father has expensive tastes. In the early days they would drive out to it with friends when the heat and dust of the city became intolerable. They would fish in the river and organise picnics. The old retainers on the estate were ready for this sort of thing. They aired rooms and drove pony traps. They cooked, and mowed the grass in front of the house. They repaired the rotting woodwork on the verandah. They had been told to do it. They owed it to the family.

They were not prepared for my father's interest in the commercial properties of the estate. It began in a small way, allowing other visitors and then charging them for the fishing. Shooting became a possibility, too, and he arranged for the breeding of partridges. The orchard was pruned for the first time in ten years, and the apples gathered instead of being left to rot. New trees were planted, cattle purchased. All this had to be done by the old servants of the estate, loyal retainers of my grandfather's who had been sent there years ago to what they had imagined would be an easy retirement. The work was not well or willingly done, and when my father introduced a bailiff, there was even greater discontent. The bailiff was a local man, an upstart, from whom my father had already bought some additional land. He took the opportunity to throw his weight around on property which had previously been irritatingly beyond his grasp, an aristocratic anachronism in a belt of cider country now being run as a business concern. It satisfied him to bring in unfamiliar machinery and to forbid old ways. But he couldn't dismiss the old retainers, whose rights had been secured by my grandparents.

When I was three we went to live there all the time. I'm not sure why. Perhaps my father needed to keep an eye on the bailiff. Perhaps he could not bear the expense of living in the city. At that stage of his career, when he was obtaining work as a soloist, he was frequently away from home travelling to concerts and rehearsals. He could use the estate as a base just as well as a town house, and the rent which he saved could no doubt be invested in more land and more fruit trees.

We hated it when he was at home.

The sound of his instrument from the upper room where he practised forbade all other activity, all other thoughts. It was a sound as compelling as the church bell tolling for service, or the cry of a creature in pain. Whatever you were doing, inside the house or out of it, you could not forget the insistence of that cello. The endlessly reiterated phrases were like a defiance of ordinary consecutive time. The arrogant arpeggios froze the will, distracted me from every pleasure. The house was cello, cello, cello. Even down in the dairy where I would go to watch Maria making the butter you could hear it, a tiny savage sound like a net thrown over the morning to prevent it from escaping. The formation of the butter in the toppling churn was a miracle to me, the glistening white curds and knobs creating solid out of liquid in a moment of time that was like a moment out of time because you could never catch it happening; but it was a magic moment tangled up in this prisoning net of tyrannical male sound, this beautiful hateful deep sound, assertive as the male voice.

I hated him because of his cruelty to my mother and because of his resentment of me. I suppose he had wanted a son. Or perhaps he had not wanted children at all. My mother adored me, and made an alliance with me in which he could not share. She may have used me as a protection against him, a preoccupation, an excuse for having no more children, which was a process that, as I came to learn, had brought her near to death. She was never perfectly well.

He forbade me my pleasures. It was as if nothing could exist that took no account of his music. I could not play with Maria's son Tamasz because I made too much noise. I could not ride my pony beyond the meadow because it made my mother anxious. And if I did find something quiet to do, away from him, if I were not present to be interrogated whenever he chose, he would also be enraged. The music would stop, and the door of the music room would open. My father would seem to be at a loss for some activity as equally concentrating as stopping the strings of his cello. He would shout at the servants, clenching and unclenching his fingers. He would quarrel with my mother, and if he had nothing better to do he would tyrannise me. Distracting as the sound of those agonised arpeggios was, I began to wish that they would never stop, for as long as they continued I was free to play without interruption. When I was six he found me one day playing with a dolls' house that my grandmother had given me. It was a beautiful little house, with no music room. Its inhabitants led gentle organic lives full of daily miracles. They made butter, gave afternoon teas to clowns and hussars, held parties in the attic, had babies. I've no idea where my knowledge of this last activity came from. I could have done with a little brother, of course, but there seemed no question of it.

My mother spent much of the day in bed, and while that is a convenient and indeed essential place for many of the preparations for introducing a new life into the world, in her case it was, though I did not know it, a preliminary to removing her own. The doctor was a frequent visitor, leaving his hat with the maid and taking his little black bag up to my mother's room. It was an ugly little square bag with a tight snap, and he might as well have been taking bits of her away without our knowing it. She always seemed paler and weaker after his visits.

My father must have known all about the dolls' house, but it suited him to forbid it me. I was now too old for such things, he said, and must have piano lessons.

I remember running to my mother in perplexity, not believing that the jolly house was to be put away. She must for once have pleaded with him, for it was not put away. However, the piano lessons began. In my innocence I boasted of this to everybody, to the gardener, to Maria, even to the bailiff when he came to go over the books with my father. But I didn't know then what they were to be like.

My father had a brass ruler, thin and flexible and very broad. It was a patent ruler for drawing staves, having five parallel gaps in it, running almost the full length so that lines for musical notes could be stencilled on the paper. This ruler therefore made a particularly thin airy whistling sound when brought down sharply on to little fingers.

At first the ruler was used for guidance, almost like its proper purpose: fingers must curl and not poke; the knuckles must be flat. How awkward those notes were! Although I knew that in reality they lay quietly side by side, little ivory lids that never opened but could be pressed down to disturb the sound that was trapped beneath, I could never be quite confident of reaching any of them accurately. If I succeeded in pressing one with my forefinger, my hand went through tortures to press the adjacent one with my middle finger. The keys were docile enough. I could hardly blame them. It was my hand that didn't behave, its other fingers waving wildly in the air, the whole wrist arched and writhing. It was not allowed to touch the ruler. The ruler was held out over the keys, lower and lower. It hid the keys from me, so that finding the right one was even harder and my fingers squirmed all the more. Inevitably my knuckles touched brass, and I learned to fear it like an electric shock, for the ruler was not only a gate and a hurdle, but a goad and a flail. My hands were trained like poor animals that have no conception of their purpose. And always the stinging mark left lines, angry red ghosts of the music I was trying to play.

So it went on for years, and the result was that I became a good pianist. Perhaps I should have been grateful to my father for that, except that when I turned out to have real talent it was something of a blow to his self-esteem. As long as he could teach me, I was only a girl. His control was a substitute for the love he could never feel. As soon as I could generate my own interpretations of the music that I now had the technique to play I was in a sense defying him. I remember the first time that this happened. I was learning the *Moonlight* sonata of Beethoven and all at once saw how the third movement should go. My father had been going on about attack and articulation, using the metronome as a cage to trap the notes that my flustered fingers could not bring to distinctness. I remember there was a vase of some frail over-coloured flowers on the piano, fuchsias perhaps, beginning to drop their petals. I felt that my performance was as gross as those flowers, watered and protected, vulnerable, predictable, short-lived. Suddenly I became as angry as I knew my father was, and ignored him completely. Without waiting for him to finish whatever it was he was saying, I played the movement through at what seemed like twice his speed and extremely quietly. It was like the pouncing of some wild animal that comes in the night and will not be denied: furious, stealthy, savage. It was certainly a denial of my father, and he was for once shocked into silence. When I had finished, the stalks in the vase were bare, and the black piano lid was covered in red fuchsia blossoms.

I ran out of the room without a word and went to lie on my bed. I was too exhilarated to sob. I was also in discomfort of a kind I had never experienced before which at first I connected with my defiance and artistic achievement, like a blush or a beating heart. In a way it was so connected, for it shared for its expression that living tide of the body which colours our excitements and embarrassments. In that hour for the first time I had become not only an artist but a full woman.

I will not bore you with the details of my life. It suffices to say that my blossoming was not as resented as it might have been, since it coincided with my father's success at Court. If he was at all bewildered at the musician his strict methods had inadvertently produced he was not required to show it. He could safely leave me on the estate to look after my mother while he disappeared for even longer periods of time than usual. The Arch-Duke's orchestra was much in demand, not only for the usual Palace occasions but also for the opera at the Winter Gardens which I have already described. He came home for my mother's final illness when it was clear that there was almost nothing left of her for the doctor to take away in his little black bag. But after the funeral he left again, having taken no interest in me except to kick my little dog Mouse when she got in the way of his feet.

I was very good. I kept my temper, and I kept out of his way. I did not want to have anything more to do with him. The estate passed to me directly on my mother's death, a far-sighted provision of my grandparents. I was able to discover some of the sharp practices of the bailiff simply through my knowledge of the way things were done on the estate, something my father and mother had never known. I was familiar, for example, with the number of barrels of cider needed for distillation into a barrel of apple brandy, and could not be diverted by the devious paperwork. When I confronted the bailiff he expected to be dismissed, but the truth is that I had fallen a little in love with his son Grigory, so I forgave him. Grigory was certainly in love with me, and had given me wagon-loads of presents (including Mouse) to prove it. I reflected that the Pyramurs had unwittingly paid for these presents many times over, but I did not think it had much to do with Grigory, who was a naive sunburned young man who would strip ostentatiously to the waist at the slightest opportunity, even to chop a day's firewood. He was studying unsuccessfully to be a lawyer, but would have made a better hussar. He adored me.

My life was at a cross-roads. I loved the country with its rolling orchards and hidden villages. I would ride for hours by the banks of the chattering river, sometimes crossing it at the shallow points where the stones broke its surface up into a glittering display, or letting my pony stand in midstream satisfying his thirst while I waved away the clouds of buzzing flies from both of us with my hat. Then I would gallop home, looking forward to one of Maria's goulashes. If I had married Grigory my life might have been entirely like that, and so might my children's. And Grigory would have made a handsome husband and father, treating me perhaps just as he would have treated his children, as charming possessions, to be laughed at and given great smacking kisses.

If I was at all tempted by such an indulgent fate it was soon put out of my mind by my music, for indeed I had kept up my piano playing. Curiously, it was what I loved best of all. Instead of associating it with my father and hating it, I associated it with defeating and transcending him, and therefore I loved it.

I went to the Conservatoire, naturally. The Principal was the pianist Kleinblut, the man of whom Busoni wrote: "If I had three hands, I could not play as well as Kleinblut plays with one." The whole corpus of music for the right hand only, commissioned by him from Brahms, Widor, Reger and others, had long been lost, destroyed by Kleinblut himself for reasons that I have already described, although some copies of a published edition of Liszt's studies, *Sisyphus*, had survived. One of these was in the Conservatoire library, in the locked section along with the undisputed treasures such as the hymn of the *Bogurodzica* in a fifteenth-century manuscript.

To begin with I was assigned to the junior teachers, the busy friendly useless ones who saw so many pupils that they could never give you more than forty minutes a week. There was very little that I could learn from them, and I began to protest. Some other students felt the same, and one of them, an Austrian called Johann Schmeck, went to the Principal to complain.

I was a little in awe of Johann Schmeck at first. It is hard to describe the effect he has on people. It's a kind of arrogance, I suppose, that gives him no need to assert himself. He would sit alone in the refectory, smiling quietly as if he understood the whole world better than it understood itself. He always wore a kind of uniform, a jacket with braided frogs, tight at the neck, and a little peaked cap. He had full lips and a thin downy moustache and eye-glasses on a ribbon. He looked very boyish, and a bit uncomfortable like a cadet, but he also had great panache, particularly when he spoke, and he had this streak of self-assurance and intolerance. He knew exactly what he was doing, and always knew when others were wrong. He was aristocratic, cruel, sardonic. Most of the students were frightened of him, and perhaps some of the teachers were, too. I was amazed to discover that he was almost two years younger than I was.

It didn't seem surprising to us that Johann was immediately successful in his interview with the Principal, because we had seen little of the Principal and imagined that he would be in as much awe of Johann as we were, and of course convinced by the justice of our case. We were delighted that he agreed to give some of us lessons himself.

The female students are always seen in pairs, but as I was the only girl among the select group of complainants, the serious ones, the high-flyers, I attended for my lessons with Johann. I was afraid that he might have minded, felt it was an intrusion that he had not bargained for, but he seemed indifferent to my presence. He almost, in a curious way, seemed indifferent to the presence of Kleinblut himself. He had a way of listening, even of responding, that made no concessions to agreement or amiability. He would simply nod. Or rather, the gesture was the reverse of a nod: a brief backward reach of the stiff cropped skull, a slight lift of the chin, a narrow glance down the aquiline nose, these were sufficient to remind you that he was not deaf. He heard, and perhaps he listened, but he kept close counsel.

Kleinblut first of all made us play to him. He invited us to perform the piece that we had most recently studied. My turn was first. He sat with folded arms not at a distance from the piano as you might think, at the point of optimum acoustic, but tightly within the curve of the instrument itself as though to catch every nuance of superfluous or accidental sound or to diagnose, like a doctor with a stethoscope, the secret causes of the likely malady of my performance.

His posture certainly did make me ill at ease. I wanted to play my Chopin, for me a recent passion. My father had so firmly grounded me in the sonorities of Beethoven and Schubert that to discover Chopin with his chromatic gasps and swooning rubatos was a kind of guilty defiance of parental authority, almost an erotic secret. It was like going to one's first dance and finding that its extraordinary breathless pleasures were not just an adolescent's dream, but part of the accepted life of society. I sat down at that battered grand and played Chopin as I had never played Chopin before.

Kleinblut seemed to be enraged.

"Where is the structure of this piece?" he asked me, quivering with his effort to remain polite. "This is a piano, not a box of chocolates. There is no structure in your playing. It is like a little girl trying to catch a butterfly, all lurches and pauses. And inaudible giggles."

His right hand was grasping the piano as he spoke, the left arm behind his back, giving him an odd air of formality as though he were not addressing a young student near to tears, but a whole auditorium of professors. This occultation of the notorious stump terrified me even more than if he had brought it down with force on the keyboard or on my wrist, as my father had brought down the brass ruler many times.

"No architectonics, no structure," repeated Kleinblut. "Now you, sir."

He resumed his seat, his right arm remaining hooked around the back of his chair, and stretched to grasp the front folded section of the piano lid. The gesture had a proprietorial air, as though to comfort the piano for its mistreatment at my hands and to support it through any further mistreatment it might undergo.

Johann took the stool, in an icy silence. The pause before he began was as long and intense as an act of prayer. Kleinblut drummed his fingers slightly, and half looked round to urge him to begin.

Johann began.

I didn't know what to do, I was so embarrassed. He played the very same piece that I had just played! He played it fast, and with a mechanical regularity that somehow gave it the tinkling blandness of a music box. I did not know where to look, and stared in a furious blush at the handkerchief I was twisting in my hands, brought out in readiness for the tears which never quite came. There was something about Johann's performance that was not merely satirical: there was a kind of deliberate savagery in it, a playful insistence that imperceptibly changed the rhythms. Could he possibly, I wondered at one point, be stressing each *fourth* consecutive quaver? It didn't seem credible, and by the time I thought I had noticed it, he seemed to have stopped doing it.

If Kleinblut had been angry before, I thought he would be likely to do violence now. He did not move from his seat, and appeared to be trembling. Over his head the imperturbable Johann Schmeck gave me an enormous wink.

"Architectonics," he declared simply.

In the next moment I thought the world was going to end, and all of it seemed to be my fault. But unbelievably Kleinblut burst out in a laugh.

"You are a jester, sir," he said. "And a fine pianist. Now play me your chosen piece."

When Johann played for the second time the whole room seemed suddenly transformed, bathed in an almost palpable submarine light. The music was very slow, very calm, full of deep soft notes and great broken chords reaching up from the piano like ruined columns or stalagmites in an elfin grotto as Johann crossed his arms to create them, almost like a swimmer. It was magical and strange and without any form at all as far as I could see. I had never heard anything like it.

Kleinblut was clearly irritated, but Johann's insouciance seemed to have somehow inoculated him against any expression of criticism or hostility.

"This French daubing," he said, "I can't think what you see in it. Does it please you, eh?"

Johann smiled at the ceiling.

"You are young, my boy," said Kleinblut, suddenly benign. "Your taste will develop. At the moment your fingers are racing ahead of your mind, I think."

He showed us to the door, patting our heads like children. I knew I was safely standing on his right, but even so shuddered inwardly at his touch.

"And you, my pretty one," he added. "Some exercises for those fingers, eh?"

I suppose I began to be in love with Johann from that day, but he was not easy to get on with at first. He was a solitary boy, even eccentric to those who didn't know him. Young as he was, he had complete independence from his family. He spent no time in cafés or chatter, practised eight hours a day, and lived on little buns, quite often yesterday's buns, which he bought very cheaply from a stall near his lodgings. I told him that the stall-owner must be ready to throw them out, and that he could have had them for nothing. I tried to give him some money myself, but he was too proud to take it. It was a long time before he was relaxed enough to talk to me properly, but I knew from his wink that day in Kleinblut's room that he must like me. Eventually we became friends, against great odds (which included our relative ages, my taste in music, his watchful concierge, money, to mention just a few).

My life was soon to become immensely complicated. At the beginning of my second year my father came to teach at the Conservatoire one day a week. Could it possibly be that he needed the money? It was one of those distinguished professorships they were in the habit of giving important people, and they must have been in need of someone to coach the string quartets that rapidly formed (and sometimes just as rapidly broke up) at the Conservatoire. I think he was probably quite good at doing this, and I heard a lot about him from my friend Ilena, who was a viola player in her third year. Whenever I met my father he asked how I was getting on, with what I could tell was a mere pretence of interest, of real interest that is, but with a regularity that almost made me think that he was there just to keep an eye on me.

At the same time Kleinblut's own interest took an unpleasant turn. He had not ceased to be critical of my playing, which he declared was sentimental. I was ready to believe it, since I did not have so high an opinion of myself as I had had before arriving at the Conservatoire. So many of us there could play well. It was something that was taken for granted. But to play better than well, to be noticed, to be admired: that was something quite different. And as for geniuses like Johann! Such playing put us all in our places. I knew I was far below the best. But if that were the case, which it surely was, why was Kleinblut so attentive to me? Why did he lean over the piano as I tried tricky runs with his suggested fingering? Why did he lend me his own music? Why did he begin to see me alone for my lessons?

There could be only one answer.

When I talked about it to Johann, he couldn't see the problem.

"You ought to be grateful for his undivided attention," he said. "Besides, he's seeing all of us alone now. He's even seeing Boris alone."

I was forced to laugh. Boris was an extremely large cheerful ugly young man, who supported himself by playing accompaniments to the photographic comedies at the kino. I had once persuaded Johann to let me take him there, so that we could listen to Boris providing glissandi from the top of the piano to the bottom when men on the screen (who were just as large as Boris, though whiter in the face) fell down flights of stairs.

Johann reflected.

"Perhaps the monster is in love with Boris, too," he said.

I was so shocked by this joke that to cover my embarrassment I blurted out:

"Well, I'm in love with you!"

Johann's eyes widened as he stared at me. I thought his glasses were going to fall off his nose. He looked at me hard. Then he smiled and touched my nose lightly, once.

"Dear Hilda," he said. "I don't think I have time in my life yet for love."

In a funny way I wasn't disappointed by this remark. Indeed, I felt quite excited. I certainly felt quite beyond any embarrassment at having made such a declaration to him. His reply had conferred on him some sort of complicity in a relationship with me. At the very least our friendship had moved on to a new plane. He didn't seem at all put out, and was just as friendly with me as he was before.

"Take no notice of Kleinblut," he concluded. "You can always scream out, and we will all come running."

"I suppose so," I said.

"Including Boris."

"Yes. Including Boris. Thank you."

Johann took his work far more seriously than I did. He practised eight hours a day, and also worked at his own compositions. Most of my other friends, like Ilena and Nina, were instrumentalists who were always late for an orchestral rehearsal. Boris was not the only one who had a job. It left me feeling exposed, idle, unserious. And when I saw Kleinblut talking with my father in the lobby one afternoon I felt alarmed. What could either be saying to the other? They both, I felt, had some reason to point out that I shouldn't be at the Conservatoire at all, that it was all a romantic girl's dream, the indulgence of an amateur with a home in the country and a small apartment on Peranski Street (large enough to accommodate my own piano, my maid Maddalejna, and of course my little dog

Mouse). But which of them was saying it? Was my father not a little bit proud of me? Didn't the lecherous Kleinblut want me to remain his pupil? Surely I was safe?

Yes, but seeing them together didn't seem at all safe.

At Christmas there was, as always, a great pretence of family affection and reunion. It was all organised by my aunt Teg, my mother's younger sister, with the assistance of her two daughters, little cousins of mine still young enough to be excited by Christmas and too young for them ever to have been cousins I played with, or even much met. There were a few other relations and friends, a great-aunt, a bachelor uncle who would always call in briefly with *rumtopf* and disappear once the tree had been lit. They were all from my mother's side of the family, of course, and like the estate itself seemed to be part of my inheritance. One year I went to my aunt Teg's, but somehow it wasn't the same. There was no room for anyone else. There was an understanding that really we had Christmas on the estate, for which my aunt Teg had an exaggeratedly sentimental feeling, to say that unlike my mother she was too young to remember having visited it as a child. It had belonged then to a great-uncle on my grandmother's side, whom nobody much remembered except for a probably invented story about his finding a bear at one of the back windows on a winter evening, firing his gun at it and hitting his own foot. My mother had never believed this story at all. "There are no bears between here and the Carpathians," she would say. "Uncle Lucasz had been drinking holly beer with the servants, and was showing off."

I missed my mother. Perhaps that was why I liked Aunt Teg so much, though they were as different as peas and beans.

Aunt Teg didn't like my father, but her idea of Christmas was to include everyone who should be included. I didn't think he would come. I knew he was living with someone now in Gomsza. I had never seen her, but I guessed she would not be the sort of woman he could bring to a big family Christmas on the estate. I would much rather have asked Johann, but I knew that he would without question be spending the festivities with his elderly parents. I had seen the little presents he had bought for them, all neatly wrapped up weeks before.

My father did come. I realised that it had been over a year since he had last been on the estate. He had had words with the bailiff, who had ended by reminding him that he who pays the piper calls the tune. I don't think my father ever forgave me for inheriting the estate. He never forgave my grandmother. I don't think he forgave even my mother. But what was there to forgive? He must have known all along that it was to be kept on our side of the family. It happens all the time. It was his own fault for putting so much into it, for building it up into a business. That was his greed.

My heart sank when his carriage drew up at the door, and it sank even further when I saw that he had brought his cello. That sound laid a kind of claim to the house that went beyond personal presence. He was going to play for us, and the floorboards, the cupboards, the rafters, the great fireplace, all would receive and send back his playing. The house became an innocent sounding-board, soaking up and hoarding his demonic eloquence. It was a kind of infection. You could never scrub the sounds out of the wood.

He hated Mouse. He kicked at her when she scampered up to him as he descended from the carriage. I felt it as though he were kicking me. He was insulting to poor Grigory, who came over on Christmas Eve. He was cold with Aunt Teg. It wasn't easy to see why he came at all.

Then I found out that he wanted to talk to me about Kleinblut, to tell me all that Kleinblut could do for me, and how much Kleinblut admired me, and what I was to do about it. He was both very unclear about this and was all too clear. It was innuendo of the most indelicate kind, and I suppose some version of it has dripped from the lips of opportunist fathers of marriageable daughters since the dawn of time. When he hinted that Kleinblut could arrange for me to give a performance at Court, I became impatient. I told him in plain terms that I knew by now that I was nothing out of the ordinary as a pianist and that I had come to terms with the fact. I told him that my feelings were engaged elsewhere (he presumed Grigory, I think, for he knew nothing of Johann) and that I found Kleinblut disgusting. When my father began to describe Kleinblut as a man of passion, a notorious romantic little short of a Teutonic knight-at-arms or a minnesinger of old, and claimed that disgust was the first sign of erotic attraction, I was compelled to laugh out loud, if only to hide my embarrassment. What father ever negotiated his only daughter in this way?

I wondered to what depths my father had sunk in other ways to obtain advancement at Court. I knew that Kleinblut had influence there, for the Arch-Duke himself had honoured us with his presence at our end-of-the-year concert, and Kleinblut of course performed at Court himself. I had seen them together at the concert where all eyes had naturally been upon them. I had thought the Arch-Duke the most glorious-looking man I had ever seen in my life. Beside him, Kleinblut seemed as suave and commonplace as a major-domo. I did not see how he could possibly have the romantic reputation he was supposed to have, and neither Ilena or Nina or any of my friends at the Conservatoire could see it either.

Then, on Christmas Day itself, my father did the most terrible thing. It was in the afternoon, normally a time of somnolence and aimlessness and trivialities, that Aunt Teg proposed that he played for us. Poor Aunt Teg. She meant well. She always wants everyone to be perfectly happy, even those who ignore or despise her. My father had no time for her, that was true, but he had brought his instrument and obviously expected to play. Someone had to ask him.

He played his favourite Bach, and I couldn't help admiring the performance. The gravity and deliberation of the unaccompanied cello is like a mathematician ruling lines, or a diver coming up with pearls.

Not everyone liked it. The great-aunt went to sleep. The girls looked restless: there was a silver dish of confectionery on the bureau that they had been helping themselves to all day, and I noticed that their eyes kept straying to it. Aunt Teg most inappropriately sat with a great smile on her face as though she were being seated on a donkey or having her photograph taken or undergoing any of the simple pleasures of life. But I knew that

Bach was not really for her one of these pleasures. The smile was pure duty.

After the slow introductory movement, my father moved into an allegro. Mouse, who was sitting in my lap with her chin thrust forward on my knee, staring at the cello in puzzlement as though a tree could not become a cow or a cow become a tree without someone having explained it to her already, pricked up her ears. My father was attacking the strings with a particular insistence and fury, born perhaps of his words to me a few hours earlier, and of my righteous defiance. At any rate, at the jab of each semiquaver the end of his bow darted towards the assembled company like a rat's sharp nose.

Such was the nature of the music that this movement was throughout as regular as the action of a loom. I noticed with some anxiety that not only were Mouse's ears cocked, but her little head was moving round and round with the action of the bow. She was becoming more and more excited.

Then she started to growl. Her growl was always very miniature and delicate, a kind of croon. But it was audible. I saw the flash of resentment in my father's eyes. He was already playing with such energy that his angry awareness of Mouse gave him a dangerous look such as I had never known.

Suddenly Mouse was pushing forward against my hands, scrabbling at my knees to get down. If only she were frightened and trying to get away! But I knew that she was seized with a desire to catch and eat whatever creature it was that lived on the tree-cow. The more I restrained her, the more her sharp claws dug into my knees. I must have relaxed with the pain, for she was in a moment on the floor and scampering towards the cello, barking and snapping at the bow.

I am sure that in that moment I could hear on the edge of my consciousness a fond little laugh from Aunt Teg, but it was not enough to defuse the tension. I suppose I expected my father to kick out, as he so often did at Mouse, but I had not reckoned on the difficulty of kicking out while you are sitting down and at the same time holding something between your knees. My father was not the sort of man to be patient in such a situation, in the hope that someone would quickly retrieve the dog. Before I had time to grab Mouse, who was making little leaps at the bow, my father had broken off his playing and stood up. This was unheard of. My father took all his performances, even domestic ones, extremely seriously. This was like interrupting the priest during the elevation of the host. But the priest would never have done what my father did. In his rage he lifted his cello and stabbed at Mouse with it. He didn't just shoo her away with it, but lifted it and brought the spike down hard on her. I've seen them standing in the river shallows, spearing salmon. It was like that. Except that those grey fishermen, who had probably been up since dawn, had infinite patience, and even a kind of devoted gentleness. My father had only their accuracy.

Everyone was on their feet at Mouse's scream of pain. There was a general confusion, a desire both to console me and pacify my father, a kind of social excitement that contained, I reflected afterwards, as much relief from the formality of the music as concern for the dog. I doubt if anyone saw at the time, as I all too clearly did, how the spike went into her side. He had to shake her free of it before she could escape, slithering and yelping over the polished floorboards. Later, after I had found her hiding in a barn, I took her to Grigory and held her while he dressed the wound. It became infected, and Mouse died, the day before I was due back at the Conservatoire. I don't think my father ever knew. He certainly wouldn't have cared.

I was now even more unnerved by Kleinblut's attentions. In so many ways it was impossible to benefit properly from his teaching without accepting a degree of intimacy. All musical techniques have, for performers, a physical and emotional context. What the fingers may do the wrist and the arm must allow them to do, and the arm reaches through the shoulder to the bowed or erect expressiveness of the head, which is the cradle of the directing mind. We could not discuss physiology without discussing feelings as well. There are tricks which the mind may perform, tricks which the mind as well as the fingers may learn. And I had not realised how many there were. I was eager to acquire all this knowledge. And sometimes, after long hours of work, grateful for enlightenment and eager for praise, I would accept the small glass of sweet wine that he would pour for me and find myself smiling at his words of encouragement.

I was not prepared for the direct approach he made. For one thing, I had never experienced anything like it, not from Johann certainly, nor Grigory, nor from any of the hot-blooded young males who had fluttered into the candlelight of my freedom. How therefore could I have feared it? He took my right hand in his right hand, quite as though to put it back on the miniature stairway of the piano keyboard like a small animal or wound-up toy to perform its mechanical paces. But he put it instead hard against the front of his trousers where I was blushingly made aware of a small animal of a livelier sort altogether. Do I say small? In that hideous instant before I drew away my hand it felt as large as did the memory of poor Mouse when I used to stroke her from her head to the tip of her adorable tail. Kleinblut was by no means put out at my horror.

"Wouldn't you like it, my dear?" he asked simply. "I'm sure you would. And do not be put off by this." (He held up the stump of his left hand.) "Ask your friends. I am a better lover with this. It makes me more resourceful."

He laughed as I ran from the room.

"You are getting on swimmingly," said Johann. His dry manner gave nothing away as usual, but I sensed that he was jealous. He despised Kleinblut and every other tutor at the Conservatoire.

"I just want to learn, Johann," I said. "That's what I'm here for." I felt guilty about not telling him everything.

But he continued to claim that Kleinblut, despite his early brilliance as a performer, had nothing to teach him. He was, Johann claimed, just another of the many stranded dinosaurs of nineteenth-century pianism. What was needed now, he said, was a new acerbity, a new classicism.

"Kleinblut's architectonics are nothing more than a simple confusion of means," he said. "He thinks the piano should really sound like an orchestra, layered and busy and full of tone. That's all nonsense."

"It is?" I asked, admiring the singleness of Johann's thin pale face and refined, if eccentric, purpose.

"Of course," he replied. "The piano is really a percussion instrument."

To prove it, he took me to one of the empty practice rooms and played to me. It was music of a kind that I had simply never heard before, and went a good way beyond the impressionistic French piece he had played for Kleinblut in its unlicensed combinations of notes. It was far from impressionistic in style, and reminded me in its dry angularities and pounding insistence of nothing so much as a sarcastic argument in a cutlery drawer.

"I can see," I said, "that you don't believe in melody."

"Ah, melody!" exclaimed Johann. "That sickness of the bourgeois soul. I call it malady."

He burrowed in his music-case.

"Try this with me," he said, pulling out a manuscript. "This might appeal to you. Take the right-hand part."

It was a piano duet. I saw that the left-hand part was black with regular note-clusters like the footprints of a chimerical beast while the right hand played mostly in unison, and played, moreover, what looked suspiciously like a tune. The opening chord, however, required a bass-note. I looked at him in puzzlement. Should I lean across him?

"Reach round my back," he said seriously.

I couldn't help giggling. He nodded us in and we played the first chord. It sounded so unlikely that I simply collapsed with laughter. A sound made me look up.

Kleinblut was standing in the doorway staring at us. I managed to refrain from snorting with laughter again, but only just. I felt quite incapable and glanced at Johann in the hope that he would attempt some explanation. His face was impassive, the head tilted, a slight smile on his face. He was simply looking down his long nose at the keyboard with a quiet sense of being in complete command of all its resources. He was waiting to resume. When I looked back, Kleinblut had gone.

It was from that moment that our troubles began. Fate linked Johann and I in more ways than one. From being so physically close we developed emotional ties that were stronger even than the rhythms of his music. And we were united in our being objects of the concentrated attention of Kleinblut.

He seemed to hate Johann with a new fervour, even as he made every attempt to ingratiate himself with me. He offered me all kinds of favours, even as he set about destroying Johann's career at the Conservatoire. How could he not see that these things were quite incompatible? The trouble with all men of power and charm and arrogance is that they cannot believe that anyone will not immediately fall in with their plans. Johann was a little like that himself.

Perhaps this similarity of character, slight as it was, led me to treat Kleinblut more indulgently than I should have done. That, and my natural respect for him as a teacher. God knows I can have done nothing to encourage any of his attentions. I should not, I know, have returned for any more lessons, but he seemed oblivious of the incident, and we were working on a new sonata. It is easy to forgive.

But Kleinblut was not to be easily put off. Through my father again I received something that sounded like a respectable offer. How could I not be suspicious? When I asked point-blank if Kleinblut meant to marry me, my father prevaricated. I thought his behaviour despicable, and told him so. I also told him that I was in love with Johann Schmeck, and intended to go with him to Dresden where he had a job at the Opera when he had graduated.

"That mad Jew?" laughed my father. "Oh yes, I've heard about him. And what job does he have at the Dresden Opera? Watering the horses?"

"As a matter of fact," I replied coolly, "he is not a Jew, and they are going to perform his opera based on Gogol's *Government Inspector*."

That made him shut up all right. His face looked like a tragic mask. But a week or so later I received a letter from my father's lawyers forbidding my marriage without my father's consent until I had attained my majority (still eighteen months ahead) and pointing out that until that date there were aspects of my possession of the estate, particularly of my enjoyment of some of the income from it, that were to say the least questionable, and that they had been instructed urgently to question them. I would be hearing more from them shortly.

Really, I thought, there was nothing to stop me from leaving for Dresden immediately. I no longer cared whether I graduated or not. Johann certainly did not, since he had long declared that there was nothing more that he could learn at the Conservatoire. I felt inclined to defy my father, and took the precaution of consulting my own firm of lawyers on all the matters about which he had been threatening me.

Johann wanted to complete the engraving of his first musical publication. From the mass of music that he had written (including many elaborate scores, ballets, songs and what not, dating back to his eighth year) he had chosen to have conferred upon it the dignity of the title of *Opus One* a series of six little piano pieces entitled *Coruscations*, and he was going to dedicate them to me. I was so proud! No music publisher in Gomsza would touch them because they looked so strange: attenuated, contrapuntal, the left hand usually playing in a different key from the right hand. So Johann was publishing them himself, even to etching the plates and running off the sheets in the basement of the Conservatoire where there were facilities of that sort for the production of choral parts. He cared nothing for his lessons, insulted Kleinblut, even insulted my father, refused to collect the Gold Medal that they were compelled to give him as the Conservatoire's most gifted pupil, and in short achieved such notoriety that everyone felt sure that some vast retribution was at hand. He, and I too, were objects of wonder, pointed at in corridors like doomed romantics.

Doomed, indeed. I was at home one morning in my apartment helping Maddalejna to finish the week's laundry (I did not trust her to iron my silk blouses), when there was an insistent ringing on the doorbell. Ilena had brought me news that Johann had been taken to the hospital after a terrible accident at the Conservatoire. She did not know how it could have happened, but it was the acid they used to make the engraved plates. Somehow it had got on to his face, and on to his hand. He had been working there alone late on the previous night. The caretaker heard his screams. Nobody else was about. He must have been tired. And careless.

I did not care that I ruined my best shantung blouse as I stood there listening to Ilena. I was aghast, knowing in my heart somehow that it was all my fault. I must have said as much to her as we made our way to the hospital.

"How can it be your fault?" she asked sympathetically, pressing my hands.

I murmured some nonsense about his poverty, the expense of our friendship, his desire to make money from his Opus One. I did not know how much she guessed, but I could not bring myself to say anything about my father's reckless pimping or about Kleinblut's shameless lust for me, both, as I guessed, the immediate cause of their jealous hatred of Johann and of his musical genius. Besides, as I looked sideways in the carriage at Ilena, at her full lip, downy cheek and haunted restless eyes, I could not help thinking of Kleinblut's leer and his words to me on that dreadful morning: "Ask your friends." Then I remembered how it had been Ilena who had told me about my father coming to teach at the Conservatoire. How much did she know about my father, and why? I decided to keep silent. She must have known a good deal in any case, but I was not going to tell her more.

And how much more was there to tell? How could either Kleinblut or my father be responsible for Johann's accident, much as they had reason to hate him as an impediment to their strange desires?

I was to learn the answer to that at the hospital.

There was my poor Johann propped in the ward with bandaged face and hand. I knew the instant I saw him that he could never have brought such a calamity upon himself through carelessness. I noticed on the bedside table his eye-glasses, the ribbon shrivelled to a burnt knot, the lens clouded with acid, and realised the horrific implications. My heart lurched. I feared for him. I knew in my heart that we must escape as soon as possible from the web of hostility I had unwittingly woven for him.

"Oh Johann," I cried. "Who has done this to you?"

He could not speak, of course. But he gave me the unequivocal and expected answer by slowly raising and holding out to me his poor damaged hand. He lifted it slightly, more than once, to draw particular attention to it, turning it into a meaningful symbol.

It was his left hand.

7

The Principle of the Purloined Sphinx

ROMUALD, RADIM AND Rudolf were silent when Józef/Hilda had finished her story. They were in some ways hypnotised by her. As she talked, she would lean forward with a gleam in her eyes, touching their hands briefly for emphasis. The old waiter had brought their sausages, and these they had eaten, hardly tasting them or knowing what they were.

She told her story with passion, continually brushing her hair not so much back, but up between her long rather bony fingers. It was impossible to imagine what her hair might have been like before she had so savagely cut it.

'So you see,' she said, 'why we had to leave.'

'Not quite,' said Romuald. 'You had a lot to leave behind.'

'Your musical career,' said Rudolf.

'The apple orchards,' added Radim.

'You could have gone to the police,' said Romuald.

Hilda looked balefully at him.

'That would have been quite hopeless,' she said. 'Don't you see? Johann is a poor student. Some of his friends are politically active. It would have been quite easy for the authorities to make him out to be an insurrectionist. The apple orchards won't get up and walk away. It's not in their nature to do so. Everyone is leaving some part of Gomsza behind, aren't they? Even you, Romuald. Not everything you love is stowed in pigskin, is it? But will Vera be the same when you eventually return? My apple orchards will be.'

Rudolf looked shrewdly at her.

'Perhaps you haven't told us everything?' he suggested. 'Is Johann in fact an insurrectionist? I can't think why you imagine you are being pursued. It would be in the interest of Kleinblut to have as little fuss as possible. Are you sure that your young friend is not wanted for blowing up the post office?'

'Johann is an artist,' declared Hilda. 'How could his friends have ever entrusted him with such an important mission. Besides . . . I never met any of his friends.'

Rudolf raised his eyebrows, and Hilda blushed slightly at her inconsequence.

'Well,' said Romuald. 'There is probably more in this than meets the eye.'

'Or less,' said Rudolf, looking at Hilda with a twinkle in his own. 'As a matter of fact, I find it rather hard now to keep your stories distinct in my mind. It is like one of those transformation scenes so popular in our parents' youth. You know, the peaceful mountain scene with shepherds ignoring their flocks in the noonday heat. You hold it up in front of a lamp and lo, it is Vesuvius erupting at night and citizens fleeing in terror. All done with cardboard, scissors and tissue-paper. In the same way we have Pyramur the timid man, the tender player, the cuckold, the cherished father. And lo, we have a cruel Pyramur, a demonic player, a rogue and a sadist. Tissue-paper. We have a dutiful son, and we have a rebellious daughter. Tissue-paper. We have the seductive Kleinblut and we have the repulsive Kleinblut. Isn't all of it, my dear young lady, accomplished with tissue-paper?'

'It is certainly accomplished,' put in Romuald. 'I wish we could have got stories like that for the *Inquisitor*.'

'I assure you,' said Hilda solemnly, 'that we *are* being pursued and that we are in the gravest danger.'

Radim thought that he could see tears gathering in the corners of her eyes. The false moustache was just slightly crooked. She looked pathetic and faintly ridiculous, like a drunk caught cheating at cards. Rudolf pursued:

‘And aren’t your disguises just a little outré?’ he said. ‘The wheelchair, the maid (who I take it is your own Maddalejna), the travesty?’

‘I was thinking that, too,’ said Radim.

‘You are forgetting the bandages,’ said Hilda. ‘How would you hide a bandaged face?’

‘How would I indeed? I’ve no idea,’ said Radim.

‘I know what I would have done,’ said Rudolf. ‘There’s a principle involved here, that of exploiting the obvious. Did you ever read about the theft of the Sphinx of Syracuse? No? It was a famous Greek coin, a common drachma, but on it a unique representation of the Sphinx of Oedipus. There was no other like it, and it belonged to the Russian collector, Count Mravetsky. It was stolen from him by an impoverished student hired as one of a band of fiddlers to play at a reception given in honour of the coin, in the very week of its acquisition. A young man not unlike your fiancé, if I might say so.’

‘You may not say so,’ said Hilda, ‘if you are implying that all poor music students are thieves.’

‘Not at all, not at all,’ said Rudolf. ‘But this young man was out of the usual run of thieves. He was something of a genius at making things disappear. This was one of his early efforts, but among the most audacious. Everyone was searched, of course, including the Count’s distinguished guests. Even their wives, perhaps particularly their wives, were searched. This silver bauble, so attractive in itself as it rested on its little baize nest, set in an ebony pedestal, was priceless. And irresistible. The Count suspected one of the ladies extremely, a woman whose teasing made him feel as Oedipus must have felt, a woman he desired who had virtually rebutted him, a woman who was something of an adventuress.

‘Well, he had her searched. He had everyone searched. He had them all searched so thoroughly that by the end of the evening he had lost not only the Sphinx of Syracuse but most of his friends as well. And the servants. And the fiddlers. He perhaps trusted his servants more than his friends, so he next paid great attention to the fiddlers. He looked inside their shoes. He looked inside their violins. He wondered if one of them could possibly have swallowed it. They all had to turn out their pockets.

'He couldn't find it. He had to let them all go in the end. But the student *had* taken the coin. It was simply in his purse with a handful of silver roubles of roughly the same size. The Count had been searching in unusual places, and in one or two embarrassingly unusual places at that, which was why he became such a social leper afterwards. He did not dream of examining the obvious place, a purse. The obvious is too often held to be of little account. This is one of the foibles of human psychology, and despite its being well-known is always liable to catch you out. This is why illusionists like myself rely on it so much. It is the first of the the basic principles of our profession.

'The poor Count was in fact triply ruined. Not only did he lose the coin, and the friendship of his insulted guests, but he suffered the mortification of finally losing a handsome woman whom he still had some hopes of finally winning. You see, the adroit student had been in the pay of the adventuress. They left the country together, and on the proceeds of the Sphinx, which they sold to a collector in Boston, they set up together in a life of crime.'

'And what happened to the Count?' asked Radim.

'Nothing happened to the Count,' said Rudolf. 'Nothing had to happen to the Count, did it? The story doesn't require anything to happen to him.'

'I feel sorry for him, that's all,' said Radim.

'You haven't yet explained,' said Hilda, 'how, according to the first principle of conjuring, you would have effected Johann's disguise.'

'Oh, that's simple,' replied Rudolf. 'Don't you see? The problem is the bandaged face and hand, isn't it? So on the principle of the Sphinx you don't hide them, you make them more obvious in order to render them comparatively unnoticeable. I would have bandaged Johann completely, and put him in a Pharaonic sarcophagus.'

'You call that unnoticeable?' laughed Hilda.

'I did say "relatively",' said Rudolf. 'Less noticeable than a black hood and a wheelchair, anyway. More of a recognisable thing, shall we say, though unusual.'

'Sometimes you don't notice the unusual thing at all,' agreed Romuald. 'Like the coal fire in August. It was staring me in the face and I didn't notice.'

'It would even,' continued Rudolf, 'have been preferable simply to leave the face openly bandaged, put him on a stretcher and dress yourself as a nurse. Or better still, as a nun. This is an important corollary of the Sphinx principle: not only do you hide things in the obvious place and make them therefore obvious and unnoticed, but you go so far as to make them more like themselves. Pursuers expect disguise, so it is a great refinement to take the thing in the opposite direction.'

Their plates were being cleared, the congealing remains of sausage and sauerkraut and boiled potatoes scraped on to one plate which the waiter held in his left hand, the other plates stacked on the left arm, the knives separated from the forks and laid at right-angles across them. But it was not the same waiter. It was not the old man who had tumbled to Hilda's disguise and been appeased with a small tip. It was a tall dark-haired young man with an extremely narrow forehead.

'Stewed apricots?' he recited. 'Stewed mirabelles? Cheese?'

'Everything!' exclaimed Rudolf, clapping his hands in mock enthusiasm. 'We'll have everything. We're still extremely hungry.'

The waiter lowered his eyelids in deference and disappeared.

Hilda bent her head conspiratorially and looked at her three companions.

'Did you,' she whispered fiercely, 'see that?'

'What?' asked Romuald.

'The waiter,' she said. 'That man pretending to be a waiter.'

'What about the waiter?' said Radim.

'Don't look at him,' she hissed. 'Don't look round, Rudolf.'

'Why not?' asked Rudolf, looking round.

'*Don't* look round, I said,' groaned Hilda.

'It's all right,' said Romuald. 'He's not there. He's gone to the kitchen.'

'Of course,' said Rudolf. 'To fetch our mirabelles.'

'I'm sure he's not a waiter,' said Hilda. 'He's spying on us. Where's the real waiter?'

'I expect the old fellow went off to the bar to spend that money you gave him,' said Rudolf. 'Or perhaps he's losing it to the ticket collector at cards. Perhaps he's off duty. Perhaps he's having something to eat himself. Perhaps he's turning into a werewolf.'

'Talking of having something to eat himself,' said Radim, 'when will Johann get something to eat?'

Hilda looked blank for a second. The young waiter was clearly obsessing her.

'Oh,' she said. 'Maddalejna is looking after him. He can't show himself here.'

'Why do you think we're being spied on?' asked Rudolf.

'You don't really have to ask me that, do you?' said Hilda. 'They're not letting just everyone leave the country.'

'Do you really think that Volo Kleinblut, Principal of the Conservatoire of Music, has a professional spy on every train leaving Gomsza?' said Rudolf.

'I'm not saying that he's spying on me,' replied Hilda. 'He could be spying on Romuald here. Or Radim. Or you. We don't know why you're leaving the country, do we? The authorities might not like it.'

'The authorities can mind their own business,' said Rudolf. 'My reasons for leaving Gomsza are quite private.'

'So are mine,' said Radim.

'Perhaps you could tell us what they are?' suggested Hilda. 'I seem to have been talking rather a lot so far on this journey. Romuald has already kindly obliged.'

'There are some things which are painful to bring into the light,' said Rudolf. 'You appear actually to enjoy telling stories.'

'Sometimes circumstances force us to give an account of ourselves,' said Hilda. 'And perhaps, if like Romuald here, and myself, you are making a complete break with the past, it would be helpful to confront it?'

'Perhaps it would,' admitted Rudolf uneasily. 'Perhaps Radim then would like to go first?'

Radim seemed to be equally reluctant.

'How do I know where to begin?' he complained. 'I do not know the real causes of anything in my life. Do you? Does anyone? If I think of the reason why I am leaving Gomsza I am immediately forced to think of a reason for that reason, and then a reason for that further reason, and so on. It takes me back into the whole past.'

'Tell us everything,' said Hilda warmly. 'After all, I have recounted all of my life.'

'In several dramatically different versions,' said Rudolf.

Hilda put a finger to her lips to silence him and turned her attention again to Radim.

'Come,' she said. 'Begin where you will, and do not mind reasons too much.'

'I will try to find them,' said Radim. 'But like the Sphinx of Syracuse they will be hidden among many other common counters of ordinary life. Like most painters I am inclined to give an equal value to everything that I perceive. But I will put into the foreground those incidents that seem to me to be of the greatest significance.'

Just then, the train hurtled into a tunnel. They had begun to leave the central Gomszan plains and were entering the rolling limestone of West Gomsza and Lower Wallenmar. It seemed a fitting moment for a new story to begin. Rudolf replenished their glasses. The lights dimmed for a moment and the sound of the train surrounded them with a resonance bequeathed by sooty brick, an enlarged thunder that was like being inside the body of a musical instrument.

'First,' said Rudolf, 'a toast. To the success of your elopement!'

'Thank you,' said Hilda. 'And if I may, I will drink to you. My three musketeers!'

They all drank, and half of Hilda's moustache disappeared completely. Then they settled down to listen.

8

The Problem of Pictorial Space

THERE HAVE BEEN only two passions in my life (said Radim). The first was to solve the problem of pictorial space; the second was a girl called Alma Sospiri.

I first met Alma years ago when I was a student at the Institute. I was very poor, just like your Johann. I remember on the day I heard that I had won my scholarship my father gave me his best suit and a little leather purse with ten gold sosti in it.

"It is the money I have saved from *barscwa*," he said. "You will need many things at the Institute, canvas, brushes, paint . . . It will be very expensive."

Barscwa, as I expect you know, is the quantity of wine left in the barrel when the wine is first piped off the lees. No one thinks that it is worth bothering with, for the filtering it would need, just a few inches of sludge. But as cellar foreman my father could lay claim to it as a perquisite if he could be bothered. He spent many unpaid evenings at the cellars, collecting and filtering the *barscwa*. It was worth no more than heel-taps, and the labour was enormous, standing in the hot fumes of the barrels, shovelling out the must. My father was proud of his *barscwa*, though, and produced it on important family occasions with a quiet air of virtue and triumph. It acquired a kind of sacred function of ennoblement or approval, like patrimony. It paid for the operation on my grandfather's leg when it was trapped in the harvester. It paid for my sister

Alizia's wedding, with twenty fiddlers playing until three in the morning.

I tell you all this not only to show you the kind of family I came from, but to make you understand what a shock it was to me to find that the *barscwa* money I had been given was no great amount to some of the students at the Institute. Indeed, the moment I arrived there word was going around that a dissolute fellow in his third year, called Arnis, had just lost such a sum at faro.

They were great swells, some of these senior students. I don't believe they ever stretched a canvas in their lives. They affected coats with great lapels and shiny buttons, and wore swords, in a bizarre imitation of military uniform. They swaggered down the street with girls on their arms. They were always almost completely drunk.

And there was I with my purse and my father's best suit.

"Take care of yourself, little Radim," my mother had said. But I think they had neither of them realised that I was no longer little. Without anyone noticing, I had pushed out to six feet, with shoulders to match, and my father's best suit made me look what I was: a country boy in the city, his clothes too tight, showing too much wrist.

I didn't mind. I was too intent on doing what I had come to do. The *barscwa* bought enough paint and canvas to satisfy a Delacroix, and my tiny scholarship (how handsome it had seemed to my parents!) was enough to pay for lodgings on Racubik Street, where most of the houses had attic rooms with skylights, and for a diet of salt buns and radishes and cucumbers.

And so it was that I set out to solve the problem of pictorial space.

The professors, of course, had no idea of it. To them it was enough to take up one's position in front of a picturesque landscape, squint at it knowingly while vigorously mixing the customary pigments, and then begin to daub. Oh, there were rules of composition. I learned about the golden section and lines of perspective. If an important oil-painting were to be produced from a preliminary sketch squared over, there was much talk about how nature's grand appearances were best to be re-arranged for the canvas. There was never any question of taking nature for granted. They could let photography do that. Art was something else.

I do believe that some of those old professors in those days were even ready to recommend the judicious placing in the landscape of a small rustic temple or heathen shrine, as if to appease the still-watchful gods of neo-classicism.

The cleverest students, those who were aware, for example, of what was being done in France, were to my mind no better. (You will forgive me for saying this, Hilda, since your Johann has more recent Gallic developments in mind, it seems.) There was one, Modor, with whom I used to talk endlessly about my problem. And he, though he reviled the professors as much as I did, could never understand what I was after. I think that was because he was himself far *too* obsessed with nature. For him, the play of light on a decanter or an orchard was enough to send him into paroxysms of excitement. The only problem for him was to capture this light in his palette.

"I don't find it!" he would exclaim, as though he had mislaid a tube. "Where is this light? I can see it, so I must be able to create it!"

For me, such effects had been quite satisfactorily achieved by the Dutch, centuries ago. I did not believe that problems of representation were anything more than a painter's routine language, or at best his parlour tricks of expression. We had all mastered these little touches of shadow and highlight. They were among the things that the professors could tell us.

But Modor still went into metaphysical ecstasies about his orchards. He would stare for days at a single apple on a plate, just a simple sour green apple on a white enamelled plate. He would stare at it until it grew brown, or until worms started to wave from it, as though they were bored with waiting inside and had come out to see what was going on.

Nothing was going on. Modor was staring at the apple, his oils still corked, his brushes dry.

I liked the fellow well enough. For one thing, he was almost as poor as I was, so we could starve and argue together in perfect friendship. For another, he lived quite alone and was terrified of women. So many of the other students had some girl in tow, pretending to be a muse or a harlot, and succeeding in nothing so much as being a giggling nuisance.

He had no wish to paint the female form, being in love with apples. And I had no wish to paint any kind of human form, being absorbed by my problem of pictorial space.

All that was to change completely, of course, but for the moment we were model students.

My problem began by being simple and ended by being complicated, quite the wrong way round for a problem if you ever want to solve it. It was not so much that I did not see where the boundaries of my canvas should be placed in relation to my viewpoint of the subject. It was that I did not see why they should appear anywhere. Not, I hasten to say, anywhere at all, but anywhere in particular.

I knew that historically such a problem had arisen because of the accumulated freedom of subject and occasion for painting it. In the beginning was the absolute necessity of sympathetic magic. The bison of Lascaux galloped across the hidden ceilings of caves in a kind of free space created by nature herself. Then art was contained in buildings that man had made. But even then the constraints were necessarily liberating: in the quarterspherical space above a chapel alcove the duologue of the Annunciation achieved its practised form, the ascending triangular shape of praying Virgin, the descending triangular shape of angel with folded wings. And so on. What upset me, I suppose, was that I was working entirely in the age of secular art and therefore liberated from these functional constraints. Ours is an age of museums, isn't it? Museums and drawing-rooms, where the dictates of space are merely cultural and financial, a refinement beyond function.

And therefore, in my opinion, reducing the artist to being the producer of a mindless commodity, a mere slave of space.

There was much in my opinions in those days that belonged inevitably to the callow iconoclasm of youth. The museum at Gomsza was, give or take a gallery or two, devoted to the pious memory of local talent, full of minor masterpieces. And I don't suppose that at that date I had ever been in a real drawing-room in my life. But this was the foundation of my theory. It was the core of a problem that was to continue to obsess me.

The first thing I did was to paint triangular canvases, the idea being, as I remember it, to deprive the jaded eye of its four accustomed compass points. This brought a certain notoriety to a student barely into his second year, as you may imagine. The professors hardly knew what to make of it, but were, I think, impressed by the purely painterly qualities of these canvases, which were nearly all concerned with the rock formations of the Wallenmar Mountains behind Szptz. I had travelled there during my first Spring vacation in the company of Modor and Koblim, another student who had already decided to become a sculptor and who had heard of these rocks and decided that it would be useful to be "influenced" by them.

In the event, at our joint exhibition in the smaller *salle* of the Institute in October, Koblim produced only one piece, and that he had had neither the time nor the money to have cast. It was an Andromeda, chained on some typically Wallenmar boulders and looking in terror at the spectator who had, in consequence, to imagine himself a monster when he had much rather imagine himself a Perseus. Modor of course showed his apples, which had become purely platonic apples; that is to say, they were tenuous performances of self-appraisal through reflection of light, maps of surface hinting at presence only, little coloured ghosts of apples. At a distance they might have been rocks . . . or shells, or teapots, or almost anything. My Wallenmar rocks were certainly rocks, and couldn't be mistaken for anything else. But that wasn't their point. It was the triangular canvases (and triangular frames) that took the eye.

There was quite a crush on the evening of the private view, even though none of us could afford to provide free schnapps or wine as many of the exhibiting students would do, to encourage their contemporaries to come along. In our case, no encouragement seemed to be necessary. The *salle* was packed.

It was on this occasion that I first saw Alma. Alma! How can I describe her as she was then?

She entered on the arm of Arnis, who had come with some of his friends to scoff at our work (work which was quite beyond his own capabilities). She did not clutch at his arm as some of the shop girls did, sluttishly, fearful of losing an impressive catch, but carried her arm delicately around and under his as though it were a large bouquet of flowers that she had just been given as an accolade for some performance of which she had already forgotten to be proud. Her nose and mouth and chin were perhaps the finest things about her, cleanly and sharply moulded, and standing in such a mysterious and meaningful relationship to one another that the only thing I wanted to do was to cover them with kisses. Since that was impossible, I could only stare.

She must have been used to it, for she looked round the *salle* boldly as if to invite attention, and when her glance met mine she stared through me as if I weren't there . . . or worse, as if I were a painting whose techniques she recognised or despised.

I asked Modor who she was, but of course he didn't know. He was not interested in girls.

"That little hunchback?" he said. "She looks pretty vicious to me."

I was outraged. Alma Sospiri was certainly not tall, and she had the habit of peering in front of her in a way that lowered her neck (I later discovered that she was short-sighted, but refused to wear spectacles in public). But to describe her as hunchbacked! I began to look upon Modor in a new light from that moment, and whatever residual interest I may have had in his apples soon evaporated. They were, like their creator, utterly sterile.

Why then had we attracted such a crowd? I was foolish enough to think that if Modor's ghost-apples could be discounted as sufficient objects of interest, then I had really hit the bulls-eye with my triangular canvases. What pathetic egotism!

It was Modor who gloomily put me right:

"It's Koblim's nude they've all come to see, you realise?"

Of course. How could I have believed in a sudden access of genuine interest in art at the Institute, knowing as I did how demoralised, dissolute and amateurish most of its students were? It was indeed the grossly naked Andromeda they had come to see, and towards which, in a pretendedly casual and indirect sort of way, they soon drifted, talking all the time and affecting not to notice any of the exhibits.

I suppose I should have been shattered, but for some reason I felt elated. Koblim's mythological piece was pure academic kitsch, and no doubt if it were not soon touched and prodded into oblivion he would eventually get it cast and it would win the Institute Prize. I didn't care. I wished him joy of it.

I stood there in a kind of manic triumph. I stood there acknowledging my destiny in my father's pathetic best suit. I knew that my collar had come open. I was hot and ruffled, and all I could hear in that crowded room was the rather high-pitched and lecherous laugh of the now doubly-hated Arnis.

My father died that Christmas, and it was discovered that the vineyard provided no pension. I did all that I could while I was at home, but there was no arguing with his employers. If my mother had been left quite alone there would have been no question but she would have gone to live with my sister Alizia and her husband. But there was also her own elder sister living at home, my Aunt Lydia, who was a bit mad and fancied herself an invalid. Alizia's husband made it quite clear that he wouldn't take them both in, even if the house were to be sold to provide an annuity for the two old women. There was nothing for it but to make my mother an allowance to enable her and Aunt Lydia to continue living in the way they were used to. That was the end of my scholarship. I searched the house all over for some hidden *barscwa*, looking in rarely used teapots, even up the chimney, but if my father had any money salted away I couldn't find it. I returned to Gomsza knowing that I now had to earn a living if I were to stay in Racubik Street. I had indeed to earn a living if I were to stay alive at all: it was what the phrase meant, I reflected grimly.

This turn of events was to have a great effect on my life. It brought me first to portrait painting, and then it brought me to Alma.

My immediate thoughts about earning money were the sort of crazy things that always occur to young people who have never earned any before. I imagined that I would buy ancient gold coins from old women on lonely farms and sell them again to dealers. I thought of inventing some quite novel article of domestic use that everyone would realise they had always wanted, and that would bring me thousands in a few months. I would join a regiment of hussars, and be promoted for bravery. It was Koblim who showed me the folly of all this.

"Why not do what you know you can do?" he said. "Why not just paint? You can paint the portraits of civic dignitaries and ask a couple of hundred sosti a time."

To my objections that I was not at all sure of obtaining a good likeness, he said that it didn't matter a bit, but that I should be careful always to include somewhere in the portrait some evidence of the sitter's wealth, taste or material success.

It was an infallible recipe. I felt at first that I had sold out like Koblim himself (who was now designing erotic lampstands) but the necessity of a regular income soon made me forget my artistic qualms. Besides, the activity itself soon provided its own interest, one not unrelated, I found, to my long-standing worries about pictorial space.

I began in a small way. I painted Koblim and Modor, for practice, and I painted some of the Faculty, those who were vain and parsimonious enough not to have already satisfied their vanity in the studio of a reputable portraitist, men like Professor Prufski, Dr Lenz, and his friend Dr Casimir of the theology department. I suppose I must after all have caught some of their appearance and character, for I soon no longer had to beg for the opportunity as a poor student. I began to be known. After only a year I was asked to paint the official portrait of the retiring Mayor of Gomsza, in preference to two or three quite well-known names who were all competing for the commission. I considered this a distinct tribute to my abilities, and began to advertise, quite discreetly, in the better papers, although Modor went out of his way to say that he'd heard that the other competing painters had merely priced themselves out of the market. The Mayor's portrait was much praised when it was hung in the Long Room at the City Hall, and I began to be approached by other civic dignitaries, and by local businessmen. It was soon after this, Rudolf, that I painted your own portrait for the Club. I remember being particularly gratified that they hung it in the dining room next to the great picture of Balatuz as the Prince of Denmark. It made a sort of exciting theatrical corner over by the buffet. Members would attack the cold goose as though fighting a stage duel.

Triangularity was a thing of the past. Soon I was able to afford the most elaborate conventional frames, heavily moulded and gilded with leaves and fruit and the occasional cupidon. And, of course, a new suit.

This activity kept the agonising over my spatial problem alive because rocks don't have eyes. The painter looks closely at the eroded pillars and scooped domes, but they don't look back at him. I realised this one day when sorting through some of my old sketches. There was one of a twenty-foot boulder veined with granite that the wind had hollowed into the shape of a skull, but I had provided it with a sinister glower and a triangular frame suited to its slightly adjusted shape. The point was that you saw it as a skull, and (I had hoped) found yourself staring at it across a crowded room. But its eyes were blank. It no more looked back at you than the rocks did. I then saw that the key to pictorial space lay not in the viewer's bearings. Deprived of his compass points, he will simply assume them. The key lay in the *reason* for his gaze in the first place. Why was the viewer there? What was his relationship with the subject of the painting? More challengingly, what was his relationship with the one person who had always, no matter how many people had viewed the painting, had a prior relationship with the subject of the painting, that is to say the painter himself?

As I looked into the eyes of Tito Sospiri, now and then squinting, stooping or holding up my thumb to provide that little bit of dramatic "business" which sitters expected and which was part of what they had paid for, I would think of myself not as the originator of his portrait, but as one of the many hundreds, perhaps thousands, of later viewers of it who would speculate on his relationship with me by examining carefully the sardonic thrust of the lower lip or the critically-appraising glint in the eye. Would that amused, half-aggressive, half-grudgingly respectful look have been *really* playing over the wealthy manufacturer's face at the time? Or was it put there wishfully by the cunning upstart painter who even then knew that he wished to marry the manufacturer's daughter, and could hardly believe his good fortune in having the opportunity to call at the Sospiris' house every day for weeks on end?

Sospiri's father had been a tanner, a stubborn Garibaldino forced eventually to leave his native Milan and make use of his skills elsewhere. The fortunes of the Sospiris had been built upon some of his traditional processes put to work on the hides of a particular kind of wild boar that roamed the Wallenmar Mountains. The man I was painting had no other skill than the business acumen which had exploited his father's secrets, but that was enough. Gomsza pigskin was famous throughout Europe: as mysteriously soft as silk, it was nonetheless tough enough to make boots. I believe that there is a tradition that the Arch-Duke's private guard wear nothing else on their feet at all times. Well, the Italians have always had a way with leather. As they also have with women.

And the qualities of Sospiri pigskin, as I was to discover, were also shared by his only daughter, Alma.

After our sessions she would appear, moody and ironic at the tea-urn, handing us pickled blackberries and sour cream, or chestnut cake and honey. I was astounded at first at how different she seemed from the assured creature of the Institute *salle* where I had first seen her, or in one or two of the student cabarets where she had turned up on the arm of Jackowski or Arnis or some other idle layabout of that time. Her father expressed surprise that we did not know each other, and I think the fact that we did not pleased him: at least *I* was not therefore one of those layabouts. She seemed resigned to having a "past", and for this to be the keynote of her reputation within the family, a subject of distant and polite concern like a skin condition or a duty that could not be shared.

She was older than I thought her, with a voice made husky by secret cigarette smoking and an assertiveness which blazed out suddenly, usually behind closed doors, at some frustrating family issue. I began to be asked to dinner, and frequently had the opportunity of long conversations with her. I would explain my ideas to her, eagerly creating hypothetical space above my untouched soup with my hands, and singeing the backs of my knuckles in the candle flames.

"It is the depth of space that matters," I would say, looking into the depth of Alma's black eyes. She would stare intently back, with a little suppressed laugh, half of admiration, half of timidity. I suppose she had every reason to think me deranged.

"But the crucial depth is not the depth of the subject itself, within it, around it, behind it."

"Of course not," agreed Alma, taking a tiny sip of wine.

"The early painters all tended to make that mistake. They were terrifically excited by perspective and insisted on ostentatious feats of distance. Every Madonna had to have a whole city-state half-seen through a window behind her, like a maze leading the eye away. The eye shouldn't be led away. The eye must be transformed."

I myself felt transformed by eloquence, and in my eyes Alma was transformed. I had thought her astoundingly beautiful at first sight, but her attentive company, her close proximity . . . ! I think those days at the Sospiris' were among the happiest of my life. It was perpetual summer, ice clinking in jugs of lemonade, the hammock strung between the sycamore trees, ready like a musical instrument to respond to the idle moods of guests who were invited to make it taut and themselves relaxed. To think that if I had been a more professional portraitist Tito Sospiri would have had to come to *me*, to my studio, for his sittings! I might never have met Alma in the easy, natural and engaging way that I did.

9

The Interlude of the Waiter's Knees

RADIM PAUSED, WHILE the waiter, who had earlier brought them bowls of fruit and baskets of cheese, came to clear their plates. Once again, braced against the motion of the train, he showed great expertise at stacking and balancing the crockery.

'Will there be anything else, gentlemen?' he asked.

'More vodka,' said Rudolf. 'Or do you have any brandy?'

'There is some Georgian brandy, sir.'

'No cognac?'

'I will see, sir.'

The waiter went back into the kitchen, walking almost as much sideways as straight ahead to compensate for the lurch of the carriage.

Hilda followed him with her eyes, openly suspicious and apparently oblivious of the lopsidedness of her false upper lip.

'Did you see his knees?' she asked, meaningfully.

'His knees?' laughed Rudolf. 'I can't say that I noticed his *knees*, no.'

'Look at his knees,' said Hilda with great intensity. 'Look at his knees and tell me what you think. And look carefully at his clothes generally.'

'He looks like a perfectly ordinary waiter to me,' said Rudolf. 'He's even rather an efficient waiter, actually. In fact I don't know when I've come across a better one. He's a great improvement on the first one, the one you bribed. I'm not quite sure *why* you bribed him. But it seemed to have the effect of getting rid of him, which is no bad thing, I venture to think.'

'Efficient, yes!' exploded Hilda. 'That's it! He's far *too* efficient.'

She nodded up and down energetically with her eyes fixed approvingly on Rudolf's. It was as though her eyes were attached invisibly to his own and the movement of her head designed to detach them. She seemed in an odd sort of way to enjoy her terror of the waiter. It was a means of thrusting her into conspiracy with the three men.

Again Rudolf was mesmerised by her. For a moment he could think of nothing sensible to say, though required to say something.

'Why don't you get rid of the rest of the moustache?' he said. 'It won't fool anyone.'

Without her eyes leaving his face she whipped off the little half-curtain of bristle and burst into a broad smile. Was she after all, thus revealed, beautiful? Rudolf could not have answered such a theoretical question, but at that moment, still hooked by her gaze, he felt the tell-tale sign of attraction, that little muscular spasm, barely more than a shiver, that runs like a drop of rain down a window from just below each hip to the area of the knees.

'His knees,' said the shock-haired Hilda, as though she were performing some formal act of somatic telepathy. Rudolf for a moment wondered if the waiter's knees were melting too.

'Look at the knees,' she itemised. 'Consider the efficiency. And consider his dress. I leave aside for now the question of his sudden appearance, just at the moment when the old waiter discovered my disguise. But you could bear that in mind as well.'

'My father used to work for Sospiri,' said Romuald, as though he had not been listening to all this. 'Or at least, he worked for a firm that had dealings with Sospiri. He was a dealer in small leather goods, mostly wallets and comb-cases, that sort of stuff. I once accompanied him to a trade fair in Lyskow when I was a small boy, and I remember him talking to this large perfumed man with waxed moustaches. They shook hands, I remember, and my poor father seemed overjoyed. "That was Mr Sospiri," he said. The name impressed itself on me. It was a name that I had seen on a card of watch-straps, printed within a black-bordered red lozenge in letters of swelling size, the central "P" being twice the size of the first and last letters of the name. Children remember things like that.'

'Yes,' said Radim. 'He was a big manufacturer at one time.'

'You don't see the name much now,' said Romuald.

'I'll tell you about that,' said Radim.

'My father worked himself to death selling watch-straps,' said Romuald. 'It wouldn't have been so bad just going round the stores in Gomsza itself, but he had to visit all the villages in the South-Eastern region of the country. He used to be away for months on end, and his horse would collapse between the shafts of his trap. It was all useless anyway. Peasants don't wear watches or carry wallets.'

The suspect waiter returned.

'Your cognac, sir,' he said, placing fresh glasses on the table. 'For everyone?'

They all nodded or murmured assent, and the waiter filled the glasses to their meniscus from a dark dusty bottle that appeared to be freshly broached. He retired.

'Did you notice?' asked Rudolf. 'Hine '82. Now that's what I call service!'

Radim was staring at his glass, with its amber liquid trembling at its brink.

'How can I drink this without spilling it?' he asked.

'How did he pour it without spilling it?' laughed Romuald.

Rudolf privately reflected that Hilda could pour out her eyes without spilling them. It was a case of direct transference, like an injection of cognac into the bloodstream.

'There you are,' said Hilda. 'What real waiter can obtain Hine '82? On a *train*?'

The three men looked at each other. Was this becoming an obsession?

'No train has such cognac. No Gomszan train, anyway,' she said. 'Everything is consumed before the train arrives here. Where did he get it from? And have you ever known a waiter on a train who could wait? This fellow is doing it by the book. I mean, if you were a political agent and had to disguise yourself as a waiter, you *would* learn how to do it, wouldn't you? And end up doing it more perfectly than a real waiter. You wouldn't *know* that real waiters never do it like that.'

Rudolf pondered.

'He might simply be a new waiter,' he said. 'Or a trainee.'

'Too old,' replied Hilda. 'And the dress, there's something wrong with his dress.'

'Quite smart,' said Rudolf. 'Neat, formal. Better than the old one, who I do believe was wearing carpet slippers.'

'*Too* smart,' said Hilda. 'I don't think he was wearing waiter's clothes at all.'

She bit her lip in concentration.

'Too smart?' laughed Rudolf. 'Too old? I wouldn't complain. And why do you speak of a "political agent"? I thought it was you who was frightened of being pursued? I don't think the rest of us, with the possible exception of Romuald here (who isn't listening to a word we're saying), *have* any political connections at all.'

'Yes I am,' said Romuald. 'And I don't. I'm not running away with any national secrets, no unpublished scandals, no confidential files. I should think they're glad to get rid of me. In another few years they'd have made me the fishing correspondent.'

'I take no interest in politics,' said Radim. 'As I believe I have said before.'

'Wait,' said Hilda, deep in thought. 'You're right, of course. I was just generalising when I said "political". The point is that he's watching someone, and I think it's one of us. In fact I'm sure it's me, because I've just worked out who he must really be.'

'Who?' asked Rudolf, Romuald and Radim, almost simultaneously.

'First tell me what you noticed about the knees.'

'Chalky,' said Romuald.

'Dirty,' said Radim.

'A mark left by a coat-hanger?' suggested Rudolf. 'A line of compacted wardrobe dust, intensified by a long-standing fold in the trousers? Half-way down, at the point where it would hang thus at the knee?'

'Oh very good!' exclaimed Hilda, clapping her hands. 'You must have been employed at one time as a detective. Do you read detective novels? My mother was keen on English detective fiction, *The Mysteries of Charlock Elms* and so on. They all take place in country houses.'

'So you think he has hired his waiter's outfit?' asked Rudolf, basking in her flattery.

'Well, no, as a matter of fact I don't,' said Hilda. 'If he had done, he would surely have hired a proper one. He has learned to carry four plates on one arm, so surely he would have bothered to hire the correct dining-room garb. No, look at the cut of the jacket when he comes back. It's formal wear, but it must be his own, for convenience. And very well worn at that. It's not dining-room, but concert-room wear. Now you can see why I felt haunted. He's a performing musician.'

'Good Lord,' said Rudolf, not knowing whether to begin to believe this or not. 'What about the knees?'

'The mark across the knees, gentlemen,' said Hilda dramatically, 'is neither chalk nor wardrobe dust. It is rosin.'

'Rosin?'

Rudolf was lost.

'Rubbed off from the bow on to the knees in savage and difficult allegro passages,' said Hilda with a decisive finality. 'Our spy is a cellist.'

'I say!'

Rudolf sat back in his seat in amazement. There was indeed a curious logic in this tortured explanation. A cellist-waiter-spy!

'Your father!' he eurekaed.

'I should think I ought to know my own father. He is a satyr to this Hyperion,' she snorted.

'I mean, sent by your father,' he said.

'Do you think so?' She pondered this as though the suggestion had come entirely from Rudolf. 'Do you really think so? What will he do to me?'

'If he tries to do anything to you,' said Radim, 'I will throw him out of the train.' Powerfully built as Radim was, he said this with such a benign and considered inflection that the others laughed.

'I'm sure we would all quite satisfactorily spring to your defence, my dear,' said Rudolf. 'Can it really be so? Is he biding his time? Is he eavesdropping?'

'If he is,' mused Romuald, 'I wonder how edifying he finds it? All he can have got so far is a rather unusual lesson in the theory of painting.'

'Don't forget the amorous interest in our friend's story,' said Rudolf. 'I was particularly enjoying that.'

'You can have more of it if you like,' said Radim. 'I hadn't got very far.'

'Yes, please,' said Romuald.

'But what are we to do about Miss Pyramur's musical spy? I must say that he has brought us a delicious cognac.'

Rudolf had nearly finished his glass.

'But you know,' he added. 'One thing suggests to me that he may be a real waiter after all.'

'What's that?' asked Romuald.

'He didn't think to provide proper brandy glasses. These little schnapps thimbles are hopeless. And just what any waiter on an international express *would* provide. Now I like a large balloon. It allows room for contemplation.'

Rudolf rolled the liquid round his mouth and through his teeth, and gave a little shiver of pleasure. Then he winked at Hilda, emboldened by the alcohol they had consumed.

'Well,' she said. 'I can see that none of you are taking this very seriously.'

'Yes we are,' countered Rudolf. 'We *are*. It's just that we are enjoying ourselves. We are quite ready to take it seriously when it comes. Whatever "it" is.'

'I'd like you to take it seriously now,' said Hilda. 'Why don't you go into the kitchen and see what he's up to?'

'Oh,' said Rudolf, taken aback.

'I will,' said Romuald, getting up. 'I don't expect he's up to anything much at all. Then we can get on with Radim's story. I want to hear more about the Sospiris.'

He was away down the aisle and out of the carriage before anyone could say anything, bumping inexpertly into the other tables as he went, and bowing theatrically to a lady in the far corner, who turned out to be the mother of the little dog Florian, whom she was feeding with pieces of ginger cake.

'Impetuous fool,' said Rudolf. 'Perhaps he'll be shot.'

'Stop laughing at me,' said Hilda.

'Very far from my thoughts,' replied Rudolf, looking at her. She moved quickly away from the subject, though not with embarrassment, merely a kind of complicit delicacy. She toyed with the stem of one of the flowers in a little silver vase on their table.

'When do you think we shall reach the frontier?'

Rudolf consulted his watch.

'Not for some hours yet, I'm afraid,' he said.

'That doesn't worry me,' said Hilda. 'All the more time to hear your stories.' She turned her gaze on Radim.

'I used to paint in watercolours once,' she said. 'Little vases of flowers just like this one.'

Radim beamed, but said nothing. What could he say?

'All women,' she said sadly, 'pretend that it is something they can do.'

Romuald appeared at the end of the dining-car and made his way to their table.

'That was quick,' said Rudolf. 'What did you see?'

Romuald sat down and took a sip of cognac.

'I'm afraid I saw our spy putting away a large jar of bottled mirabelles,' he said. 'They belonged on a rather high shelf in the galley, and he was having to kneel on one of the working surfaces to put it away.'

'Oh,' said Hilda.

'And this working-surface seemed to be covered with chopped cabbage-stalks, potato-peelings . . . and flour.'

'Flour,' said Rudolf.

'Oh,' said Hilda again. 'Oh dear. Kneeling on the edge of a table covered with flour. I see.'

There was a thoughtful pause.

'And what did you do?' asked Rudolf.

'Well,' said Romuald. 'I felt a complete fool, of course. Our old waiter was sitting in a corner, cutting his corns. You were right: he had been wearing carpet slippers.'

'I suppose,' said Hilda, 'that's what a corner is for.'

'What?'

'Cutting your corns.'

She giggled. Romuald didn't seem amused.

'I thought I'd better say how much we liked the brandy,' he said. 'Then I asked for the bill.'

'You didn't ask for some more brandy at the same time, I suppose?' asked Rudolf.

'I did, as a matter of fact,' said Romuald.

'Good man,' said Rudolf. 'Now, having disposed of our illusory spy, perhaps we can have the rest of Radim's story.'

10

The Trick of the Transformed Spectator

MY COURTSHIP OF Alma (continued Radim) seemed as natural to me as sitting down to a meal that had been prepared for me, and to which I had been freely invited.

We played tennis, at which she beat me easily. She would laugh and tousle my hair and call me a great bear. Her parents looked on all this with more than tolerance. They even seemed to be encouraging me. It never occurred to me to wonder why. It never occurred to me to wonder where all her suitors might be; all those eligible Captains, Italian cousins, favoured sons of colleagues urged by their fathers to make a match, pigskin with lace, pigskin with cotton, pigskin with tobacco, pigskin with anything, pigskin with plain banknotes – but pigskin with pigment? I could understand that Alma's Bohemian life had been suddenly purged, without lasting recrimination. The family, like that of so many Italians, was close and affectionate. Alma's mother, a knitting version of her daughter some twenty kilos heavier, was forever bringing her cold drinks, stroking her cheek, looking at her, looking at me, laughing. It was a household full of laughter and perfume, full of cakes, jokes, smoking. Alma was an only child, rebellious no doubt on that account, somewhat indulged.

It was not until after we were married, and Alma bore a child within five months, that the truth of the matter came home to me. Sospiri had paid for our honeymoon, at Interlaken in the Bernese

Oberland. The excitement of travel and the unbroken proximity to Alma, combined with mountains, light and rich food, had made me dizzy with happiness. I fondly thought the child mine until the early accouchement produced a three-kilo infant, fully mature. But it was not mine. It was a child of Bohemia. It may have been anyone's child, Doranyi's, Sortz's, the insufferable Arnis's. It could even have been Koblim's for all I knew: several of his athletic or ecstatic bearers of table lamps, all lifted knees, throats and camisoles, bore a striking likeness to Alma in my eyes. Perhaps I was simply besotted with the female body, as a young husband must inevitably be. I would see these lamps in the parlours of the nouveaux-riches I was commissioned to paint, small men of unnatural means, agents for the property of others, smelling of aniseed, and I would seethe and growl and hum with fury as I painted them, as though they, too, merely in the fashionable possession of a Koblim ornament had therefore known my Alma too intimately for my comfort. It made no difference that there had been no opportunity for Alma to have known Koblim during her months of social experiment at the Institute: my jealousy was vast and irrational.

What a fool I was! It must have been a conspiracy of the whole family to legitimise this child of sin. And to think that I had not arranged matters so that my mother and Aunt Lydia could attend the wedding, because I was ashamed of them! The Sospiris were not fit to polish their shoes.

You may wonder how Alma came out of all this. This little girl with olive skin and a direct stare, whose kisses were like the nibbled quarters of freshly cut figs! In her case I was a double fool.

I was expected, you see, as a young painter of humble origins full of talent and ambition, to take Alma and her bastard in my stride. Why should I care? I had the girl I wanted. I had the support and respect of her family for coming to her rescue. But from my point of view I was an object of derision, you see, and in my pride I turned down every opportunity of accepting largesse from the Sospiris, until they gave up trying, imagining me such a genius (or at least so stubborn) that I would prefer to forge my career on my own and be entirely responsible for Alma and little Tito. That didn't worry them in the slightest, and when Sospiri died after five years or so I discovered why. He was mortgaged to the hilt, had a mistress in Prukow on whom he had spent literally tens of thousands, and left barely enough for Mamma Sospiri to live on. At all events, having refused an allowance for years (refused it, that is to say, on Alma's behalf) I discovered that in the end I had nothing. I suspected that Alma had been well supplied personally while her father was alive, but I was not in a position to know much about that, or to do anything at all about it. As far as I was concerned we had nothing and I was content to have nothing. I wanted to have as little to do with this family as possible.

They had played on me the oldest trick in the world, and I raged and sulked like the cuckold in a farce. All it needed, as I came to see, was a little rueful acceptance on my part, a shrug, a graceful acknowledgement that I had been duped, something of that sort. If I had been prepared to take the rough with the smooth in this way, I dare say we should have settled down well enough, Alma and I. But I was not prepared to be so philosophical about it. I retreated into my shell.

And so, having just for a moment (one blissful moment!) almost got her, been on the verge of a quiet sort of triumph, turning out to be someone she really could, after all, trust, despite the initial deception, someone who was, indeed, her great "bear", a bestower of kisses, someone prepared to endorse his clumsy professions of undying love with real down-to-earth daily loyalty, I was revealed in one instant in my true colours as a romantic opportunist, a time-server, a hurt betrayer, a lover of self.

Oh, we got along in our way, Alma and I, since in the nature of things we had little alternative. I was not going to abandon her and the baby, after all, and she had already chosen (or, with whatever protracted family debates and consultation, had been induced to choose) this particular solution to her little "problem". We had made our bed, and we both knew that we had to lie in it.

Somehow, in the midst of our fury and shame, we created something like that sacred space that is the definition of a family life, and for my part I created it defiantly, in opposition to anything that was Sospiri – the Sospiri caution, the Sospiri sensuality, the

Sospiri secrecy, the Sospiri appetite for little cakes at three o'clock in the afternoon. I was reckless, untidy, single-minded and puritanical in my renewed artistic quest, and I threw the life of the emotions to the winds. I was through with all that for ever. Alma, little Alma! Like a bruised yellow peach, still firm to the touch, still not absolutely spoilt, a child of gravity and of the sun!

I looked away, and when I looked back the years had intervened as stealthily and certainly as creeping and conspiratorial children. Her son, from being a creature as in need of attendance and anointment as a dying man or a corpse, grew to a monstrous independence which grieved Alma, who for nearly half her life had had no care but his. She lived for him, only for him, and I let her. Once he had grown up and begun to look beyond her world, only then did she take an interest in me.

For one thing, she discovered that basically, in Sospiri terms, we were poor. We could only keep one horse, who was frequently out of sorts, so that our diligence rusted in the mews. We could afford sole, but not lobster. There came a day when haddock appeared more often on the table than sole. Alma urged me to expand my range, to seek new commissions. Why was I not chosen to supply the murals of the new Opera House? Why had I not painted the Arch-Duke and his family? Why was I not better known? Even Modor was now well-known in avant-garde circles, famous in particular for leaving patches of his canvases bare, as though to indicate an unquenchable honesty in the face of the mysteries of vision.

I was not jealous of Modor, or of anyone else for that matter, but I would have liked to please Alma. I had only to see her beautiful rounded shoulders and the curious thrusting angle of her neck to be seized with the twin desire of making her perfectly comfortable and happy, and of covering them with half-savage kisses, like a cat nuzzling its fur.

But I could no more rationally connect our material happiness with my innermost ambitions as a painter than I could connect my passion for Alma with the biological future of the human race. If she had neglected me for little Tito, it was perhaps only as a response to my neglecting her for my studies in pictorial space. Did she give up on me, or did I give up on her? I shall never now know the answer to that, I suppose.

I wanted to find a satisfactory medium for my ideas, as a lover wants to find some fulfilling means of expressing his love. I suppose I was in fact in both positions; both of them theoretical, impossible, frustrating. The painter is dissatisfied with the bounds set upon his art; the lover frets at the limitations of the body. Both are a claim upon space.

I wasn't content, you see, with symbols, with conventions. That figure reclining in the bottom left-hand corner of a pastoral scene might be a shepherd resting in the heat of the day, or he might represent the painter himself viewing his own landscape, but what he really signifies is something to do with the shape and composition of the painting. He is saying in effect: 'The painting is going to come to an end down here soon, and I am looking out and away up there in order to distract you from the fact.'

I was not sure how I could conquer space by doing away with such symbols. I studied something of the psychology of vision, and observed how the eye scans whatever lies within its field. This helped me to see that the way the eye behaves is precisely the key to whatever the painter chooses to present to it – rather like training a dog to do certain tricks. The eye glances here, and there, and over there, and back again but not quite in the same place. It is the ocular mapping of that frontal arena which the body, by facing that way, must be prepared to act in, to defend, to control. Now, if we had eyes all round, like flies! What would fly art be like, I wondered? I even tried to sketch a landscape with a 180 degree span. My method, crude as it was, was borrowed from certain geographical projections. I would have done better to have bent the paper.

Modor returned from Paris, and told me at dinner of a new French painter who composed his paintings as artlessly as if a camera's shutter had been released prematurely, before the subjects had composed themselves within its lens. His subjects were bathers, actresses, ballet-dancers tying their shoes in the wings of the theatre, and the effect was that of voyeurism, the subject seen at a squint, as it were, because the onlooker should not have been there in the first place.

Modor looked so tired, and thin. And yes, old. Alma insisted that he took a second portion of honey cake and fussed around him in a way that irritated me. It was my old jealousy, I suppose, even though I thought of Modor as an entirely passionless creature. Perhaps for this reason I became irritable.

"Your libertine painter doesn't interest me," I said. "It's typical of the French to find new ways of dignifying the erotic."

"The French have found new ways of seeing everything," he replied.

"And I suppose you are eager to return to Paris to play your part in this new revolution?" I retorted. I thought I saw him glance at Alma briefly before he gave his enigmatic reply.

"I shall have to see," he said, taking up his slice of honey cake. I loathed the way he ate this cake. We had, after all, provided forks. It was one of the ingrained Sospiri traditions that had survived in our family. Not that I used one myself. But I would have expected a guest to use one.

He lifted the dripping wedge high in the air in his bony fingers, higher than he needed to in my opinion, higher than his mouth. The result was, that to bite it he had to bite upwards. It was quite disgusting. Just as disgusting as I imagined his friend's ballet-dancers to be, clutching their toes and exposing their soft white bottoms, skimpily clad in tulle.

"And what are you working on now?" he asked. "What is your plan?"

The question was so professional. So direct. I realised that it came with the artless intimacy of old friendship. And I also realised that in spite of all my obsessions, my continued consciousness of problems that needed a radical solution, I did not have anything like a "plan". Most of my work suddenly seemed of little importance, mere violation of Institute rules, mere caprice, no more mature than the triangular canvases of my youth. And in a way, yes, working on not dissimilar lines from his balletomane friend, in the sense that I had discovered ways of ignoring the formal limits of the area of canvas at my disposal.

Alma was pouring coffee. The thin black stream with its comforting aroma induced me to make some confident reply that would be an equal sign of my affluence. Lighting a cigar with much display of fire and judicious sucking, I replied:

"My plan . . . my plan is to increase the angle of vision. My plan is to maximise space."

"And how do you do that?" asked Modor. He had eaten and drunk rather too much, I could see, and was likely to be argumentative. I was forced to extemporise.

"Why, by bending the canvas, of course," I replied.

"A panorama!" exclaimed Modor, with a sort of leer I had never seen on his face before. "A peep-show!"

"Not at all, not at all," I said. I refused to say more but fetched the schnapps. A few more glasses and Modor would be unfit for debate, and I would be relieved from the necessity of explaining any further a project that I had not yet thought through at all.

Modor stayed with us for a while. Despite my irritation (and I suppose I had always in some way or other felt irritated by Modor) I was in a strange way excited. Not so much by his news of the latest Parisian excesses as by the feeling that I could now define my own intentions more clearly by taking quite a different road, even perhaps (in Modor's scornful terms) the road of the "peepshow".

Something of that kind had occurred to me when I was producing my fly sketches, when I did once or twice bend the paper to see what happened. Now, after Modor's visit, I felt suddenly quite confident that the panorama had fresh possibilities.

Its history belonged to romance and the pure wishfulness of trompe l'œil, although the stage sets and peep-shows of the Baroque period had prepared for it. In 1785 an Irishman called Barker was incarcerated in a tiny prison cell lit by a fanlight and hit upon the idea of painting a semi-circular *veduta* of Edinburgh. He later had a productive career as a purveyor of battle scenes, views of the British fleet of Portsmouth, and other excitements, in a small building in Leicester Square, London. By 1800, similar displays could be seen in Berlin, Paris and Vienna. Daguerre produced three-dimensional dioramas with cunning lighting effects. It is still a popular form of display, as you may know, at exhibitions and trade-fairs. I could understand Modor's incredulous amusement.

But I remembered an example I had seen at Aeschen on our honeymoon, a panorama of the city of Thun painted at the beginning of the last century by Marquand Wocher. It was in a circular, domed wooden structure over twenty metres high, and one entered through a dark corridor leading to a dais which looked out upon this extraordinary spectacle. Even Alma had gasped with pleasure at this bird's-eye view of a small Swiss town as it would have been seen by Goethe and Kleist. The freshness, the quality of light, the variety of human experience to be glimpsed from Wocher's rooftop all round the spectator, made it an unforgettable experience. Why had I not at the time been fired by its techniques? And why had I not remembered it before? I suppose the answer is obvious. I connected it too closely with my feelings of betrayal by my young bride. It symbolised a brief moment of elevated hope and vision, ruined by the commonplace sordidness of life.

Perhaps now, though, I could face this vision with equanimity and build my own artistic quest upon it. I spoke of the family as a kind of sacred space. I'm sure I really believed it, and that to image such space in painting was the noblest artistic endeavour possible.

Are all enclosed spaces areas of enchantment? Does the fact of enclosure allow infinite control of the interior? Hardly, you would think. What is the commonest form of such a space? A room? Do you have power over the space of even the most familiar room? You imagine that the curtains, the lamp-fittings, the furniture and so on, represent the charting, even the creation of the space they inhabit. But no: these objects are intrusions from outside, property of third parties, obeying physical laws that always lead to one disastrous implication: breakdown, stubborn refusal to function, independence, past lives that are nothing to do with the space that they ought to have been created for. And if you try to clear your space of all this historical luggage, what are you left with? The work-space, the studio? The stage of play? Purely potential space? Never: for you are in it yourself, trailing your own pedestrian lumber.

Can you imagine your enchanted space as properly and fruitfully empty? No. Because you always imagine yourself inside imagining it. Think of being outside, on the other hand, and the space might as well not exist, like the inside of a tennis ball. It wouldn't matter what shape it was. The interior space of that spherical shape might be octohedral for all you could tell. And the real space that we inhabit, mundane as it is, full of small models of all likely spaces that its nature and physical laws prescribe, is in fact quite shapeless, a universal space of limitless extension in any direction, without sides or corners.

Sideless and cornerless painting! For me, a canvas did have just these magical qualities that were lacking in any actual space. It was an imaginary and hypothetical space. And because it was imaginary, or at least because what it contained gave it this imaginary status, it could have any actual shape it liked. It had sides. It had corners. That was obvious. And these sides and corners could appear anywhere. So much for my triangular period and my circular period. I could see that all those oddly-shaped canvases had only the point of emphasising the primacy of the imaginary. Suppose the sides and corners need never appear at all? Wouldn't that really be preferable? Wouldn't the imaginary and the real then become as one? All that effort spent on ignoring the edges. All those problems of framing, when by drawing attention to the limits of the enchanted space one helped the spectator to concentrate his attention within it; all such difficulties (including the difficulty of hanging the canvas, the problem of the relationship with other canvases, all irrelevant distractions of display and status) would promptly disappear. You'd be inside the space as man finds himself inside the universe! Or as the artist is inside his studio, but with the artist miraculously absconded! The artist would have been transformed into his work, like a stage illusion. The spectator's sympathy, his aesthetic act of possessing the artist's vision, would be the sole principle of the transformed space. The artist in his vision, the onlooker in the work: both would disappear, and the work of art would become its own world. It would be a way of entering the ball, or of being inside it from the beginning. The work of art is painted for the spectator, who is there from its conception, like the worm in the apple, ignorant of anything that is outside.

So I set about my panorama, which was to show a view of Gomsza from the roof of our house, just as Wocher had represented Thun from the roof of that little house in the Kreuzgasse, all around, a complete 360 degrees. It was lucky that we were not so well off, or we would have been living in one of the suburbs, with a view of nothing at all of interest. As it was, I had simply moved further down Racubik Street when I married Alma, into an apartment which contained not only the attic studio, but the floor beneath it. All I needed was access to the roof, or at least to the flattest part of the roof, for the large skylight was set into the steeply sloping surface of tiles at the front of the house, too dangerous to climb out of.

In my immediate enthusiasm I hacked through the ceiling myself, showering the studio with plaster. There was a tiny roof-space, perhaps part of an older loft, before the houses had been subdivided. It became an obsession with me to create a perfect area of work, within which was contained, in the closest proximity to the view of the subject itself, a ready-made circular mounting of struts and lathes to which would be affixed the sixteen panels of linen, each three metres in width by twenty-four metres in depth, the central twelve metres of each panel being fixed to the battens and stitched together to form a kind of drum lining my studio. I used linen for ease of handling, for there was some fine construction necessary. Six metres of the panelling at both top and bottom were for the moment left unattached. Those at the top simply lay loose over the struts; those at the bottom were already carefully measured and each trimmed to a tapered point. The idea was, you see, to go one better than Wocher and paint not simply a cylindrical panorama (cutting off the landscape at top and bottom in what in effect was an automatic deference to just that tradition of the lateral boundaries of a canvas that I was trying to escape from) but an entire globe of vision, including the zenith of the heavens and the very spot on which the painter is notionally standing. My canvas was finally to be stitched into the shape of the interior of a sphere and entirely covered with pigment.

In the roof space I found a wealth of natural life I had never suspected: scuttling spiders of unlikely size moving as awkwardly as carnival giants; blanched tendrils of the creeper that was more familiar to me in the mature green version that bearded the brick front of the house; the layered papery citadel of a wasps' nest, long vacated. I pushed through all this in my excitement to reach the view that I had never seen before, savouring the anticipation of the future spectator who would pay his fifty copecks to have it recreated for him. I cut through felt cladding, sawed through two joists, dislodged tiles, until I could thrust out my cobwebbed face over the rooftops of Gomsza like an exultant chimneysweep. I shouted with joy at the view, which was better than I could possibly have imagined: to the South, the green copper roof of the Town Hall and the elegant façade of Peranski Street; to the West, the dome of St Nepomuk's, the stone tower of the Institute, the floral ironwork of the railway station; to the North, the tumble-down roofs of the metalworkers' quarter, the Post Office, and in the distance towards the North-West the surprising outline of the nearest range of the Wallenmar Mountains; to the East, the tram-cables stretching in a long L-shape down August 5th Street, a jumble of slum tenements surrounding the granite crenellations of the Penal Institution. That evening it rained, and the next day I called in a builder to do the job properly: a watertight trap-door, a railed platform mounted on the sloping tiles, a fixed ladder on to the roof, and a moveable tower of scaffolding within the studio which gave me equal access to every surface of the panorama and to the brief laddered exit to the roof.

I was aware, as I set about this great enterprise, that I was being observed from a distance, critically. No one knew about it, of course, except Alma and Modor. That knowledge seemed to me to have brought them together, as privileged onlookers, or perhaps, in their view, as the patient guardians of a madman.

Modor would sometimes be in the living-room in the evening when I came down from the studio, obviously eager to inspect the progress of the panorama. I fended him off without difficulty, pouring myself a last trickle of tea from the urn and sinking back on to the sofa with a grunt intended to forbid sympathy or curiosity. I kept Alma away, too, as I wanted it to be a particular surprise for her, a reminder of her delight at Wocher's panorama on the occasion of our honeymoon, perhaps even a kind of gift that might symbolise our reunion. And she would have to be its centre. My vision would be translated into hers, its first spectator.

I did not reckon on Modor. I had become so used to the domesticated Alma, the forgiven Alma, the household dispenser of tea, medicines, cake and dutiful, wifely affection, that I was not ready for the raised ghost of the Bohemian Alma. Modor, lounging in our apartment as if he were in a *boîte* on the Left Bank, inspired in her the distant enthusiasms of her wild youth at the Institute. I remembered all the occasions on which she had urged me to move West to seek my artistic fortune. When I protested that the nature of my profession and the contacts that maintained it absolutely demanded that I stay in Gomsza and accept the civic fruitfulness of that provincialism, she had sulked. How unreasonable women are! She knew perfectly well that portraiture depended upon a local reputation. Our marriage itself was founded upon the fact. But Modor was a reminder of the freedom of her youth. And I do believe that he set out deliberately to encourage her.

Months, years went by, and he showed no intention of returning to Paris. He even contrived some kind of part-time professorship at the Institute, goodness knows how. They must have been short-handed to allow such a wraith to haunt the place, twenty years on; actually to pay him so many sosti a month to demoralise a drawing class with his indecisiveness. I couldn't imagine how he could ever bring himself to sully a sheet of paper with a piece of charcoal, particularly not in front of an apple, and certainly not in front of students. Perhaps at the Institute they believed him to be distinguished in some way.

But an odd thing happened, and it was some time before I really noticed it. And even when I did notice it, I don't think I fully realised the significance of it.

It occurred to me that Modor was a changed man. He no longer seemed quite so drawn and thin. He was older, certainly, as we all were, but not thin any more. He was fleshing out. And at the same time Alma, whose embonpoint over the years had come more and more to resemble Mamma Sospiri's, was now looking unusually trim for her age.

It was only when I happened to see them walking together with our dog (they were just turning the corner into Racubik Street, by the wine shop) that I experienced the full shock. Alma was wearing what I thought was a new blue dress, until I discovered that it was an old one that she had not been able to get into for ten years. Modor was carrying a walking-stick (he may have always carried one, I suppose, leaving it in the hall when he came to see us, but I had not seen it before) and was twirling it in an insouciant manner which I thought quite out of character.

Their transformation was like a conspiracy. They were secretly becoming like each other. This illusion seemed to pass when they set eyes on me: each reassumed the role that they knew I would expect of them. But I had seen enough. Modor represented a dream of escape for Alma, a real starving painter marvelled at for his eccentricities, and she had fed him up into a suitor.

I was amused at this, but thought no more about it. I was too intent on completing the panorama. I had reached the climactic point where I had to remove myself from my own painting and replace myself with my hypothetical spectator.

The problem was this: my perspective was not static, so that any element of horizontal scanning shifted the relationship of the objects within my sight. There was, of course, a practical way to get round this, and in effect each of my sixteen panels had its own perspective. At eye level there was no problem: the eye's natural narrowness of angle of vision allowed the illusion of uninterrupted unity of perspective as it scanned the interior of the globe. But within the area of my feet there was indeed a problem: there would be an absolute conflict between the real platform on which the spectator would inevitably have to stand, and my representation of the rooftop I was seated on in my view of the scene. I could not portray anything of myself or I would become a meaningless revolving blur. I had to paint myself out of the picture altogether.

It was, in those final stages, a most satisfying disappearing trick.

But it was a trick I felt to be real in some way. Every artist disappears from his canvas. In the case of my Gomsza panorama I intended the spectator to *become* the artist, by placing himself entirely at the core of the painter's universe. The spectator will be like the apple-worm, metamorphosed by vision, but paradoxically confined within the globe rather than released from it.

The instant the last stroke of paint was dry I called Alma and "Professor" Modor into the studio and made them climb under the looped and trailing bottom ends of the panels on to the platform inside. Then I sewed the panels together into a perfect sphere around them, while they admired the panorama in silent wonder.

A perfect disappearing trick! To be enclosed entirely from the world outside while at the same time being more completely exposed to an ideal version of it! The illusion was so complete that they would after a moment have no thoughts of looking for a way out.

To lose the will to escape, to be totally absorbed in a confinement, is as certain a barrier to freedom as a lock to which there is no key. But I, the originator, was now truly liberated. I was no longer chained to a passion which was unrequited. I no longer had to make a living to keep up appearances. I no longer needed to suffer the agonising suspicion of having been, or being about to be, cuckolded. I was free to leave!

I carefully folded and packed my panels in the largest container I could find (which happened to be a basket from the hospital laundry in August 5th Street) and made arrangements, as you see, to travel with it to Paris, where I will exhibit it and astound the world.

11

The Rashness of the Pious Prisoner

'BRAVO', CRIED RUDOLF, bringing his hands together in delight. 'That was, if I may say so, an illusion worthy of the theatre. And speaking as a seasoned illusionist, it mystified even me.'

'It's sad that you had nothing to stay for,' said Romuald. 'A whole life evaporated, just like that.'

'You could have left Gomsza long before,' said Hilda.

'But you see,' said Radim, in whom the unusual effort of talking had created a spark of responsive alertness, fuelled by the brandy, 'life isn't like that. It isn't a stagnant pool to persist or not to persist at a whim of the weather. It's more like a river that finds its course. And I had to find my own course and nobody else's. Yes, I could have left long before, but that was what Alma was forever urging me to do, on her terms, to make me successful so that she could feel important. I have never confused artistic success with social success.'

'Forgive me,' said Romuald. 'I simply meant that you appeared from your story really to have loved your wife after all.'

'Love?' said Radim with a laugh. 'What is that?'

Romuald was confused.

'Everything you have said about your wife implies that irrational pattern, that indissoluble link. I'm sure we all felt it in what you said, as we have felt it in our own lives.'

'Links are not indissoluble,' said Radim. 'The keys that lock us together are as easily lost as the keys which keep us apart. They are man-made. So are the chains and locks and closed rooms that they are made for. You yourself were defeated for want of a key.'

'Don't remind me!' cried Romuald. 'It's a disaster! I know it is going to be the greatest regret of my life.'

'Whereas,' said Radim. 'I have at once found the key and thrown it away. You might be said *not* to have found it *and* to have thrown it away. We are both liberated.'

'Liberated?' said Romuald.

'Of course,' said Radim, 'that's why we are on this train. It is obviously the supreme vehicle of liberation, one for which no return tickets are available.'

'We have all seized this single opportunity,' said Hilda. 'And you are quite right. Out there in the dark is another pair of railway lines running silently by the side of the ones rumbling away beneath us. Those lines in theory return to Gomsza. They return to Casimir and Vera, to Modor and Alma, to my father and to Kleinblut. But despite their parallel presence, curving when we curve, ascending when we ascend, ours is after all the one train that can't, as we stare out at those lines, be travelling on them.'

'Indeed not,' said Rudolf. 'And in fact, as we curve to the right, they are curving to the left.'

'And as we ascend,' agreed Hilda, 'they are descending.'

'And as we enter a tunnel,' added Rudolf, 'they are leaving a tunnel. Since we have just done so yet again, and since the dining-car appears to contain a number of partly-open windows, shall we escape these smuts and return to our compartment?'

'A good idea,' said Radim. 'It will symbolise the limit of the returning we are able to accomplish, which is to the truth of our own situations, in particular to the truth of Miss Pyramur's situation. I shall look forward to making the acquaintance at last of the brilliant Mr Schmeck.'

'Ah,' said Hilda, thoughtfully. 'That may not be possible.'

'Not possible?' queried Radim.

'Not yet,' she said.

The roar of the tunnel did not diminish as she smiled at them, and they felt the hectic precipitation of the train as a dramatic back-drop to further secrecy, the dimming of the lights and the rattling of the windows as a sympathetic extension of the wild danger of her smile. What was this smile really like? It had none of the eager conspiratorial frankness of the smiles that had accompanied her stories. It was a smaller, more baleful smile, and the light that played about her lips was intermittent as though her soul were troubled. It was a challenging, even ceremonious smile, inviting alert but submissive responses.

Rudolf was put in mind again of the tissue-paper story of the faithful Hilda's commitment to puzzling genius and to a misbehaving lap-dog. He could not help feeling the disparity between the character of the tale and the character of the teller, the ingénue music student, whose sufferings as a daughter had been met with stoicism, and the nervous adventuress, resourceful in will and deceit. They were as discrepant as the two elder Pyramurs she had created in her two stories, and quite honestly tended to cancel each other out. Such cancelling seemed to lead to the impossibility of believing either. Well, neither story need be true, even though the smiling girl in the pale linen suit was no apparition.

When they returned to their compartment they found the corridor partly blocked by the waterseller's trolley, apparently abandoned. But as they tried to enter the compartment, the waterseller himself came out of it.

'What are you doing in there, you rascal?' said Romuald, gripping him by the ragged collar of what seemed to be an ancient military tunic.

'Nothing, sir, nothing,' said the waterseller, managing to appear at once sullen and outraged.

'You were rifling our belongings,' said Romuald. 'Turn out your pockets!'

'I was seeing if anyone wanted water, sir,' replied the waterseller. 'I haven't taken anything.'

'You could see that the compartment is unoccupied,' said Romuald. 'You had no need to go in. You are not allowed to go in.'

'There's no such rule,' said the waterseller defiantly. And then, encouraged by the absence of contradiction, he foolishly added: 'Besides, all your cases are locked.'

At this, Rudolf burst out laughing. Having played the host, he now felt entitled to take upon himself the leadership of their little party.

'You rogue,' he said. 'Let him go. He can't have taken anything.'

'How do we know?' said Romuald angrily. 'Turn out your pockets!'

The waterseller turned his aggrieved face towards Rudolf, his unexpected protector. His expression, locked into the shiny bony little features, implied a lifetime of persecution, deviousness, stubborn argument and hurt.

'You're quite right, sir,' he said. 'I haven't taken a thing.'

Rudolf, attempting to defuse the situation, reached across to the waterseller's left ear and produced from it a small paper cup.

'What then,' said Rudolf, 'is this?'

Hilda clapped her hands with pleasure, but the waterseller seemed to be unimpressed. He barely glanced at it before replying.

'That's mine, sir,' he said. 'It's one of my cups.'

Rudolf appeared to throw the cup into the trolley, and then reached to the man's ear again to produce another cup. He did it again. And again.

The waterseller's face maintained such a solemnity as Rudolf began to use both hands to produce what seemed to be an impossible number of cups showering from the man's ears into the trolley, that none of the party could stop themselves from laughing.

But when the performance was finished Romuald made him turn out his pockets all the same.

The result was pitiful: a worn leather purse containing a few copecks, a chipped and blackened pipe with a pouch of tobacco that smelled of horse manure, a piece of bread and a cold boiled egg wrapped in a torn red handkerchief. Rudolf looked away. He did not want to expose the man's life in this way. But Romuald persisted.

'Aha! What's this?' he said, after a foray inside the waterseller's tunic. He had in his hand a small tablet with a gilt frame, a varnished image of the Virgin and Child radiant in fawn, vermilion and gold on an umber background, dark-eyed and serene. 'You're not going to tell me that this belongs to you.'

A tear was trickling down the waterseller's nose.

'Sir,' he said. 'That is the one possession of mine that keeps me sane in this wicked world. It is the one thing that has any value for me. And not because of its value to anyone else, I might say. I know nothing of that. I dare say it is hundreds of years old and should be in a museum. But it belongs to me. It was given to me by the bravest man I have ever known.'

They were somewhat chastened by this dignified speech, and Rudolf, who had been preparing to release a stream of small change from the man's nose, slipped the palmed copecks back into his pocket, and instead invited him into their compartment.

'It sounds as if you have a story to tell, my friend,' he said, gently. 'Do tell us how you came by the ikon.'

The waterseller perched himself on the edge of the seat and blotted first one eye and then the other with his handkerchief before folding it and putting it carefully away with the rest of his belongings. He looked at them each in turn, as if to judge the profitability of recounting his story. Suddenly he was no longer cringing: he had in a moment converted his distinction as the focus of attention from the abject to the indulged, like a child pacified or bribed with sweets. He was evidently as practised at judging his audience as a huckster in a Saturday market. It was a moment of pure theatre.

Romuald had thrown himself into a window seat with one arm and elbow against the glass, toying with a lock of his hair and looking at the waterseller with such a gaze of suspicion and critical displeasure that anyone who was less of a real rogue (or, perhaps, less of a truly outraged innocent) would have quailed and faltered into silence. As it was, with Rudolf and Hilda eager for the story, and Radim ready enough for it, though perhaps readier for a doze, the waterseller clearly decided that there was something to be gained from telling it, and proceeded to do so.

There's some point to this story, as a matter of fact (said the water-seller). I heard your political talk in the dining car. Your toasts to freedom and all that. Long live the Arch-Duke, death to the Tsar, and all that sort of talk. I'm sure I don't understand a word of it. As far as I know (correct me if I'm wrong) the Duchy of Gomsza was a part of Russia long before my grandfather was born. My mother was Russian, and I'm as Russian as they come around here, *istniy russkiy chelovek*. I was one of the first platelayers on the Great Siberian Railway in 1891. Ask me who set up the Great Siberian Railway? Do you know? It was Tsar Alexander. The whole world would be nothing but little pieces of this and that without the Tsar. What has the Arch-Duke ever done? Why does he try to go it alone? He must be a stubborn fellow, the Arch-Duke. Well, I know he is. I was there when that anarchist tried to do him in on the platform at Brodcow. I was on maintenance then, greasing the couplings of the royal train. It was the first Gomszan royal carriage, a lovely job by Ringhofer of Prague, walnut panelling, Hensenberger lighting, the lot. The Arch-Duke was just about to get into it when the bomb hit him. But it didn't do more than that. It just thudded into his back like a turnip and fell to his heels. The anarchist was a young chap, rather fat, sweating like a pig. Nobody did anything! I remember thinking that there should have been someone there to do something. The only hussars for yards around were dressed in animal skins and playing some Kraut march with drums and clarinets. Well, the Arch-Duke didn't turn a hair. He just looked over his shoulder as though someone had made a smell. He has this profile like a race-horse. He gave the bomb a little kick with his heel, just like that! It might have been a lap-dog snapping at his heels! It still didn't go off. All it did was trickle along to the edge of the platform and fall underneath the train. You probably remember what happened. It killed the chap who was sent to fish it out. Blew his arms off and split most of the cast-iron bogies. Of course, the Arch-Duke was miles away by then.

I'd love to know what they did to that anarchist. Considering the things they can do to their own troops when it takes their fancy, he can't have been a pretty sight when they'd finished with him. Torture isn't just a profession, it's a frame of mind.

I saw all that when I was a young man on the Eastern Front in '71. It's what I'm going to tell you about.

We could put up with a lot in those days. Most of the lads had been on the land, tricked into the army with drink, fed up with the bad harvests. The comradeship seemed worth a lot then, worth almost everything. All the drill, all the marching: at least it kept you warm. It was better than grubbing in frozen soil for root crops. And there was a billet and a stove at the end of the day. Even when we got near the front it wasn't so bad. A barn instead of a billet, and even bigger fires. Sometimes they got out of hand and the barn would burn down. Or the lads would find the farmer's store of spirit. The farmers were paid well enough for it, anyway. And if the Tsar had been that way before us we were very welcome indeed. Quite a hero's welcome we might get, believe it or not.

It didn't seem a bad life, and we didn't think much about what we were doing. That is, until the villages we came to began to be wholly Russian and the fires and drunkenness led to other things, and there was no compensation. I saw things happen to village girls that I'd be ashamed to tell you about.

Not that there were that many rabid nationalists among us. It was a matter of honour to preserve our frontiers at that time and it was all explained to us ten times a day. You'd be too young to remember any of that. It wasn't as if we were doing any actual fighting. It was all a question of keeping lines of communication open, always had been. The armies passed backwards and forwards. I don't know whether they ever engaged or not. You could imagine the Chiefs of Staff moving little flags on maps laid out in the halls of provincial castles, quite content with the theory of it. It suited the old Arch-Duke to put up a show. Probably it wasn't about frontiers at all. I heard later that it was all about constitutional concessions that the Tsarist bureaucracy wasn't prepared to consider. And if you ask me, the Tsar knew all about it and allowed it to happen. I mean, if the Tsar hadn't allowed Gomsza to have an army, we wouldn't have had one, would we? And there's a limit to what a toy army can do. It can play band music on railway stations, and it can organise farming lads into licensed marauders, but that's about it, isn't it?

Still, when you're hundreds of miles from home and get the rule book thrown at you, the army is the army for all that. Without some sort of discipline it would have been chaos.

I don't pretend to be a saint. I drank my share of looted vodka with the worst of them. I avoided duties. I was insubordinate. And maybe, yes, I was a trickier customer than many. I didn't like a lot of the things I saw, and had less reason than a lot of the lads to hold anything against the Russians themselves.

I honestly don't remember what it was that got me in the guardhouse one day on a serious charge. I'd been in a lot of scrapes, but we all mucked in together and were loyal to our sergeant who was a real old professional who knew what was important and what wasn't. It was the officers mostly who had no sense of proportion. They were pig-ignorant, the lot of them, and made most of it up as they went along. All they cared about was their record. They could buy themselves in and out, you see. It was just a part of their career.

Well, I'd insulted some officer. They kept themselves in the background usually, and if they came around poking their noses into what didn't really concern them they were often surprised at the reaction.

I was sent back to Blot, a small town within Gomszan territory where they actually had a proper prison. We'd passed through it some weeks previously. I don't know what happened to the civilian prisoners. Perhaps they were released. The inhabitants of Blot were a cowed lot. There's money to be made whenever the army sets up headquarters, but no one showed any interest. Things could have been humming, but they seemed ready to abandon their town to the army.

It was very cold. I remember that the cart I was sent back in under armed guard was full of sacking that had frozen. It crackled when I sat on it. The corporals in charge of me were quite friendly. They allowed me to smoke, and talked freely. For them it was an enjoyable change of scene.

It was only when I had been locked up that I began to get the wind up. I'd expected a routine court-martial in front of a senior officer, you see. A chance to show him my harmlessness, my goodwill. My only fear had been the likelihood of his not knowing much about conditions further up the line. I knew that the free-and-easy behaviour of front-line (well, nearly front-line) troops might not cut much ice with some pen-pusher playing it by the book. But there wasn't any sign of a trial. I was shut up with a crew of desperadoes in the heart of this provincial jail.

No one was in very good health that winter. I mean, you had to be fairly fit to survive in the army. It was just a question of putting up with the atrocious conditions. As long as you didn't catch anything, you'd survive easily enough. But we'd all caught things. You had to watch it. You had to keep as clean as you could. I'd better not go into details, but you can use your imagination. The least that I had was a kind of foot fungus. It itched, like anything. If you were lucky you could get some fumigating powder from the MO. They used that powder on every part of the body you can think of. It didn't do a lot of good, but it helped with the toes.

There was nothing like an MO in the prison, so my toes were terrible, all split and raw. But it was nothing. As long as you could still stand, you were all right. In fact, as long as you kept on the right side of Kronblatt you were more or less all right. I mean, you might die in the night, and no one would turn a hair, but at least you'd die of natural causes. Probably from dysentery.

Kronblatt was the young officer in charge of the prison, and he was a careerist if ever there was one. He'd trained in a Prussian military academy. Perhaps he even was Prussian himself. I don't know. I certainly didn't know why he was joining in this particular escapade, teasing the Tsar a thousand miles from the sort of life he obviously valued. Oh, he liked the good things. Word went round about the wine, the meals, the cigars. He was always perfectly turned out, his buttons gleaming, his uniform freshly pressed. There were regulation creases in his tunic that even the compilers of the regulations had forgotten about. He'd probably looked exactly like that ever since his passing-out parade. What was he doing in the Gomszan army? You could just about imagine him as a household officer, in admin, hoping for a political career. But out in the field? On active service in the provinces? In winter?

The answer seemed to be the way he enjoyed himself with the

prisoners. Since there were no trials, there was no military justice. It seemed as though no one had the energy for it. Any trouble-makers were just sent back to Blot, where Kronblatt had energy to spare for making their life a misery. He enjoyed it.

He knew we couldn't get out. That made his world complete. There might just as well have been nothing outside that prison as far as he was concerned, and because he had total control over the prison that put paid to any of our hopes. We gave up all thought of getting back to our regiments, let alone to our families or our wives. The real world was nowhere.

One of the men in our cell was a big baby. Lem, he was called. God knows how he'd got into the army. He couldn't do anything right. You know the type. Slow on the uptake. Clumsy. Ready to believe anything you told him. Kronblatt really had it in for him. He could never fold his gear properly, never keep anything clean, you see, and that was one of the things that Kronblatt insisted on. All we ever did was clean things, particularly floors and latrines. Over and over. And our gear. It all had to be cleaned. We had to clean it, fold it, parade in it. We had to show it off all the time, every few hours sometimes. We'd have to be on parade in the middle of the night. Clean and shining. Lem just couldn't do it. I don't think his uniform had ever fitted him. None of us still had the full regulation kit, of course, but you'd somehow make do. Soldiers have a natural pride, and we hung on to our little tins of blacking like relics. There was a black market in buttons. I've seen baldrics made out of harness and buckles out of soldered pewter tankard handles. The point was believing in it. If you believed you were smart, you were smart. You'd always get by. Lem didn't believe in anything. He couldn't even stand up straight. He couldn't carry anything without dropping it.

Kronblatt went for him like a snake goes for a mouse. Lem was always in so much trouble that the rest of us got off lightly. I didn't know how far Kronblatt would go. He gave all his attention to Lem. He seemed to want to catch him out all the time, to force him to commit worse and worse mistakes, perhaps to make the worst mistake of all, the mistake that would provide Kronblatt with the excuse to do away with him. We all sensed this, and feared the worst. We didn't know how Kronblatt would manage it, how he would get away with it in the end. I mean, we knew you weren't allowed to just kill prisoners. The prisoners had to be accounted for to someone, we knew. But there we were, on the other hand, miles from anywhere in a place that no one ever came to inspect. None of us were sure we would be missed. We all felt sure that Lem wouldn't be missed.

We watched it all with a kind of fascination, and a kind of horror. But we weren't prepared to do anything to stop it. After all, while it continued we were safe. There was even a thrill of satisfaction in it. Satisfaction that we were not Lem, I mean; that everything rotten that happened was happening to somebody else, not to us. It's a common enough feeling, isn't it? You must have felt it at school. There's always someone who gets into trouble.

Then Piotr arrived. We didn't take much notice of him at first. He was an insignificant-looking bloke, a bookish type. None of us took to him. For one thing, he wouldn't tell us what he was in for. We thought that was strange for a start. And then he was inclined to pray. Well, I don't mind a man praying now and again. We had a lot of reason to pray, after all. I can't say I didn't have moments of quiet despair myself. But this bloke prayed all the time!

Kronblatt naturally soon had it in for him, too. He was quiet like Lem, and Kronblatt couldn't deal with that. If you were smart and kept your gear in good shape you could more or less get by. If you were ready to talk, even at the right moment to answer back, then Kronblatt could be amused by you. There was a kind of respect. But with silence he didn't know where he was. He didn't know what a silent prisoner might be thinking and that unnerved him. Lem's silence, the silence of idiocy, was manageable. That great face with its hooded eyes and hanging mouth was simply too stupid to be a challenge. But Piotr's silence was aimed to protect himself. Kronblatt couldn't be amused by Piotr. There was nothing he could condescend to. On the contrary, he must have felt that Piotr was judging *him*.

Life didn't seem quite so threatened when Piotr was there. He let everything continue for all of us just by behaving throughout as if nothing really mattered, as if nothing could be changed. He would slowly light his pipe in the face of the worst tirades. His response to insults was quietly to puff upon it. If it were knocked out of his mouth he would simply smile, sitting there with his arms on his knees. Short of hitting him directly, Kronblatt couldn't do anything else. I mean, there are some people, aren't there, who for mysterious reasons are quite safe. Piotr did have the air, unlike Lem, of being someone who might be missed. He had a kind of invisible rank. It was authority, really, I suppose. Not the kind of authority you're given, the kind you already have. Kronblatt hated him almost as much as he hated Lem, but there didn't seem to be anything he could do about it. So he took it out all the more on Lem.

I'll not trouble you with the details. I can hardly remember what finally triggered it all off, in any case. Even now it seems like a dream to me. I remember it all only as the unconnected scenes of a nightmare. Some of the scenes don't even belong to the story. There was something about a kettle being broken. I don't even know whose kettle it was. It can't have been Kronblatt's, and we were hardly allowed to have possessions ourselves.

I also remember the shrews that crept in through the cracks in the stone walls for warmth, though God knows it barely seemed warmer inside than out. Little feathery things they were, scurrying over the flags. We were hungry enough to eat them, if we could catch them. You broke off the tail, and skinned them by peeling them back from the rear end, like pulling off the finger of a glove. If we had the end of a candle we could roast them, but they weren't more than a mouthful.

Come to think of it, I don't think Piotr ever ate the shrews. He didn't seem to care much about what happened to him.

The disaster, the final moment that everyone had been expecting, was suddenly happening. Life is like that, I've found. It's the way that you remember things. Things that happen, like islands in a big sea of nothingness.

Kronblatt had drawn his sword. Lem was backed into a corner, its point at his throat. No one knew how many misplaced millimetres of folded blanket had caused this assault, but despite our continued fear of violence it was a novelty. We were used to our hardships and punishments, and we had this feeling that Lem was doomed. We expected it and in a way we helped it to happen. It gave a kind of satisfaction to know that the weakest of the herd could be left behind, a lame calf like a sop to the wolves.

"Leave him alone," said Piotr. I can't be sure if I remember this right: could he have said these amazing words without looking up from his little book of devotions? We were shocked at the unnecessary interference, this reckless drawing away of the scent from our scapegoat. I remember how Piotr used to sit, square on the bench with his right ankle rested on his left knee, the book propped against his thigh. He never spoke much in any case, but when he did there was always some reason for it.

"Leave the poor bugger alone."

The words were like a kind of signal. They seemed to announce the very crisis their meaning was meant to avoid, almost in a way to cause it. They cleared the air for a new stage in our confrontations with our tormentor.

Kronblatt gave a kind of disbelieving shout, something between exasperation and triumph. The point of the sword, which had been barely touching the underside of Lem's chin, had now alarmingly disappeared and a dark trickle of blood was inching down his neck.

You couldn't tell whether it was deliberate or not. It might have been defiance, a response to threatened self-respect. It might have been an involuntary jerk of the hand, a tiny lunge of surprise. Perhaps he had been going to do it anyway, having more or less decided that he did after all have the power to go so far without recrimination. How can you cut a man's throat by accident?

The sword had been so much a part of Kronblatt's torments that it was strange now to see it in use. He had used it to poke at our badly laid-out equipment. He had lifted dirty articles of clothing with its tip. The points it made were those of outrage, regulation and punishment. Now that its real point had been used we were reminded that it wasn't just a sergeant-major's baton or a lecturer's rod. It was a weapon. And I can tell you, once you have used a weapon you are ready to use it again.

Piotr was standing up.

"You have gone too far," he said. You had to hand it to this man. There he was, still holding his prayer book in one hand, with his finger between the pages to keep his place. He might have been telling someone off for some petty infringement of the rules. He had this authority, you see, as though he belonged to some kind of club with Kronblatt, despite their difference of position, and as though Kronblatt would understand.

But I don't think that Kronblatt wanted to understand. Having gone too far he was now ready to go further. He said something, but I don't remember what it was. He turned and slashed out at Piotr with his sword.

This was pure rage. For a moment I thought it was a calculated stroke. A cut appeared in Piotr's tunic, running from the shoulder right across to the waist on the opposite side. You could imagine a skilled swordsman doing something like that to demonstrate his finesse, cutting off a row of buttons with one flash of the blade. If it had been something like that perhaps everything might somehow still have been all right, with Lem's throat patched up like a shaving-cut and Piotr's shabby uniform neatly stripped from him in ribbons in a display of swordsmanship that would have salvaged Kronblatt's dignity. But it wasn't like that. Blood welled out into the breach in the tunic, drenching the cloth which now drooped wetly like the strange outer skin of a wound.

Had Kronblatt called the guards? Suddenly they had appeared, uncertain at first of their role in the mayhem that ensued. For they were too late to prevent Piotr stepping up to his assailant and, with that last surge of strength that the fatally wounded are often able to summon up, seizing the sword from him and bringing it down with great force against the wrist that had so recently wielded it. The hand was practically severed.

Two deaths in as many minutes! You might say that it cleared the air. The only noise was Lem's snivelling, as he stood there clutching his throat as though he were trying to strangle himself. The guards, deciding that they couldn't deal with everything at once, simply carted Kronblatt away, his hand dangling like a lady's wrist-purse and leaving a trail of dark drops falling as thickly as a sower casts seed. We were locked in, without medical aid, and Piotr died that night, after bequeathing his personal possessions among the rest of us.

He gave me the ikon and the prayer book. He must have thought I looked the most spiritual of the bunch. Well, I am quite spiritual as a matter of fact. To the others he gave pieces of equipment, items of clothing, anything they thought worth taking as being better than what they already had. There wasn't much. He gave Lem his pipe, and that didn't look as if it would be much use. There was stuff bubbling out of Lem's mouth that wasn't going to make room for anything to be put *in*.

Piotr didn't make a sound all this time, though he was cut to the ribs. Now that's what I call a brave man. He died to save someone else who couldn't defend himself. Quite unnecessary, I thought at the time. But now I'm not so sure. I've taken a look in that book of prayers. Many a time I've been curious as to what it said in there, and it said some pretty strange things. I gave it to my wife a few years after we were married, just after she'd had our first child, and she thought it said some strange things too. I let her keep it. Women know more about such things than men do, after all. Like the ikon, there, the Madonna. She looked just like that with little Piotr. Pure innocence. She'd even let me have a good suck if I asked her nicely.

12

The Authority of the Absent Arch-Duke

THE WATERSELLER APPEARED to have finished his story. Or rather, though he was still talking, he appeared to have lost the narrative thread. Rudolf leaned forward eagerly in his seat.

'Who was this Kronblatt?' he asked the waterseller. 'What happened to him?'

'How should I know?' replied the waterseller shiftily. 'He was a goner, I expect.'

'But you don't know that he died?' said Rudolf. 'Do you?'

'I never saw him again,' said the waterseller. 'They hushed it all up, of course, but I was months in Blot. The campaign was almost over before they released me, but I never saw him again.'

'Which hand was it?' asked Rudolf intensely, glancing at the others as if for support, requiring them to focus, like himself, on this crucial question.

'Which hand, sir?' asked the waterseller in puzzlement. 'I don't really believe I remember.'

'Of course he doesn't remember,' laughed Romuald. 'He's making the whole thing up.'

'Making it up?' said Rudolf angrily. 'How can he be making it up? Don't you see? This Kronblatt must be the same person as Kleinblut.'

'Hilda's monster of the Conservatoire?' said Romuald. 'I'm not so sure that she didn't make him up, too. He may have had time to double as the international genius of the Winter Gardens, theatrical producer and the most physically resourceful pianist of all time, but he can hardly have had the opportunity for a career as a sadistic martinet on the Eastern Front in the campaigns of '71 as well. Life is too short.'

'Life *is* short, sir,' said the waterseller. 'That's certainly true. And now: can I have my things back?'

Radim, who had managed to keep awake for a good deal of the story, shook him vigorously by the hand.

'Of course you must have your things back,' he said. 'We've all been affected by your story. It shows that it is right to speak out against the injustices of the world. It shows that the truth will be heard.'

Romuald looked quizzical at this.

'A great deal *besides* the truth is always clamouring to be heard,' he said. 'And what's more, often gets a hearing.'

'You're absolutely right, sir,' said the waterseller, pocketing his possessions once more. He stood up, suddenly dry-eyed and determined. 'There's no stopping it sometimes.'

He left the compartment, touching his brow to them with one dirty forefinger and with something like a wink.

'Good evening to you, gentlemen,' he said. 'We'll soon be at the frontier, and there I shall have to leave you.' He paused and looked round at them all before he disappeared down the corridor with his trolley, adding these last words carelessly, but with conviction:

'It was the left hand.'

When he had gone, Rudolf looked enquiringly at Hilda.

'Well?' he said. 'What is the explanation of this extraordinary coincidence? Could this be your Kleinblut?'

Romuald joined him silently in his enquiry, and even Radim turned to her in expectation of an answer.

Hilda looked at all three for a moment before she nodded briefly and put a finger to her lips conspiratorially.

'Yes, of course it is,' she said. 'But then again, it isn't at all. I thought you would have guessed sooner or later that Kleinblut isn't who I said he was. He's not any of those things, though most of the things I said about my Kleinblut are true enough of him.'

'You're still speaking in riddles,' said Romuald. 'You've been speaking in riddles since we met you. Has anything at all that you've told us been true?'

'Yes,' said Hilda doubtfully. 'Some of the things.'

'Your name is Hilda Pyramur?'

'No.'

'Your father is the cellist Cyprian Pyramur?'

'No.'

'You are escaping to Dresden with your lover, Johann Schmeck?'

'No.'

'What about the earlier story? Any of that true after all, perhaps?'

'No.'

'Oh dear,' said Rudolf. 'You have been leading us up the garden path, haven't you? Why so?'

'Because, my dear friends,' said Hilda, touching Rudolf and Radim on the sleeve and nodding towards Romuald in the corner as if to draw them all into a new alliance, a new pact of complicity, silence and loyalty, 'I am on this train with a very dear and important mission. It is of far greater significance than Józef's burial of his mother or Hilda's escape from her father. This is no romance. I told you those stories to gain your sympathy. Now I must tell you the truth in order to gain your loyalty as citizens of Gomsza.'

She looked at them with solemnity, as at the swearing of vows.

'You see,' she said, 'I am the Duchess Beatricz of Lower Gomsza. I am the daughter, the youngest daughter, of the Arch-Duke. The man in the inner compartment there is the Arch-Duke himself, and we must make sure that he escapes from Gomsza. I am rapidly discovering that I can barely do it by myself with what little help I have. I need your assistance desperately.'

Rudolf looked back at her with equal solemnity, and then giggled.

'There is something delicious about these charades,' he said. 'It's quite surprising how at every turn, at every surprise, there's no sense of their ever coming to an end. They could quite clearly go on for ever. I congratulate you, my dear.'

'I have never been more serious in my life,' hissed Beatricz with whitened face and her hand clutching Rudolf's sleeve as if to save him from falling. 'I might have told you everything when we first met, certainly when my disguise failed me, if I had been sure of your belief and your readiness to play the part of patriots.'

'Are you sure of us now?' asked Romuald.

'Least sure of you,' said Beatricz frankly. 'Journalism is the richest seed-bed for opportunists. And yes, I have read your things now and again in the *Inquisitor*. I knew that if you would not stay for your Vera you would not stay for the Arch-Duke. And you, Radim, clearly haven't a political idea in your head. Rudolf, dear, you are perhaps the most realistic.'

Rudolf blushed.

'I thought what you said earlier about federalism very true,' continued Beatricz. 'It is indeed to confuse nations with empires. But I noticed that you could come up with no solutions to our problems. Quite understandable. I don't know that there are any solutions. But when you proposed that toast to freedom I was cheered by the thought of your loyalty to the Duchy.'

'But why,' protested Rudolf, 'did you not then tell us the truth? Why the lengthy fabrication about Kleinblut and Schmeck at the Conservatoire?'

'I nearly told you, of course,' replied the Duchess. 'But something made me draw back from the truth.'

'We knew it, I think,' said Rudolf. 'There was something too bizarre about your story.'

'Ah, but it's in the nature of stories to be bizarre,' said Beatricz. 'Surely? Or otherwise they would never become stories. Besides, its elements were true enough in their way. My musical education has meant much to me, and there *is* someone called Johann Schmeck.'

'And you two are . . . ?' enquired Rudolf delicately.

'Of course not,' said Beatricz. 'He is much too arrogant to

dream of paying any attention to a lady of the Court. He was my tutor for a while. Our opportunities for intimacy were practically non-existent.'

She paused, and then directly addressed Romuald who was gazing at her with a fixed stare that unsuccessfully suppressed a yawn.

'You still don't believe me, I suddenly realise,' she said. 'Here, perhaps this will convince you.'

She drew a small object out of the pocket of her linen suit, something attached to a chain, and went into the tiny sycamore-panelled toilet. She soon reappeared, now with two objects in her hands attached together. She pulled them apart, with a conjuror's ostentation.

'There,' she said.

The ring had pressed into the soft underside of the tablet of soap a credible impression of the ducal insignia of Gomsza, familiar from such representations of it as the seal of approval proudly displayed by purveyors of goods and services to the Court. It was, however, a finer version than these, with the hairline flourishes only possible in the fine incuse carving of garnet.

'Yes,' said Romuald slowly. 'We believe you.'

'Never doubted for a moment,' said Rudolf.

'Deeply honoured,' agreed Radim.

'You see,' said Beatricz, 'all power is finally dependent for its existence upon a sign that it *does* exist. At the centre of politics lies this little circular argument. It's a matter of trust, like banknotes. Take this ring, which you recognise as bearing the highest authority. Obviously it is in itself only a sign of something else. But what is that authority which it represents? It is hardly anything at all without its embodiment in something which represents it. I don't just mean that decrees couldn't be put into operation without the ducal seal squeezed at the bottom, though that's true enough. I mean that the authority is dependent *on the Arch-Duke himself*. Without him the authority is nothing at all.'

'And he chooses this moment to leave Gomsza?' asked Romuald with incredulity.

'Of course,' said Beatricz. 'Can't you see why?'

'Pure funk, I expect,' replied Romuald. 'The country's cracking up and he can't stand it.'

He suddenly sat forward, and pointed at the inner compartment.

'You mean to say that he's actually in there? The Arch-Duke?'

'I can hardly make myself plainer.'

Romuald shook his head and smiled wonderingly.

'What a merry dance you've led us,' he said. 'I can't quite take it in yet.'

'Well,' said Beatricz, 'perhaps when you *have* taken it in you'll have the goodness to ascribe a better motive to this journey of the Arch-Duke's.'

'Yes, of course,' put in Rudolf. 'A journey does imply a reason. What could it be? I'm sure we're not dealing here with a simple matter of self-imposed exile, the manifold attractions of retirement?'

'If the Arch-Duke were to abdicate at this moment,' said Romuald, 'it would be a tragedy for the country.'

'And yet you yourself have "abdicated", haven't you?' objected Beatricz. 'You are not in a position to make such a criticism. However, I assure you that this is not a question of abdications.'

'I thought perhaps he might have a fortune salted away in some Western bank,' said Rudolf.

'The Arch-Duke's wealth,' said Beatricz, 'is entirely invested in the cultural life of Gomsza. As you must surely know.'

'Can he have allies in Germany?' pondered Romuald. 'Germany itself seems ready to pounce. If he has, I doubt they are trustworthy. They would simply use him as a handle against the Tsar and before long the whole of Gomsza would turn into a playground of war between the major powers. As it is, there is still a chance that Minski's insurrection can be controlled.'

'And what about the anarchists?' asked Rudolf. 'Can Korn control them?'

'Minski could control them,' suggested Romuald.

'You mean play them off against each other?'

'Why not?'

Beatricz interrupted them in exasperation.

'You don't understand,' she said. 'Of course Korn can control the anarchists. He does control them, and always has. Who better to be leader of the anarchists than the Chief of Police? It's the perfect smokescreen. Who is really behind the bomb attempts? He uses the anarchist movement to consolidate his power. Why do you think he has never called in the Cossacks to deal with the rioting? That's because the riots were pretty well orchestrated by Korn himself. Korn has almost complete executive power, and that's not much of a secret. But what would happen if Korn were to gain control of the First Army? An alliance with General Zemlinsz is entirely possible, since it's perfectly credible that the only way through the current crisis is for the police and the military to work hand in hand. Zemlinsz would certainly fall for that. He could be made to believe that Korn is loyal to the Arch-Duke, and before you could turn round he'd be conniving at an anarchist takeover. A republic would be declared, and then after a wave of executions Korn could declare himself President. And there's not much that the Tsar would be able to do about it either. In fact, when it comes down to it there are precious few hopes for Gomsza as we know it. One of them is to expose Korn *now* before he makes a decisive move with Zemlinsz.'

'Or to hope, after all, that Minski will take charge?' asked Rudolf.

'Minski's quarrel with Gomsza is obscure,' said Beatricz. 'But at its core is a professional grudge. If he fails (and surely he will fail) the army will close ranks and become an impeccable military machine. Minski is one of yesterday's men. His impulses are generous, rhapsodic, like musical overtures. He couldn't possibly recognise his own motives, but it's precisely *because* he is such a romantic that he has never been trusted. There is not enough cruelty in him to allow him real power.'

'Oh Lord,' said Rudolf. 'Do we have to believe that cruelty is a necessary adjunct to power? What about the Arch-Duke? Do you believe that your father is cruel?'

'Luckily, as I have been trying to explain,' replied Beatricz, 'there is no question of my father being corrupted by power because he has never had to struggle to attain it. Minski is a peasant, punishingly humiliated as a young cadet and bewildered by his own subconscious desire for revenge against the aristocratic officer class. Zemlinsz is an icy careerist with cousins in every government department. Korn is pure Hun. He does everything by the book, and he can recognise the value to him of a man like Zemlinsz. They all need power like a drug. They've all in their way had to work for it. My father doesn't possess power in that sense. He possesses authority. He is like his signet ring. He is a symbol. The ring is a symbol. The wax seal that it makes is a symbol. Even the documents sealed with it are symbols. The Arch-Duke is a ratifying symbol of the power vested in the Duchy of Gomsza, and as the head of state it is not power as such that he possesses. It is authority. Without his authority, executive power in the Duchy would be seen for what it is: the muddled greedy acts of men who have material possessions to protect, or who want to obtain more. Remove that authority and the greed and muddle would have no rationale and no effectiveness. The position of a spurious man like Korn would be immediately untenable. He would be howled down by everyone like him who would suddenly see no reasons for his privileges. Now do you see why the Arch-Duke is leaving Gomsza? It's the only way to undermine Korn's position. It's the only way for the present chaos to resolve itself without undermining the Arch-Duke's position. Without authority, Korn will be seen for what he is: a ruthless seizer of unlawful power.'

'But won't there be even worse disorder than there is already?' objected Rudolf. 'The country will grind to a halt.'

'Nothing ever quite does that, does it?' said Beatricz. 'Those worst fears have never been realised. Life goes on.'

'Without the Arch-Duke?' said Rudolf. 'Suppose no one gets round to asking for him back? Suppose they are happy with the spurious?'

'That is a risk we will have to take.'

'And of course,' said Romuald wryly, 'there are always the positive advantages of exile, aren't there, provided one has the money and the admirers? The Mediterranean estate, the deference, the circuit of Grand Hotels, the nostalgia? If they don't want you back life could be perfectly pleasant. The life-style without the responsibility.'

The Duchess sighed, and rolled her eyes.

'There will be a great deal to *do*,' she said. 'As you yourself correctly guessed, there are political connections to be consolidated.'

'We understand well enough,' said Rudolf. 'You are, as they say, drawing back in order to spring forward all the more vigorously. Like a tiger.'

Radim shook his head. He had taken in very little of all this. Was this wiry young tiger in the cream linen suit who had shared all her false adventures with them and who had been chattering away almost non-stop really what she now said she was? While he was telling them about the panorama, she had nodded with absorbed assent, rapidly shifted her position for expedient comfort, and generally encouraged him with the glitter in her eye. He had hardly done the same for her, but he had been interested nonetheless. And was even the second Kleinblut an invention, a passing fancy designed to put them off the scent? He put the question to her.

'Kleinblut an invention?' she exclaimed. 'You did not recognise him? How could I invent a man like that?'

'He is also Kronblatt?' asked Rudolf.

'I did once know something of Korn's early life,' she said, 'and even without the hand it would all fit. He was brought up in Prussia, as the old waterseller said. His father was a small farmer who had left Gomsza after the Russian invasion having lost all his land. He was brought up to hate everything Russian. That was why he returned to Gomsza to make his fortune on the Eastern Front. I didn't know how he lost his hand. I didn't think anyone did. Of course, everyone at Court liked to guess. They hate him. It was my aunt's idea that he had chopped it off deliberately. I always liked that idea.'

'And he has nothing to do with music, after all?' asked Rudolf.

'Well,' smiled the Duchess. 'He is in his way a civilised man, though his taste does have a tell-tale streak of the Biedermeyer in it. He likes to give musical soirées, you know. Sentimental lieder, and little puffing wind quintets. It must relax him after a day spent tearing out fingernails on August 5th Street. Johann Schmeck has performed for him, I can't think why.'

'I find this all very odd,' said Rudolf. 'Were we supposed to know that Korn has a missing hand?'

'I knew,' said Romuald. 'I think. I think I did know. It is not a fact that is allowed to be publicly acknowledged. But I had heard something about it. It was one of the details that vaguely disturbed me about your stories. But then, your stories were so circumstantial.'

'I had always been fascinated by that hand,' said Beatricz, 'ever since my aunt pointed it out to me as a child. It was not a hand that gave good dreams, I can assure you.'

'One might even say that you seem obsessed by it,' said Rudolf.

'Who wouldn't be?' replied Beatricz. 'It's a strangely precious possession for a Chief of Police. The original ivory one was designed by someone who had worked with Fabergé and therefore insisted on jewelled excess in addition to the practical clockwork. A key at the wrist set various grasping positions, for example, but its fingernails were slivers of translucent coral. It was strong enough to loop and control the reins of a pair of horses, but the fourth finger unscrewed at its emerald ring to reveal a small glass chamber for opium. The machinery was very advanced. More recently he had it all reset in celluloid for flexibility: where the ivory had to be jointed, giving the inevitable impression of a Chinese automaton, the celluloid was cast in one piece and is flesh-coloured. At the same time the machinery was improved. A very fine spring allows for up to a minute and a half of simple repetitive movement in three of the fingers, and on a good day it is said that he can play Schumann. Rather badly, of course, but well enough for it to be a matter of wonder.'

At this moment, just when they were beginning to think that the girl's fantasies had once again gained control of reality, the train gave a shudder and there was a strained tightening of metal beneath them. So identified had the compartment become with the continued motion and onward impetus of the train, that at first it seemed as if some mechanical argument had arisen between the two, as if the one were shaking off the other like a horse unwilling to be ridden.

The train was braking.

Immediately there was activity in the corridors. People who had been lying down sat up. People who had been sitting looked out of the windows. One or two people, who had been already looking out of a window, shouted.

'What's happening?' asked Romuald.

'I don't know,' said Rudolf. 'It's completely dark outside. We can't be at the frontier yet, can we?'

'Then why do you think we're stopping?' asked Radim.

A guard was shouldering his way down the corridor. Rudolf opened the door and called to him.

'What's up?'

'No idea, sir,' was the reply.

'We're not due to stop, are we?'

'Not here, we're not,' said the guard over his shoulder. And he disappeared into the next compartment.

13

The Imprisonment of the Paris Express

BY THIS TIME the train had screeched and jolted to a stop. There were speculative murmurs up and down its length. One or two doors slammed.

Rudolf opened the window and lowered the sash.

'There are people getting out,' he said. 'Shall we take a look?'

'Supposing the train moves on without us?' asked Radim.

'I doubt it will do that,' said Rudolf. 'Coming?'

'Yes, I'll come,' said Romuald.

They jumped down on to the gravel and looked about them. It was hard to be quite sure where they were, since the light from the compartments didn't reach very far. After a while, as their eyes grew accustomed to the dark, they could see that the track was running by the side of a pine forest. They walked towards the front of the train.

'What do you make of her latest story, then?' asked Romuald. 'Can you believe a word of it?'

'Hard to, isn't it?' replied Rudolf. 'It seems to be so outrageous that it has stopped the train dead in its tracks.'

'But is it possible?'

Rudolf pondered.

'None of its elements make it impossible, but then that was true of her other stories. The Arch-Duke does have three daughters, doesn't he? Anna, Christina and Beatricz? Anna's the active one. I was once presented to her at a charity performance. Christina's practically a nun. And no one knows much about Beatricz. I thought she was still very young.'

'Could she be Beatricz?' asked Radim.

'Whoever she is,' said Rudolf, 'she's the most extraordinary young woman I have ever met. Don't you think she's fascinating?'

'She could petrify a cobra,' said Romuald.

'Isn't she rather *thin*?' asked Radim.

'Real thinness trifles with the grave,' said Rudolf. 'Isn't it simply that we are accustomed to corpulence? She seems to me to possess the perfectly economical body. Look at her when she talks. You can almost see every muscle doing its particular job. If it's true of her face, I'm sure it will be true of the rest of her.'

'Not much chance of ever finding out,' said Romuald with a laugh.

Rudolf glanced at him sternly, but they could barely see each other's faces in the dark. A man came towards them swinging a lantern.

'Get back,' he was saying. 'All passengers back in their compartments.' It was the German conductor.

'What's the matter?' asked Rudolf. 'Why have we stopped?'

'The line is blocked,' said the conductor. 'Covered with boulders.'

'An avalanche!' exclaimed Radim. 'It's a good job we weren't all killed.'

'No avalanche,' said Rudolf. 'The country just here is as flat as a lake.'

'Quite right, sir,' said the conductor. 'Those boulders were put there deliberately. And contrary to what you might think they were not put there to derail the train.'

'I can't think what else they were put there for,' said Radim irritably. 'The students at the Institute these days do things like that and call it sculpture, but we're rather a long way from the Institute.'

'They were obviously put there to stop the train, sir, weren't they?' explained the conductor wearily. 'And not to derail it, because of that big fire lit on top of it to warn the driver. Very nicely calculated, it was. He just had time to stop with about ten yards to spare.'

They moved a little further from the train and looked up the line. The conductor was right. A beacon flickered.

'How long will it take to clear it?' asked Rudolf.

'We can't clear that,' said the conductor.

'Why on earth not?' asked Rudolf.

'We haven't got the manpower, have we?' said the conductor. 'Haven't got the manpower on this train.'

'Good Lord,' said Romuald. 'There are hundreds of men on this train. What do you mean?'

'You're suggesting that we ask the passengers to do it?' asked the conductor.

'Why not?'

'It's against company policy,' said the conductor. 'Passengers are not allowed off the train except at stations, so please sir, would you return to your compartments?'

'What's going to happen?' asked Romuald.

'The driver intends to wait and see what they want,' said the conductor.

'What *who* want?' exclaimed Romuald in exasperation.

'Whoever stopped the train, of course,' replied the conductor. 'Now, *if* you please.'

He went on his way, herding the passengers back into the train.

The night air was close, without wind. A faintly fungoid resiny smell came from the forest. Ahead of them the engine of the train released its superfluous head of steam with impatience, long dragonish snorts that hid the front of the train from view.

'Do you think this has anything to do with our young friend?' asked Radim, as they returned to their compartment.

'Almost certainly,' said Romuald.

Rudolf was silent.

When they re-entered the carriage they found that the Duchess already knew what was happening. The news had travelled quickly down the corridors of the train.

'There would be panic,' she said, 'if most of the passengers hadn't already bedded down for the night. As it is, those who *are* awake and are most anxious at the prospect of being searched at the frontier, are now momentarily relieved of their anxiety.'

'Does that include you?' asked Rudolf.

'He agreed to be under heavy sedation for the duration of the journey. He felt it would be safer. Maddalejna is under instructions to admit no one without a special knock. I can't tell him. It is better that he doesn't know.'

'Perhaps you should wake him,' said Rudolf. 'Perhaps indeed you should leave the train, for your own safety. We can't be far from the frontier.'

The Duchess wasn't worried. She had shown greater anxiety about the waiter who was neither a cellist nor a spy.

'Can you provide two, or perhaps three, horses?' she asked. 'No? And can you tell precisely where we are? I thought not. We shall just have to wait and see what happens, shan't we?'

Romuald let out a short bark of laughter. His face was unsmiling, though.

'I'm not sure that we aren't quite near the town of Morsken,' he said. 'Famed for its mediaeval castle and for its salt. An anarchist stronghold, if I'm not mistaken, ever since the saltwork strikes of eighteen months ago. Perhaps we've all been captured by anarchists.'

'Anarchists?' exclaimed Radim, in alarm.

'A trainload of aristocratic refugees would be quite a coup, wouldn't it?' said Romuald. 'Or do they have something more specific in mind? Can our young friend's latest story possibly contain an element of truth?'

Before the Duchess could reply, and as if in response to his speculations, they all at once heard a strange but familiar sound behind them. At first they could not tell what it was. Then the stillness of their bodies told them.

It was a sound that should have been accompanied by motion, a sound that they were used to as a condition of their travelling, a whole environment. It was a train.

Another train!

Would it crash into them? As the sound grew nearer they could tell that it was not an express. Its laboured chugging and lightness of locomotion suggested that it was some stalwart of a branch line, a dogsbody of a little train, used to being sent on errands. And it certainly sounded as if it were coming for them.

Rudolf could not help feeling that Beatricz's calm and the quiet purposefulness of the train had some connection. He couldn't quite work out what this might be. Still in his mind the images of loyal son and victimised music student overlaid the latest image of aristocratic political adventuress.

It wasn't long before a jolt told them that the new engine had coupled with the rear of the fourgon which itself was immediately behind their carriage. Soon after that the outer doors of the carriage were locked.

They rushed to the windows in time to see the dark shapes of men with kerchiefed heads and rifles slung over their backs moving up the tracks.

'Are we just going to sit here and let them do this?' asked Romuald.

'Where do you think they got the key to the carriage doors?' wondered Radim.

'I give up,' said Rudolf. 'We are being kidnapped by bandits, and it all seems more perfectly organised than the schedule of the train itself.'

Just then there was a scream further down the train. Nothing hysterical, something closer to a shout or remonstration. They heard angry voices, and then a shot rang out. There was silence.

'I've never thought,' said Rudolf after a moment, 'that there was any point in undue heroism.'

They all looked at one another.

'I mean,' he continued, 'if anyone feels like going to see what that was, they are welcome to. But I don't think I shall go myself.'

Nobody said anything, and shortly afterwards the train started moving slowly backwards.

Beatricz's composure unnerved them. Invading her compartment, patronising her, hanging on her words, humouring her, protecting her, now all seemed like a game. If they were all being kidnapped, then perhaps it was the Arch-Duke who was being kidnapped. But Beatricz didn't look as if she was being kidnapped at all.

What's more, the train didn't feel right. It didn't somehow feel like the same train at all. It felt lighter.

After a while, Romuald was appointed hero, and agreed to go and see what was happening.

He wasn't sure what to expect. Cowed passengers, certainly, with armed men standing by like the ones they had glimpsed locking the train doors. Perhaps someone wounded.

He found nothing.

The compartments beyond theirs were now empty, except for the heavier belongings of the passengers who had been there and some evidence of hasty departure: a little travelling silver billy-can on a window-table with a half-eaten stewed pear in it, a glove on the floor. When he went through to the next carriage, the next carriage wasn't there. He found himself staring out at a disappearing perspective of railway track, unrolling steadily with an air of cunning like a line playing out a prize fish. He had to grab on to the sides to prevent himself falling. He could hardly believe it. The emptiness and the twin shining rail leading away into the dark was after a while as natural as the flashing night view from their window had been. But where was the Paris Express? It had disappeared as if it had never existed. It had been swallowed up by an anonymous pine forest, all of it, the driver and his bierwurst, the passengers with tickets, the passengers without tickets, the waiters, the guards, the brass urn of the waterseller, everything. They were now effectively on a completely new train, going in a different direction for a different purpose.

Romuald reported back to the others. They took the news gravely.

'How ironical it makes our recent conversation about the impossibility of returning!' said Rudolf.

'Liberation with a vengeance,' said Radim.

'It's not liberation at all,' said Romuald. 'We're prisoners, aren't we?'

'It certainly looks like it,' said Rudolf. 'But, you know, being a prisoner is the greatest release of responsibility of all. At the very instant of closing your options, it offers the arbitrary possibility of a new one, a future in which your own lame intentions and failed decisions need at last have no place. What a relief! I had an uncle who went bankrupt. He was never happier. He adored prison.'

'Don't be an idiot,' said Romuald. 'Where's the virtue in that?'

'I didn't say there was virtue in it,' replied Rudolf. 'Do you happen to find much virtue in life in any case? I'm sure I don't. No, it was I suppose an absence of virtue, but it was an absence of vice, too. He was simply relieved of the necessity of making choices. For him it was idyllic.'

'I don't imagine his creditors took the same view,' said Romuald.

'Well, of course,' said Rudolf, 'it was they who had effectively put him there. What else could they do? They got back as much of their money as they could, and I suppose they felt that it was better than nothing.'

'Better to have let him go on making money,' said Romuald.

'But he was losing it!' exclaimed Rudolf. 'That was the whole point. He'd failed totally. I don't think he had any desire to carry on at all. He wanted to creep into a hole and hide. He wanted to disappear. And prison was a form of designed disappearance. Imprisonment is a sort of calculated conjuring trick on society's part, isn't it? If you turn a walking-stick into a scarf you deny the walking-stick its function. It was the same with my uncle. He'd failed as a businessman, so they turned him into a prisoner, the very opposite of a businessman. Hey presto!'

'A prisoner isn't actually anything at all,' protested Romuald. 'If you turn a walking-stick into a scarf, at least you've got the scarf.'

'In my act,' said Rudolf, 'the scarf then turns into a dove which disappears into the audience.'

'That's the illusion,' said Romuald. 'I'll bet it was trained to fly to your assistant, who then locked it up until the next performance.'

'Quite right,' said Rudolf. 'And there you are again, you see. Prison. That dove had no problems at all.'

'The absence of other doves?' suggested Romuald.

'*Other* doves?' exclaimed Rudolf. 'The greatest trouble of all!

Especially for a dove. Do you think it's all billing and cooing? Doves are vicious creatures.'

'What did your uncle do?' asked Romuald.

Rudolf paused for a moment.

'He was an undertaker,' he said.

'An undertaker?' repeated Romuald.

'Yes,' said Rudolf. 'You might say that he also made people disappear in a way. Though he could only do it with those who had already lost all interest in life. He was a kindly man, good at his craft but with no head for figures. He helped me a lot when I started out, you know.'

Radim groaned.

'How you two can chatter on like this when we're in such a mess, I've no idea,' he said. 'Shouldn't we be doing something?'

'What do you suggest?' asked Rudolf.

Radim looked at him helplessly. 'Quite,' said Rudolf. 'All this seems predetermined. We can hardly jump off. The train is going too fast. And even if it weren't I doubt you would want to leave your panorama behind. I certainly wouldn't want to abandon my equipment. I could have it built again, naturally, but I wouldn't want its secrets to fall into the wrong hands. I'm quite comforted in a way that it's all there safe behind us in the fourgon. Or I suppose I should now say in front of us.'

'Rudolf is right,' said Beatricz. 'There is nothing we can do. I imagine we are being taken on a branch line to Morsken. We shall have to see what happens after that. Are you tired?'

This seemed to be addressed to Rudolf.

'Absolutely exhausted,' he replied with a flashing smile that contradicted what he was saying. 'But I think it's too late now to pull down the couchettes, don't you? Besides, there aren't enough for all of us, and I think we should keep awake.'

'We should indeed,' said Beatricz. 'And I can think of an ideal way of doing so.'

So can I, thought Rudolf, if the others could be persuaded to move into one of the empty compartments. He looked at the Duchess's hand resting on her knee and wondered what it would feel like if it were holding the back of his neck. His own was large enough to allow it in that position to command one ear-lobe with a thumb and the other with the middle finger, a delicate erotic grasp that could so transfix a woman that his other hand could move where it willed, unhindered as a mountain goat.

'We have heard Romuald's story,' she continued, 'and we have heard Radim's. What about yours? It is clear by now that none of you are serious political refugees, and so far we have the clearest evidence that whatever a man's vocation may urge him to say to the contrary, the true springs of his actions are wound by the gentler passions. What do you say?'

Rudolf bowed.

'If you like,' he said graciously.

'Romuald and Radim have lost the love of their lives,' she went on. 'In one case it seems to have been due to insufficient loyalty. In the other, to insufficient decisiveness. Do you have such a tale to tell? What is your insufficiency?'

Her dark eyes gazed at him as if intent on drawing out secrets from his own.

He smiled, and half looked away.

'Oh,' he said carelessly. 'Insufficient seriousness, I suppose.'

The abbreviated train rattled on.

14

The Embarrassment of the Empty Coffin

FOR AS LONG as I can remember (said Rudolf) I have had cousins to impress. Older than me, tremendously energetic, quarrelsome even, beautiful, all girls. It was a law of nature, my needing to impress them.

I was an only child, but never one of the brooding solitary ones. My parents were perfectly sensible people, neither too busy to neglect me nor too indulgent. For some people their children become toys or religious idols: little working models of their own lives, apparently untroubled by the calamities of passion. Wind up a son, and watch him act out the elusive perfection of your own muddled career! Light candles before the image of your daughter, and love itself might be restored to its first purity!

I'm glad to say that my father and mother would have nothing to do with any of that nonsense. Their approach to all aspects of family life was rational and humane. Even the fact that I had no brothers or sisters was a deliberate choice on their part. I got the impression that far from being the natural product of an undying and sanctified love for each other (which might, you would have thought, have issued in further such products in the course of time) I was merely their calculated contribution to the stock of Gomszan nationals, indeed to the species itself, merely a biological duty fulfilled, a sign that their marriage had a social as well as a personal function. I was clothed and fed without that excessive drama, ritual or regulation that so often accompanies the fond mechanics of nurture, and then quietly educated on liberal scientific principles. Intellectual family friends applauded this as being very advanced, but I think you wouldn't be far wrong to say that I was neglected.

My mother and her brother were very close, and because Uncle Anton was a generous man he did a great deal for us. My grandparents had died when I was quite little, so that Anton had inherited the family house at Mavrinka. I think he felt guilty that he should have so much and my mother so little. My father was a laboratory assistant at the Institute, on a small salary and with unexciting prospects. It was his brother, incidentally, who was the unsuccessful undertaker. Uncle Stefan was like my father in many ways. Both were dogged, rational men, both without real ambition. Curiously enough, their professions were alarmingly related, for whereas my father cultivated live cell tissue in gelatine, my Uncle Stefan disposed of dead cell tissue in oak. Rank on rank of glass saucers; rank on rank of six-foot boxes. I can't believe that either of them were very excited by their work.

Our way of life was perfectly decent, but it must have seemed modest to Uncle Anton. He was used to having the space to live in style and was quite ready to spend his inheritance on doing so. He kept a carriage and a groom, and would send it round to us whenever we needed it. He bought my mother a grand piano. He took us all on holidays. He was always giving us treats, and parties, slapping my father on the back and pouring him large drinks. I suppose my father hated him, though I think he could never have dared say so to my mother. Mama of course adored Anton. And as for me, I dread to think what my life might have been like without Uncle Anton and Aunt Zizzie, and particularly without their three daughters.

Those cousins! Xanthia, Georgie and Delecta, all arms and legs, all brown wrists and knee-lace, all nibbled nails and sandy toes. Why do I remember those limbs, those extremities? I suppose I wanted to share in their speed, their freedom, their activity. They were always running in from the garden, or hugging each other, or standing on shoulders to pick apples. I really admired the way they did that, not sitting on shoulders and holding on to the head, but standing right up like an acrobat with the one below clutching the ankles as though steadying the foot of a ladder. Delecta was the smallest, and she would hold the basket. Apples thundered down, on to heads, into the grass, sometimes into the basket. It didn't matter if the apples got bruised, because they didn't last for long. Those girls were always eating apples. I couldn't think of an apple without it having the white cave of a bite out of its side. The shape of the bite reminded you of the shape of the mouth that had bitten, the green serration so exact a contour of the teeth that you could almost feel them with your own tongue, the white hollow in the flesh like something you had yourself devoured.

That house at Mavrinka was always associated for me with the smell of apples. It was perhaps most powerful at Christmas, when we used to be sent into the attic to fetch the finest red pippins for the sideboard displays. The apples were kept in wooden slatted racks, specially built and lining the whole length of the attic. Although they were perfectly crisp, dry and fresh, as though they had been picked that afternoon and not ten weeks earlier, still there was something mysterious about them. Many of the apples still had twig or leaf attached, and the leaves had withered, lending the concentrated moisture of the fruit a greater surprise. It was like picking them all over again, reminding us of the exploits of the summer.

While the girls were as steady as real acrobats, I had all the rashness of a monkey. It seemed quite obvious to me that I had to climb high into the branches of the tree to bring them apples, even though they could pick as many as they wanted through their own devices. I thought it seemed right that a boy should climb higher than they did, and so I would disappear into the topmost branches in search of the perfectly ripe apple, commenting on my precarious progress as I did so, calling down to them at frequent intervals to draw attention to the danger I pretended to be in. By the time I came down they would inevitably have become bored and gone inside. They never did any one thing for long at a time.

I said that they were older than I was, but that isn't strictly true. Xanthia and Georgie were older, and the most beautiful and the most intolerant, but Delecta was actually just my own age. To me, therefore, at the height of my boyhood passion for sturdy thighs wading in the stream with skirts kilted up, for the sight of the slight swell of early breasts in muslin as arms reached into a tree, for the heady privilege of being allowed to plait long brown hair already rich with its sebaceous promise of the animal, the presence of their younger sister was for a time the least stimulating. And it was natural that as time went on I would more frequently find myself left with Delecta when the two older girls went off by themselves.

The thing about Delecta, which I should have known about from the beginning, was her short attention span. It wasn't that things held no interest for her. On the contrary, she had the most intense curiosity about the world and all its wonders, but this curiosity was soon satisfied with the first coherent set of facts about the matter that she could assemble. Once something was explained, whatever fascination it had previously held for her evaporated. If she understood it, it was simply no longer interesting.

I began to think that the finer experiences would pass her by, and go thudding unnoticed into the grass.

I will keep my story as brief as I can, for I don't suppose you can be much interested in my life apart from the relationship with Delecta. It's enough to tell you that although I had, under my father's frequently rather stern tutelage, a distinct talent for the Mathematics and was expected to study to an advanced level at the Institute and even perhaps to make it my career, I turned instead to one of my earliest obsessions: conjuring. I was a disappointment to him in this respect, though I'm quite sure that he is now grateful for my success in the art, since it has saved him from a penurious retirement and gives him something to talk about with his drinking friends, none of whom are at all intellectual, but for whom the theatre and its magic have a perpetual fascination.

For me, the development of my skills went hand in hand with the development of my love for Delecta. For of course I soon came to love her with an intensity far beyond the distant romping flirtation I had with her sisters. The latter, after all, was born simply of a generalised animal passion, a holiday companionship freely indulged in like a drug, as surprising a disruption of ordinary life for an adolescent as holidays always are. Particularly in the long summers, when clothes are lightly abandoned and small adventures freely undertaken. The whims of holiday can make a very young man quite dizzy. But whims lead to nothing very much, and Xanthia and Georgie already had their own lives: friends with whom they corresponded; household duties to remind them that they were now young women; even, soon enough, the visitations of other young men, some to my fear and shame not so very young as all that, men with small moustaches who would put me in my place by giving both Delecta and me chocolate to make us disappear.

She was shrewd enough to sense my fury.

"You don't care to be bribed like this, do you, Dolfie?" she would ask, sucking the soft chocolate from her teeth. "They think that we're children. They think we don't know."

I was in a high old sulk, I'm sure, refusing to eat mine. What did Delecta know, anyway? What went on behind that narrow brow and tumbling hair? Her eyes looked into mine, themselves as dark as chocolate, looked right into mine as if for the first time ever.

"They've no idea," said Delecta, carefully considering the last sweet brown morsel cornered in its foil before dabbing at it with her long tongue, "no idea at all that in fact we aren't children any more now and won't ever be again."

I remember even being slightly shocked at this, while pretending not to know what she meant. I thought I had learned to dictate our recreations and to guide our friendship into the patterns that suited me. I made her wade after me through ponds while we logged the fragile hours of the mayfly. She it was who carried the sandwiches, or kept time in the lower reaches of the piano while I uncertainly deliberated my extemporised octave melodies. Above all, she was to be my conjuring assistant, my stooge, my first audience.

I think it was science that made me truly appreciate the beauties of conjuring. You may think it a form of theatre, and indeed it has long been so. The pure wonder at things turning out to be other than they seem to be is the source of all drama, and it is the essence of conjuring, too. But science, a younger art, intends to show us things as they are. And the history of science has in its relatively brief course revealed greater wonders to us.

Why are we not content with these real wonders, transformations with ascertainable laws that describe, rehearse and predict their own occurrence? Why is it never sufficient, this breathtaking natural teleology of matter?

It is power, my friends. We require the power that belongs to the possession of secrets. When my father began to explain to me the calm accountability and coherence of Euclidean geometry, I remember being impressed. But the theorems for me were tainted with authority. Not my father's authority, of course, for he was a man without any will to command, even within his own family, but tainted with the dull authority of the inevitable. How could one continue to be impressed by such logical assertions, assertions always unfailingly verifiable? It was the same with nature. Wonderful, of course, in its way, but not so wonderful as if the apple-orchard had produced pears, or the larvae that Delecta and I collected in marmalade jars had turned into water-lilies rather than mayfly. I loved nature, and I loved the house at Mavrinka, but this acceptance of the settled order of things could never satisfy my soul. My soul craved power, the ability to surprise such a settled order of things, to upset nature, to win applause, to win the adoration of the girls.

I lacked then the imagination to perceive that it is perfectly possible to do all these things simply in the pursuit of the truth. When my father pointed out to me that the genially tyrannical propositions of Euclid fall utterly to pieces when put into operation on the most familiar and practical surface we possess, the surface of the globe itself (on which it may easily be seen that a triangle can possess three right angles) I was not impressed at all. It simply suggested to me that there existed somewhere a new tedious set of theorems applicable to the spatial charting of curved surfaces. Indeed, if I had possessed the stamina and inclination for scientific study, I would have encountered at the Institute the work of Gauss, Lobachevsky and Riemann, who have developed a non-

Euclidean geometry for volumes. And now such purely mathematical developments are being exploited in order to construct a physical theory which will affect our whole notion of the nature of space, indeed of the universe itself. Ever since Kepler, the empty space of the solar system has provided a Euclidean field upon which the paths of the planets have been described. Flat space geometry works perfectly well in those areas so remote from the earth, except for one small distortion which cannot be accounted for: the nearest planet to the sun, Mercury, possesses a tiny variation in its orbit, not more than 43 seconds of arc per century, and unaccountable in terms of the gravitational pull of any other body. I understand that a young genius called Einstein has accounted for this distortion by the simple means of a re-definition of gravity along non-Euclidean lines. Space itself, my friends, is, as it were, curved!

Forgive me, however, if for the reasons I have already given I cannot be much excited by this news. I would certainly not have been excited in my adolescence. What most excited me then was the window display in a little curiosity shop called Bella-Bella's in an alley behind Peranski Street where was laid out a glittering display of strange objects. One of these was labelled "This egg will disappear, 50 cop." It looked to me a perfectly commonplace farmyard egg sitting in an egg-cup without a thought in its head, and it started me wondering how such a thing could be. I went into Bella-Bella's and bought it, and was shown how it worked.

While I practised the business of making it disappear, that egg was my universe. Within its surface were subsumed all the wonders of orbits, all complexities of systems. I was happy in my secure knowledge that no audience would propose theorems to explain its disappearance. They could only gasp with amazement.

I neglected my school work in order to perfect my tricks. Night after night, with my exercise books unopened, I would stand before a mirror manipulating that small spheroid with a fixed smile on my face, a smile of arrogant self-congratulation and oily ingratiation. It was like a trick performed by an automaton. It takes time, you understand, for novices to realise how much the art of conjuring depends not on pure prestidigitation, but on the psychological manipulation of the audience, the narrative context of the trickery. I've always liked to develop a scenario for my illusions, sinister, comic, mystical, it doesn't matter, but it is the scenario which controls the emotions, and carefully directs the attention, of the audience. The audience is there to be outwitted, to be plainly deceived, frankly, to be bullied. You have to despise your audience, that's the essence of the matter.

And of course I couldn't despise my audience. My audience was Delecta.

When the holidays came, my routine was faultless. My mother and I arrived at Mavrinka a few days before Delecta was due home from school, and I remember making a great fuss about borrowing things from Aunt Zizzie in order to have everything quite ready: a small table, some bowls and lamps, a tasselled shawl. Aunt Zizzie complied readily, but with great amusement. There is something very pompous about a boy-conjuror, and I suppose I was no exception.

Whenever I meet members of the public they are always eager to know how I achieve my illusions. Of course, I hate to tell them. If I do, it spoils for them the most satisfying illusion of all – that there *can* be no explanation, that whatever they have seen is so totally mystifying that there really can be no known human means of achieving it. I like that. I thrive on that borrowed power of the mage, because really, in all honesty, I am a simple fellow and I know well enough that our ordinary transformations and transactions are sordid affairs for the most part, little biological performances that both dazzle and disgust us according to whether we are performer or spectator. Oh yes, life itself can be a very sorry spectacle indeed.

So, no explanations. But while we are about eggs, and the eager infancy of my career, I can see no harm in satisfying your curiosity with a few principles of the art. How may an egg disappear? How may it reappear?

An egg is a solid object. It is also a liquid object. And therein lies the dual problem.

But there is always a dual solution: preparation and psychology.

Manipulation of objects and manipulation of the audience. Usually these go hand in hand.

Take the egg-in-the-tumbler trick. I put an egg into a tumbler and cover it with water. I cover the tumbler with a cloth and give it to you to hold. When I remove the cloth, the egg has disappeared. How is it done? The tumbler is, of course, no ordinary tumbler. It is a bottomless tumbler with a slight inward lip at the base. Inserted in that base, and stiff enough to support the egg, even stiff enough to be tapped, is a circular disc of gelatin. The water is warm. Within a few seconds it will have softened the gelatin so that I may palm the egg. Where does all the water go? First of all, since the egg fits so snugly into the base of the tumbler, there is room for only a very little water. Secondly, it isn't water. It is alcohol. I guide the tiny trickle down my wrist and it evaporates. The egg is palmed. Yes, you need to learn to palm an egg, one of the hardest objects to palm. And you need to be able to talk your audience into not noticing.

If you are skilled at palming and substitution, then much may be done with the three-quarter egg. One performer I knew pretended that he had a whole egg, but in reality had only a partial egg, the inside of which was painted red. He pretended to swallow it, and to prove that he had swallowed it he would open his mouth. The audience saw no egg there because the inside of the egg matched the colour of his mouth. He was then able to reproduce the egg. I myself perfected the art of introducing a fine silk handkerchief into a blown egg. Also of soaking a blown egg in vinegar to remove the shell and leave only the skin. You can imagine what sort of trick might follow.

Enough about eggs. Needless to say that Bella-Bella's egg was a crude affair of painted wood and elastic. But it was sufficient for a parlour trick, sufficient at any rate to gain the admiration of Delecta.

She raised her hands delightedly as if to repel the emanations of the supernatural from my own.

"Come, Dolfie," she said, her voice rising to its rare pitch of drama and decisiveness. "This is a fine *enterprise* you have found! This could be your business in life, surely?"

She had a way of becoming excited by her own improvised thoughts, and uttering them as if in quotation marks. There was something a trifle roguish about it, coming from a girl who was normally so silent and grave, issuing as it did from a mouth judiciously pondering, while she thoughtfully twirled a strand of her hair, directed as it was with a friendly twinkle in the eye and a strange kind of complicit insistent shake of the head followed by her usual smile, half critical, half joking, and it thrilled me to the core of my being. If I had not been quite sure till then, I at once knew that I did want to be a conjuror. I knew also that I believed in Delecta, and I believed in whatever I found in her response to me that ratified my attention to her. I don't suppose that what she said mattered very much. It was the physical circumstances of her saying it to me in the way she did that was important. She might even have told me that my performance was trifling and demeaning so long as she did it with that same ironical intensity and friendly merriment.

That phrase of hers, "They think that we're the children", haunted me. A sober thought, indeed, challenged by her chocolate-smudged chin. If, as she implied, the courting games of Xanthia and Georgie and their strutting little beaux were after all not grown-up but childish, how then were we to behave? What were the rules for two who were no longer children, though thought to be so by the household and by the whole world? Even, frequently, by ourselves? The transition to maturity was imperceptible, an invisible moment between the falling of the blossom and the swelling of the fruit, though the moment seemed during that summer to be stretched to a painful infinity. Could it have been within one and the same year that she kicked me for not giving her a serrated crimson triangle from Madagascar when I had two identical ones, and that I found myself one day when we bathed almost choking with the wild thudding in my heart when I saw for a moment the long declivity of her spine, oddly concave as it entered the bunched haunches of her skirts, and heavily downed with hair?

This gift of hers, the physical gift, I mean, of arousing the passion of men, was one that she must have been taught to expect.

She had the example of her sisters, after all. But she had received it coolly, graciously and without real interest. She carried it around with her like an unopened letter whose handwriting promised the most sensational news. She knew it would keep. It was pure theory to her, the envelope in her hand, a passport of sorts ("They think we're the children"), but not requiring immediate action.

I knew this well enough. Suddenly I sensed that physical contact was forbidden. Stroking the cat together, my hand stroked hers. The pleasure ran, cat-like I thought, right up the underneath of my arm in prickling lurches like the spread of flames in dry grass, finishing in a small blaze behind my ears. At that moment if I had touched those parts of her own body I think I should have died. There was no acknowledgement on her side, and her own contact with me continued firm and businesslike, the grip on the forearm when climbing over a stile, the cousinly kiss on greeting. But no longer did we romp. If there were transformations in her body which forbade it, there certainly were in mine. There were times when the effect was quite as surprising as any conjuring trick I could then perform. As surprising, but infinitely more embarrassing. This was my gift, and as is the way with the male, I had peeped into the envelope many times, speculating about the contents. That anticipatory knowledge was beyond sharing, and I had no idea what I could do with it.

I was grateful, almost relieved, to fall in with the myth of her encouragement of my career. I really believed that she was interested. And I thought that if I could be successful and please her with my success, then in the course of things we should marry. She would become my assistant in the theatre, we would buy a house very like the house at Mavrinka, and we should have babies. In my enthusiasm for our future life and for the olive downiness of her jaw and forehead I explained to her the trick of the disappearing egg.

It was a mistake. She let out a howl of rage and disappointment.

"Is *that* all it is?" she said, stamping her foot. "Well, I declare! And you say it cost you only fifty copecks? Rather costly at that, I dare say. Hmph."

But she soon smiled at me to prove that it was all a little comedy that she had been playing. My responding smile was uncertain, both because I knew that something of her disappointment and irritation was real and because when she stamped her foot all I really wanted to do was to bury my lips in the loose strands of her brown hair to find the smooth column of her neck beneath. And I did not dare.

I should have dared! I know that now. What was it that made me resolve even more strongly to pursue my world of shadows and mirrors? It was defiance, timidity, erotic sublimation, aesthetic excitement, despair.

I could not persuade Delecta to take an interest in it, even though we had shared so much in the past. She was polite enough.

"Whatever will you find next?" she would exclaim, at each new trick. "You must go on surprising me, Dolfie."

But I couldn't get her to practise any illusions herself. She seemed to prefer not knowing how they worked. A sniff, and a toss of the head:

"So disappointing," she would say. "Is that really all it is?"

Everything in the world is only what it is! Although I didn't want to accuse my little Delecta of being cynical, I sometimes felt that she needed enchantment. I realised that after all it was she, not I, who had always proposed our entomological expeditions. I would have been happier playing at Cossacks. We should have been exchanged at birth, perhaps: my father would have found her a responsive pupil, and I could have indulged all my dreams at Mavrinka. Perhaps we *had* in fact been exchanged, I once wondered. It would have been a strange experiment conducted by my mother and my uncle, the result of a pact made in childhood between a sister and brother too close to imagine ever being really parted through marriage. "We will bring up each other's offspring as our own, so that through many mysteries and adventures they may find themselves, their true parents, and so each other, whereby our proscribed union can be fulfilled in them!" Such are the romantic dreams of youth in those wild drifting minutes before sleep. How I could ever imagine such a proposal being agreed by my merry Uncle Anton I've no idea. It was true that he didn't seem to mind my continued intimacy with his youngest daughter, when he perhaps might have had much to be anxious about, but no doubt he was simply used to my presence. Perhaps he guessed that I was too timid to thrust my ripe attentions on her. Besides, though Delecta in particular had inherited his rather dry brand of jollity, she was in full possession of Aunt Zizzie's nose and forehead. That was a fact of biology that put paid to romance. But even when things are clearly what they are, they are not "really" only that. The world is at its best when it is what we want to see. And we want it to be marvellous.

To me, the illusionist is like the poet in his creation of artificial marvels. Not only do these add, in an absolute sense, to the existing stock of the marvellous, they also enact in a pure form our own admiring wonderment. They are symbols of our valuation of the world, signs of our consent to mystification, tokens of the human, the purest form of drama.

My perfection of the illusion of the egg is like this. In my act now it is an episode that represents the most sublime miracle of nature. The egg is produced, as if from nowhere. The hand reaches out, a gesture of wistful expectation, and the fingers pluck the egg out of the air. It is the source of life, a gift. Cradled in my hands, it becomes a dove, which I caress before allowing it to fly away. I reach for another egg, which also turns into a dove. Another egg, another dove. Another, and yet another. The stage is fluttering with wings that reflect the glittering light. The music soars. It is like the birth of angels. No matter that the egg is the same egg, palmed and reproduced. No matter that the birds are gently clipped into my sleeves and into the tails of my evening suit in readiness. The illusion is everything. The illusion is what reminds the audience of their innocence. The routine is now a classic, and has been imitated all over Europe.

It has come a long way from the wooden spheroid on its piece of elastic.

The conjuror may work without apparatus, but he can't work without imagination. I could entertain you with a card or a coin (see, Radim, the number of copecks you conceal in your nose: they cannot be good for it. How can you breathe?) but even these small party tricks are tedious after a while. The best illusions will need specially constructed properties, but they must be simple. They may use a certain costume or setting, but these must never distract from the accomplished effect. Too much rigmarole and the audience cannot be sure of what they have seen. Too little perhaps, and they may see too much. But if it is too easy to guess how a trick is done, no amount of hocus-pocus will turn it into a better trick. The very best tricks require unusual dexterity or physical skill. The worst can be bought by anybody at Bella-Bella's.

One of my favourite illusions is a simple transformation performed in full view of the audience within seconds. The basis of the trick is, I confess, borrowed from Harry Houdini, but even that master of escapology uses a screen for greater freedom of operation. In my version there is, as you will see when I describe it, every appearance of there being practically nothing between the audience and the transformation itself, though you will also see that in reality I have merely converted Houdini's screen into a kind of portable curtain. That small adjustment (a psychological adjustment, I would emphasise) makes every difference.

A carpet is rolled out and a large trunk first displayed and then placed upon it. No trapdoors, you see. Mind you, a trap door would not be remotely necessary, but the audience likes to have such safeguards. They are never the right ones, or the illusion could not take place, but they satisfy the audience's sense of objective scrutiny and appear to narrow the sphere of operations. A member of the audience is asked to provide his jacket, a precisely identifiable garment, which I then put on myself. I am manacled and put into a sack which has been placed in the trunk. The sack is tied with rope and padlocked. The jacketless member of the audience is given the three keys to hold. He holds them, grinning like a delighted baby. A drum rolls. My assistant leaps on top of the trunk with a roll of cloth which she holds above her head and releases to form a curtain covering the area in front of her body and the trunk. The audience, expecting a protracted drum-roll to accompany lengthy writhings and manipulations, is dumbfounded when the cloth is immediately lowered.

It can't be! The cloth has not been lowered by my assistant. It has been lowered by me! I smile at the whoops and yells of disbelief and roll up the cloth. I jump down from the trunk, reclaim the three keys from the gentleman in the audience, unlock and open the trunk, unlock the sack padlock and help my manacled assistant to step out. She is wearing the gentleman's jacket!

Of course, every little element of this apparent miracle is easily explicable. None of the equipment is examined. It does not need to be. There is too much of it and the whole illusion is performed at immense speed. The point is that the audience will subconsciously know that I use prepared equipment and yet will still wonder how everything can be done so quickly that the transformation appears to be instantaneous. The manacles can be slipped off by a simple repositioning of the wrists. I am free of them by the time the rope is being tightened above my head. It only appears to be tightened, of course: from within the sack I pull down a length of rope, while from outside my assistant pulls together the two looped ends and padlocks them. When the lid of the trunk is lowered, the length of rope I pulled down into the sack is enough to enable me to get out of it before the first trunk padlock is snapped shut. The trunk has a double inward panel at the rear with a release catch worked from the inside. I am out of both jacket and trunk by the time the second trunk padlock is closed and the keys have been given to the man from the audience. As soon as my assistant has dropped the cloth I am up on the trunk beside her, crouched and ready for the whole process to be reversed. Far from making the procedure at all difficult, the rigmarole with the keys is essential to allow enough time for all stages of the escape and replacement to be effected. The point is that the audience does not make sufficient allowance for this as usable time. The transposition of human bodies thus gives the illusion of being instantaneous.

I said no explanations, didn't I? But I don't mind telling you all this. The principle is hardly a secret, and wouldn't in any case spoil your enjoyment. I saw acts like it in my youth, in the period when I had left school and was studying all the effects of the illusionist. Needless to say, my dream was that Delecta should join me on the stage. As soon as I had achieved any sort of success, as soon even as I had found regular employment, I intended to spirit her away from Mavrinka and train her as my assistant. I had a vision of her in white tights, white leotard and pantaloons, with white roses in her hair, collecting on her gracefully curved wrists and arms a whole aviary of doves which I would bring to their mature birth from a single egg. As it was, in all my early illusions I had to rehearse as my own assistant, which was not the same thing at all. While she, staying on at her school far longer than I had at mine, or than she would ever have been expected to, was achieving distinct academic success.

Did I expect her studies to keep her wholly occupied? Did I imagine that she would remain in an abstracted purity of emotional attachment while I embarked on my career and travelled all over Europe? For although I soon had the chance to appear in the varieties in the Turkish Hall in August 5th Street I was not content there. The audiences were noisy. The hall was full of smoke, and people broke glasses. During the delicate build-up to my best tricks someone was bound to shout: "Bring on the dancers!" I needed a more sophisticated audience even though I could hope only for a very undistinguished position on the programme. This at least I could find in theatres abroad, in Paris, and in Munich. Much later I was to blossom in my own show at the Aquarium.

While I was on tour I wrote to her every week. My letters were about nothing very much, or nothing very much that would interest her, anyway. They were like little reassuring glances behind me. I had to make sure that she was still there. But how would I know, if she never replied to me? How could she reply when I was moving about from city to city? Yet I continued to send off my letters regularly, inventing all sorts of reasons for doing so, like pretending to myself that she still collected foreign stamps.

It's so strange, isn't it, that parting intensifies our attachment to those we love? I don't mean estrangement, of course, when absence is a necessary precondition of cutting our losses. I mean the suspension of a relationship that hasn't yet come to a conclusion, where the absence of the beloved allows us to forget completely all the small shortcomings that qualify our appraisal of her real presence. In my mind Delecta continued to exist in all her better moments, quizzical, physically graceful, even-tempered, uncritical of me. The reality I knew was not consistently so. But even if I chanced to think of them, which was not often, I could find excuses for all her failings. Even the fact that she did not write to me I could turn into a noble resolve, a vow of self-deprivation, as though I had left her in a cloister while I went out to fight dragons.

Those little reassuring glances back, my letters, were hectic bulletins of the absurd and trivial. I collected every scrap of obscure information or gossip that I thought might please her, and cast myself in the role of the unprotected innocent, a kind of travelling buffoon. What an error! I suppose it's a side of my character that is always lurking there, ready to bubble up when least needed. I suppose, too, that I thought of her as an innocent child who needed to be entertained with innocent prattle. What were the alternatives? I'd let myself in for the role I played through my timidity. If I had reached out that day and run my fingers slowly down her spine, if at any time at all I had taken her in my arms and let my mouth show my serious hunger for her, then I would at least have been unable to relapse into playing the jocular elder brother. We would have known where we stood. My letters were love letters of a sort, and I've no doubt she understood them to be love letters, but at the same time I knew that I was play-acting. And surely she knew that too, but what else she thought about I had no idea.

Meanwhile I was making a name for myself. Or rather, in the craven manner of the tyro I was making a name for the Great Tartini. Everything exciting has to be foreign, doesn't it? Did you know that Houdini's name is Eric Weiss? Well, that's a foreign name, too, and I suppose there aren't in fact any foreign names in America. They're all foreign. I used the name Tartini because I based my act on a violin. I was a demon fiddler and I conjured all kinds of demonic things out of my violin. Including the Devil himself, whom I then had to make disappear. I somehow had the idea that Tartini belonged in the Middle Ages, so the set was the dungeon of a castle, and the Great Tartini was also an alchemist. What a hotch-potch! The lugubrious setting was very useful, though, to disguise the raw edges of my illusions. The stage was in almost complete darkness, and the spots had green filters. It gave me greater confidence with my Brazen Head and Flying Alligator. It wasn't until much later in my career that I had enough confidence to call myself Rudolf Gromowski, and to work in a bright stage light that acted as a challenge to the audience to outwit me if they could – a modesty so natural and so casual that it seemed like effrontery. By that time I had also learned to be able to do without equipment if I wished. I could do anything I wanted to, and even reintroduced the Great Tartini, as a comic turn, pretending to expose the tricks but making them quite extraordinarily marvellous in the process.

But for a while I was entirely dependent on my first constructions, not only such classics as sawing the young lady in half, but more individual effects developed by me as being appropriate to the Great Tartini, effects such as those I have mentioned, along with the Dismembered Suit of Armour, and the Empty Coffin.

I was particularly proud of the Empty Coffin, because it was one of my first major illusions, built for me to my own design by my Uncle Stefan. I had no idea, when I first approached him with the request to build it for me, that he was already in severe financial straits. Later I felt guilty that I may have contributed in some way to his bankruptcy, distracting him from his business with impossibly complicated technical requests.

Dear Uncle Stefan. He was a superb craftsman. There were aspects of the design of my coffin that were purely his inspiration. I knew the effect I wanted to produce, and I had the basic idea, but there were frustrating problems in the details of the specification that hardly gave my uncle a moment's hesitation.

The result was beautiful, and quite original. The principle was a sliding panel, of course, and that was by no means new. But the design of the coffin itself made use of false perspective in the interior, based on a seventeenth-century peepshow that I had found in a corner of the Gomsza Museum. The eye was deceived, since it looked absolutely as shallow as an ordinary coffin and you would take little notice of the unusually thick sides necessary to support this impression. After the grotesquery of the Flying Alligator and the mind-reading interlude of the Talking Head (not to mention the pure comedy of the Dismembered Suit of Armour, which was largely worked with wires), the Empty Coffin brought my act to a striking climax. It was a perfect example of the simplicity necessary for the best illusions.

So when I returned with some sense of personal triumph to Gomsza I resolved that it should be the one trick that I would take with me out to Mavrinka to present to Delecta in a private performance that would not only commemorate my return but remind her of that earlier performance with Bella-Bella's egg. And because it needed an assistant, I would use it as an excuse to involve her. I would, in the course of astounding her with it, let her into its secrets and make her a part of their working.

The house at Mavrinka was more bustling and alive than I think I had ever seen it. Xanthia and her husband David were visiting with their new baby. I had never seen Uncle Anton so happy: he held it in both hands like a crock of gold that he'd just turned up in a ploughed field, beaming all over his face. A Professor Hannlich from the Institute had come for lunch, and Georgie and Aunt Zizzie were busy helping the cook in the kitchen. I was welcomed with little swooping cries of delight, as if by birds.

"Ah, Rudolf, your mother said you had grown thin but she didn't say how handsome. Give your Aunt Zizzie a big kiss."

"Where is Delecta?" I asked.

"Give her a moment," said my mother. "She'll be down. Anton, give the baby back to its mother or you'll drop it. Why don't you find some vodka?"

I was introduced to the baby and to David, its father, a young man whose facial expression was possibly even more infantile than his offspring's. Xanthia offered me her cheek. She had entered the charmed palace of motherhood, and was bestowing spells. Georgie was friendly enough to give me a floury hug, but of course I was uneasy about meeting Delecta again and wondered why she hadn't come running down. I was ushered into the living-room like an ordinary guest and had to endure a stiff conversation with Professor Hannlich, holding our brimming vodkas in front of us as though in competition for steady hands.

"I hear you are to entertain us this evening, young man," he said.

"I am," I said, looking around me and wondering why everyone seemed to have disappeared again. There were crucial events occurring in the kitchen, and some kind of staunching had to be done to the baby, but where were Anton and David, and what was Delecta doing?

"And you are an illusionist?" asked Professor Hannlich.

"I am indeed," I said. The professor smiled gently, and with a slight air of self-satisfied complicity, as though the mere knowledge of my profession gave him access to my most secret life. He was a tanned, raddled, saturnine man in middle life, looking less like a professor than a successful wine-grower. I did not know what he might be a professor of, but he had the air of not so much knowing theorems as being proud of a fine baritone voice.

"And you are . . . Dolfie?" he asked.

I did not know what to say to this. Of course I was Dolfie, but not to him. I stood there stiffly and bowed slightly.

"I am the Great Tartini," I said.

He should have laughed at that. Really, I shouldn't have minded a friendly response to my pompous formality. I was quite ready to laugh myself. In fact I had to bite back a giggle. What an idiot he was to be embarrassed: all he did was raise his head in half a vague nod, while his eyes glanced away as if to search for a hiding-place.

Why had I taken such an instant dislike to Professor Hannlich? For all I knew he felt insecure in his new relationship with the happy family at Mavrinka and was simply getting his bearings, having heard so much fond chatter about me. Or perhaps he knew my father at the Institute, and had heard him talk of me. I stupidly asked him if he knew my father, a laboratory technician! He said he didn't, and we were silent, looking into our already empty glasses.

When Delecta came downstairs she was fiercely brushed and scrubbed, as if for an outing, and at the same time looked as if she might have been fast asleep ten minutes previously. I thought her clothes seemed unusually severe: a coat and skirt brown as old bibles, and high buttoned boots. She looked as though she ought to have been carrying a small whip. It was only after she had given me a kiss, holding on to both my shoulders as though she were lifting me down from a wall, that I realised that she had been crying.

What was I to do? Should I go away? Should I never have gone away in the first place? All my better feelings were hovering as ineffectively as mayflies above the stagnating pool of my emotional life. But better feelings must always make way for the onward machine of daily life, and at that moment we were called to lunch. I sometimes think that the Last Trump itself would have to be postponed for lunch.

I picked up no useful signals during that babel of a meal. Really I could hardly have told you if it were the baby asking me about the night-life of Paris or Uncle Anton making political jokes to Xanthia's pocket husband or Professor Hannlich howling incessantly. All I knew was that Delecta said nothing at all but smiled valiantly round the table like a convalescent. I was suddenly a traveller in a foreign country, learning local customs for the first time. Even Georgie, the most relaxed of the girls as I remembered, dealt me conversational gambits from a much-pondered list in the far side of her brain, like a journalist.

I knew, of course, why there was such a large gathering for lunch and why (as I was proudly told) the Priuts were coming over after tea and bringing Mstislav Priut's old aunt, who was a cousin of the Arch-Duke's: Anton and Zizzie were drumming up an audience for me. I ought to have been pleased, just as I ought to have recognised my favoured position when I was first to be helped to a second serving of goose, but I wasn't. No, not at all. I had wanted Delecta to myself. I wouldn't have minded if everyone else had chosen to go away for the day. I would have been happy if those three corpses of geese glossily snug in their steaming bed of red cabbage had still been white birds hissing in their orchard freedom.

I was allowed to have Delecta during the afternoon to rehearse as my assistant. The long drawing-room was set up as a tiny theatre, with tables and two standing lamps, and a screen brought down from upstairs. All this had been arranged, as had Delecta's participation. Anton helped me in with my properties. Only the coffin was really too large for me to manage on my own. As we carried it in I reflected that they might just as well carry me away at the end in it. I felt that my position was hopeless.

The others couldn't keep away. Xanthia brought her baby in to be shown the pretty things even though the little red creature seemed as blind as a kitten. At one crucial moment, when I had just taken Delecta by both hands and spoken her name in that strange formal tone that goes beyond the vocative into a drama of tender annunciation, in swept Georgie with dishes of bon-bons, whistling slightly between her teeth.

"Whoops," she said, stretching her mouth at us in a smirk of mechanical geniality. I knew it couldn't be a genuine smile, for a genuine smile would have revealed to me whatever she understood to be the reality of Delecta's feelings for me, which surely they had discussed often, far into the night. She swept out again.

There was nothing for it but to get on with the rehearsal. I showed her the cups to be passed and the awkward objects to be disposed of. I planted prepared playing cards on her person. Shades of Bella-Bella! I explained the rigmarole of the coffin.

"Why must I say 'Hey Presto'?" she asked.

"Because I'm inside the coffin and can't say it myself," I said.

"What does it mean?" she persisted.

"I don't really know," I replied. "It must be Italian. If it's 'e presto', I expect it means 'and quickly', or something of that sort."

"In the twinkling of an eye?" she offered.

"Yes," I said.

"Well?" she said, looking at me with a twinkling in her own eye.

"Well what?" I replied, my heart sinking at the prospect now of her forcing the issue.

"There are many things that can happen in the twinkling of an eye," she said mysteriously. She touched my cheek briefly.

I felt the initiative passing from me. I felt suddenly drained and helpless, yielding that initiative. It was a feeling I remembered well from years and years before when, for example, she had insisted on finishing a painting for me. She would lean over and colour-in key portions of my landscape, her tongue just showing between her teeth in concentration, sometimes curling up to touch the lip in a glistening mime of the moving pencil. Despite her kindly effort her colouring would always be just that little bit less careful than mine would have been. The delicious powerlessness, the consent to lose my will in hers, was a precise physical sensation to which I willingly abandoned myself. The sense that the painting might be spoiled, and that I would allow it to be spoiled, irrevocably, sent a deep wave of cold shooting down my back and brought a ringing to my ears.

This was my moment, I fully recognised, but it had also become her moment too. I could not speak. My heart was full of all that I wanted, and I could say nothing for the hope that it would be she who would say it.

I became aware of the old grandfather clock by the fireplace standing erect in his perpetual alertness to the passing of time. The space between each leaden heart-beat seemed prolonged, a small limbo of silence perpetually on offer, perpetually being snatched away. That sound was like the insistence of death, tolerated as the pronouncement of a familiar social machine. The hour displaced on its moon face was twenty past three, a time when the human heart is itself at its lowest ebb. Was this all that we had had? Was it all that we had left? You will say that it was only a convenience, an innocent time of the day, but I knew in my silence that it was a time of trial.

I was actually in the coffin. Her hand had been at my cheek. Was it still at my cheek? Grandfather Time in his own coffin told me that I could still act as if it were.

Could I ask her why she had never written to me? I wanted her to confess it herself.

Could I embrace her frankly, as a lover, not as a cousin and a conjuror? I wanted her to embrace me.

She had to acknowledge herself as chosen. The princess had to condescend to the fool.

I thought of moving my hand to her hand, to keep it at my cheek. I could approve that gesture as a beginning of something that she might be induced to continue. But her hand was leaving my cheek. At the very next tick of the clock it could fairly be said that her fingers were no longer quite in contact with it.

I might have been timing a race with a stop-watch, except that it was myself who was running it. Real time isn't quite like that. It's more like a great glacier nudging along the frozen mammoths of one's long-dead intentions: they glare at you through the ice as though still alive. Everything is still and deathly cold. But moving. Imperceptibly moving. So you are conscious that there is some sort of goal.

What a trick it would be to turn linear time back on itself, so that it needn't have any goal at all! Not simply to *go* back, since that would be to succumb to the fascinating but fatally improper temptation of the second chance. One can never go back. No, I mean to play a trick on time, turn it inside out. You've seen the Möbius strip, the loop of paper with the twist so that the wandering fly moves from inside to outside not aware when the one becomes the other because there is no point where it does so. The Klein Bottle is the three-dimensional version. It looks like a cucumber swallowing itself. Can't we imagine a version that includes the dimension of time? If we could, then going back would be the same as going forward. The whole of history would have its tail in its mouth. All time would be theoretically present, just as the whole of the Klein Bottle is one surface. You could never pour anything out of it. Or into it, for that matter.

I could imagine a dance of a sacred liquid, neither still nor moving. A medium for true life.

Whereas there I was, frozen in my glacier, lumbered with emotions that were extinct as soon as they could be identified. I was a kind of paleontologist of love, finding names and labels for states of being that barely existed.

There was a label in question just then, I suddenly felt, that wasn't only to do with me and my feelings. It was something to do exclusively with Delecta, and her state of mind, something I had taken too little account of. It was a label for her wistfulness, her puzzlement, her weepy mood, her twinkling challenge, her disappointment, her rage (I could see the rage gathering in her dark eyes with every tick of the clock). What was it? It was like a riddle suddenly becoming clear to me in that moment when I saw that there was a riddle to be guessed.

It was choice. Delecta was having to make a decision. I had

returned after a long absence and thrown her into a quandary. In the instant before the full answer to the riddle came flooding in upon me I felt relieved, grateful, flattered: she did have feelings for me, I was indeed to be seriously considered, I had moved her, I was a possibility. But against what or whom was I being judged? For what was I being assessed?

At that moment I recollected something that had been said at lunch. It had been part of the general hum of conversation that had arisen about myself and conjuring, and so I had in my nervousness suppressed it. Now I could see that there had been other reasons for suppressing it. The smirking Professor Hannlich had picked up a remark which for once seemed to interest him.

"You ask," he had said, waving his fork in the air, "why these stage illusions involve disappearances?"

"That's what I was wondering," said my Uncle Anton. "Isn't it more surprising if strange things unexpectedly *appear*?"

"Not really," I said. "Anything appearing unexpectedly is strange, isn't it? But the disappearance of something that you've already had time to get used to is much stranger. Best of all is the combination of both, the transformation."

Aunt Zizzie was passing tureens of baked onions and parsleyed potatoes. David was trying to get Xanthia to produce more cider, not daring to ask for it himself, and Xanthia was confiding something very terrifying and intimate about babies to Georgie. The conversation was taking place in a mild hubbub, and no one was taking it very seriously.

"Thank you," said Uncle Anton. "I think I could manage to transform another baked onion."

"That is not the answer," said Professor Hannlich. "The real answer is deeply involved with the whole development of the mediaeval drama. What is the great disappearance in the culture of Christendom? It is the disappearance of the body of Christ from the sepulchre. The women at the tomb were your first audience."

Had I detected at that point a faint snort from Delecta? Was it a suppressed laugh, or had she choked on a sprig of parsley? If it had been a response to the professor's theory, was it an amused cry of approval, felt to be undignified? Or was it a more intimate sound, critical but tolerant, as of something heard and argued many times before? Or was it pure impudence, suppressed derision? I had barely focussed on the sound before I was myself, distractingly, faced with a hot tureen of pungent caramelised onion.

"Why did the Greeks only have transformations?" continued the professor, speaking with his mouth full. "That is because the metamorphosis is a myth of aetiology. We have the miracle of disappearance, and the ritual development of the Corpus Christi play. The Greeks have tragedy, the transformation of the hero through the recognition of origins. For the Greeks, psychology; for the Christians, magic."

"My goodness," said Uncle Anton. "I thought the Church was against magic."

"I don't think you quite understand the level of analogy I'm applying here," smiled the Professor. He had looked round the table, trying not to seem annoyed that not everyone was listening. "This young man's hocus pocus is ultimately built upon the model of the resurrection. The priest and the magician share a celebratory . . . syntax."

More ambiguous sounds from Delecta.

"Why," concluded Professor Hannlich triumphantly, "'hocus pocus' is itself a clinching example of what I mean. It is the vulgar, that is to say unlatined, interpretation of the priest's creation of the miracle of the Eucharist, 'Hoc est corpus . . .'"

"In that case," said my uncle, "it's surely an appearance, not a disappearance, and we're back to where we started." He had laughed heartily at that, and tucked into his fresh helping of goose.

Within the space of another tick of the grandfather clock I was in full possession of my precarious intuition. I had not, even in my ambition to present my skills at Mavrinka like the suitor in a fairy-tale returning to the king after completing impossible tasks, bothered to discover that Delecta had left school and was already studying at the Institute. This lewd professor, so easy in his presence in the house, so confident in his views, and so unnaturally diffident with me, who must have been presented to him as some sort of rival, was her teacher and clearly, then, her admirer. God forbid the thought! How could it be so? How could my aunt and uncle not realise? More particularly, how could Xanthia and Georgie not realise? Why had his effrontery not been challenged?

And to what degree had Delecta encouraged it?

She was aware of it, that was certain. No doubt she was flattered. Perhaps in a flush of intellectual self-esteem she had made some response. And then, as usual, lost interest. Or perhaps she was slowly being won over, a patient seduction by a practised villain, his presence here at Mavrinka today of all days forming a subtle and calculating ultimatum.

This was the poor girl's choice. That was why she had been up in her room, crying. And here was I standing in my futile coffin in an agony of postponed action, as though forced to perform a trick I had never practised. But real life is just like that. We never get a chance to rehearse it.

In this second of realisation, my leaden heart slowing to the remorseless warning of the pendulum, my wits buried in speculation, my face an idiot gawp, I at last confronted my fate.

'Hey presto!' said Delecta, shutting the coffin lid upon me. The last clear view I had of her was of a pair of decisively pursed lips and a pair of interrogative eyebrows.

It was no wonder I disappeared.

There are emotions that destroy one as surely as obliterating calamities like war, disease, earthquake. My shame, frustrated passion, inadequacy and jealousy fuelled a wish to be swallowed up utterly. And so I was. I was literally flattened by the predicament I was in.

When she opened the coffin lid almost immediately, she was astonished. She could not see me, but I could see her. She hadn't expected me to do the trick there and then. To her the coffin was suddenly utterly empty.

She retreated a little, as if afraid of this wooden shape that had (even with warning) swallowed me up. She took two or three steps backwards, and bumped into a small table. Turning to steady it, she saw that it contained one of Georgie's dishes of bon-bons. As if in a daze she reached out and put one in her mouth. Then she sat down, the knave of hearts falling from her blouse to the floor.

She didn't look as if she were waiting for anything to happen.

She was neither audience nor accomplice. And what about me? What did I expect to happen? I did not know whether I was her lover or not. I didn't deserve to be.

I didn't deserve to be an illusionist, either. For with the coffin lid open I couldn't reappear.

I thought I had explained how she must shut the coffin lid again before I could be released. Perhaps I had, but she certainly showed no sign of doing so. She sat there deep in thought, moving her mouth and tongue again and again over the little drop of boiled sugar until it must have dwindled to the size of my hopes.

Why hadn't she thrown her arms about me, and welcomed me with extravagant affection? I could imagine how it might have been done, descending the stairs at a run, a bounce across the hall, slightly displacing a rug, with "Oh, Dolfie, Dolfie, you don't know how glad I am to see you! Didn't you get my letters?" And I would have silently twirled her in my embrace, the scent of her hair full in my nostrils. Why was she such an odd girl? What was it that put her off me? It was as though I unwittingly terrified her.

My story is to all intents and purposes over. There I was, deep in my personal Klein Bottle, a master of confusion himself confused. And there was Delecta on a sofa, already looking less confused than bored.

Scowling slightly, she took another bon-bon. Her booted ankles were crossed, her hands lightly grasping the sofa cushions as if she were about to leap up again. Did she know that I could see her? The extreme beauty of those who think they are unobserved is a rarely seen phenomenon. The mind has been released from the duty of managing the muscles of the face in its articulation and communication of emotion. It is withdrawn and serene, the primary human mask with no demands made upon it. She wrinkled her upper lip as if to get rid of an itch, and after a second or two smoothed her skirt.

It wasn't long before someone came into the room again. I heard the door, and the tread, as feet moved from the floorboards to the carpet that covered the centre of the room. The first clue that I had to the person's identity was a large hand that came over the back of the sofa and grasped Delecta's shoulder. It was a male hand, the gesture familiar, intended to reassure, to convey unspoken thoughts. It was the kind of gesture a husband would make to a wife who had something on her mind that she didn't want to talk about. It was not her father's hand. It was Professor Hannlich's.

His voice was cautious, as though he had looked everywhere in the room and seen no one, but was still not quite sure:

"Where is the Great Tartini?" he asked.

"He's gone," said Delecta, dully.

"Gone?" I thought, incredulously. How could she say I was gone? Did she really think, could she possibly have thought that I had really disappeared? For a moment I didn't know whether to be amused at her incredulity or alarmed at her deviousness, thinking that she might be ready out of revenge to get him to talk about me in my presence. Then I realised that she was referring not so much to my corporeal presence as to my soul in relation to hers. I had not effectively made contact. I had not stayed to meet her on her own ground. Was this a sort of comfort to me? I was ready to seize on anything, even the fact that her own hand had not (as any wife's would who was not, for example, stupefied by mourning) reached up to touch or grasp Professor Hannlich's hand when it was pressing her shoulder. Small comfort! Soon he was seated by her on the sofa and his hand was upon her again and it was not on her shoulder.

I knew that I deserved my imprisonment and my agony. I had brought it on myself. I was ready to suffer it to its fullest extent.

To be fair to Delecta, she did make some kind of demur.

"Don't worry," said Hannlich soothingly. "Your mother and Georgie are up to their ears in puff pastry, Xanthia is feeding the baby, and your father has taken David to see the horses. Presumably the Great Tartini has gone with them. No one will come in."

She looked at him searchingly through her daze, and I saw in that look the history of enough intimacy to exclude my frail projects and imaginings. She had not removed his hand from its outrageous resting place. She hadn't even finished sucking her bon-bon. His own mask was a mask of ardent, knowing attention. To my eyes it was nothing more than a priapic leer.

In a moment she would, I was sure, bring herself to explain that I was still in the coffin, apparently empty as it was. They could go no further, could they? I had seen enough. My ruin was complete.

And all this, of course, was years ago. Whenever I have returned to Gomsza it has been with the hope that she will have found it in herself to be able to keep her attention on me long enough to realise that we were made for one another. Some sort of vision of her has always sustained me in my travels, always in the end brought me back to her. A strand of her hair brushed impatiently back from her forehead. Her bottom lip sucked in and chewed in doubtfulness or vacancy.

But on this last visit it was too late. She has married a fat grocer from Reznik.

15

The Transformation of the Mayor of Morsken

PUFFING EXTREMELY WITH the effort of pulling its oddly abbreviated backward load, the little train arrived at the station in Morsken. So laboured had its journey been that it hardly seemed necessary to apply the brakes. A mild tightening squeal brought it quickly to a stop, and two of the men who had captured the final carriage and the fourgon of the Paris Express leaped from the driver's cab, smirking and spitting on the platform. The third (for there were only three of them to commandeer the whole train, emboldened as they were by drink and the possession of keys to both locked carriages) sat on the roof of the train with crossed legs and a rifle across his knees. He rose slowly, as if cramped, stooping to pick up the striped rug he had been sitting on, and at the same time let off his rifle with the other hand into the night air. He might have been signalling the arrival of the train, but there was no need.

Ranged along the platform beneath its crenellated wooden canopy was a line of policemen standing formally at ease as though guarding a funeral route. Their blue serge uniforms were far from new, the red facings worn or eked out with patches of a different shade. Their leather belts and bucklers were worn, and only some of them wore the regulation kepi. But each of them had at his hip an enormous holster containing a gleaming black pistol, sticking out like a key designed to wind up a tin soldier. The station was poorly lit by one or two oil lamps.

When the bandit on the roof fired his salutation, some of the policemen turned and grinned at each other, and one of them adjusted his pistol in its holster. The shot was a reminder that something exciting was afoot, a dangerous little welcoming committee for which the armoury had been opened that very afternoon and the weapons issued. The bandit unlocked the main carriage door and tossed the key casually to the officer in charge.

What had they expected? The officer in charge was a red-haired bully called Von Bergen, pacing the platform like a child with lead soldiers, positioning men so that no one could escape from the train. At his side was the almost tearful Mayor of Morsken, a former cobbler called Milo Muszmek. He followed Von Bergen with indistinct pleading, approached him as if to stroke or fondle him into a concession that was now in reality a foregone hope. For the most part Von Bergen ignored him, stalking smartly up and down, peering between the carriages to make sure that his men on the other side of the line were spaced efficiently, signalling to others to close in on the end of the train, to step down on to the track to encircle it completely. Once or twice he turned and breasted Muszmek away with a resistant squaring of the shoulders and aggressive jerks of the head. Muszmek was hardly cowed by this, but several times he attempted to leave, only to have his way barred by one or other of the armed police.

'This was your little piece of theatre in the first place, Muszmek,' said Von Bergen. 'You'll have to see it out now.'

Muszmek was sweating.

'It's treason,' he muttered. 'Bare-faced treason.'

Von Bergen smiled.

'We shall see,' he said. 'If your prize is on board the train it's the end of the road for you. You're finished in any case. The tide has turned.'

'Who has paid you to do this, Von Bergen?'

'Freedom has no need to bribe her servants, Muszmek.'

As they faced each other on the platform it seemed as if they might come to blows, but some mysterious force kept the men from touching one another. Mutual reproach, and a long history of antagonism, acted as a bond between them. It was as though what either threatened the other deserved, as though what each had done the other was ready to undo. The overheated little engine was sending exhausted sighs of steam into the track-well that erupted in clouds between the carriage and the platform. When these cleared the carriage door was open and stepping down from it was a young man dressed in a white suit.

'Well?' asked the young man peremptorily, making little effort to disguise the fact that he was a young woman. 'Which of you is the Mayor? Which is Muszmek?'

'I am,' said Muszmek and Von Bergen simultaneously. They looked at each other.

'I am Muszmek,' said Muszmek defiantly. 'And this is Von Bergen, the Chief of Police.'

'No,' said Von Bergen. 'I am now the Mayor. I appoint myself Mayor. Muszmek is under arrest on the charge of treason.'

The bandits who had driven the train roared with laughter at this. The one who had been on the roof unbuttoned his waistcoat and spat on the platform, treading it into the dust.

'They'll kill each other before long, you'll see,' he said. 'They were like this at school. They can't bear each other, but they can't let each other out of their sight.'

'Be quiet, you,' said Von Bergen to the bandit.

'I'll be as quiet as tobacco once I've been paid, my friend,' said the bandit. He pulled the bolt on his rifle and caught the bullet as it was ejected. He looked at it briefly, smelt it as though it were a cigar, rolled his eyes, winked broadly at everyone, and fed the bullet back into his rifle, snapping the bolt ostentatiously.

The line of young policemen stirred excitedly at this, and one of them was heard to laugh. The bandit waved at him in careless greeting.

'How are you doing, Franz?' he called out. 'Pity they couldn't find a uniform to fit you.'

'Silence!' cried Von Bergen, whirling round to his men. 'Attention! Draw your arms!'

The line came to attention, and the pistols were produced. Some of the men seemed to be familiar with their weapons, automatically taking off the safety catch. Others simply held them by their sides, slightly away from the body, as if they might go off by chance.

'You, you and you,' snapped Von Bergen. 'Arrest this man!'

The policemen looked uncertain. The bandit, who was by now fingering a real cigar and hunting for matches in his waistcoat, laughed again and pointed to Muszmek.

'There's your victim, friends,' he said. 'It looks as though your chief's got all he wanted. A little trainload of voluntary captives, the tables turned, his rival's job, what next?'

'What are you waiting for?' said Von Bergen. 'I'll have you on a charge.'

Three of his men came forward and took hold of the Mayor, gently enough, as though removing a drunk from a restaurant. Muszmek looked at them sorrowfully.

'You don't know what you're doing,' he said, shaking his head. 'Von Bergen, I don't understand this at all.'

The bandit laughed again, puffing on his cigar.

'Von Bergen knows which side his bread is buttered on, that's all,' he said. 'And so do I. I'd be still slaving away in the salt-works if I didn't.'

'You'd still be in jail if there was any law and order in this town,' said the Mayor, trying to free his arms from the grip of the young policemen.

'There's a new order of things, Mayor,' said the bandit. 'Haven't you noticed? This is the twentieth century, at last. The millennium. All the jails are empty.'

'The criminals are on the streets,' muttered Muszmek.

'On the streets?' said the bandit. 'Most of them are on this railway platform taking orders from your old friend Von Bergen there.'

'I've had enough of this from both of you,' said Von Bergen. He turned back to the puzzled young figure in the white suit, but she had disappeared. He looked up and down the platform.

'Got back on the train, sir,' called one of the policemen helpfully.

In the carriage, Beatricz looked in agonised appeal at her three travelling companions before giving her coded rap on the door of the schlafzimmer.

'It's all gone wrong,' she said. 'Do you have guns?'

'Of course we don't have guns,' said Rudolf. 'What do you mean "gone wrong"? What's right about kidnapping in the first place?'

She looked at him, white-faced.

'It depends on who's doing the kidnapping, doesn't it?' she said.

The inner door opened and the maid appeared.

'It's no good,' said Beatricz. 'It's chaos out there! Muszmek's under arrest. We've been found out.'

They were on either side of the little door, each holding a handle. There was a moment's indecision, a wavering, when it was not clear whether the maid should come out or Beatricz should go in before they could lock the door against Von Bergen and his unexpected reception. There was no time to lock the door. Von Bergen was in the carriage, closely followed by his men.

'Keep away from that door,' he cried.

Beatricz turned defiantly, but he caught hold of her wrist and flung her into a corner, into the arms of Romuald and Rudolf.

'I say,' said Rudolf, in mild objection. 'This is an outrage.'

Von Bergen had one foot in the door and one hand on his pistol. One of the policemen was just behind him. He caught hold of the maid's wrist to pull her through into the compartment, but found her strangely resistant. He used both hands to pull. The maid produced a small gun and fired at him. It made a pert little snap like a firecracker.

'What the devil!' muttered Von Bergen. The bullet had missed. He struggled to produce his own pistol. The maid fired again, and this time caught the accompanying policeman in the fore-arm. He let out a bellow like someone who has just hit his thumb with a hammer, and fell back heavily against Radim.

Von Bergen levelled his pistol and fired. The maid fell heavily forward on to her knees, reaching for Von Bergen's weapon which went off again, splintering the panelling.

'Get back!' shouted Von Bergen to Radim, Rudolf and Romuald. But they had no intention of coming forward. Rudolf felt for Beatricz's hand and squeezed it as if to say: 'Whatever happens next, however terrible it is, I'm here!' It's not clear how useful the message might have been at that point, but strangely enough Beatricz's hand squeezed back. In another context, in a dream of heroism perhaps, such a response would have been a signal of faithfulness, a stimulant to brave deeds, a sudden pact. In this case, sadly for Rudolf, it was merely a reflex. The maid Maddalejna lay on the compartment floor, and Beatricz was calling out. She moved forward, whether to attack Von Bergen or attend to her maid is not clear, but Rudolf restrained her for her own good.

In the inner compartment the figure in black lay on the bed, in a funereal stillness.

Would they now shoot the Arch-Duke? thought Rudolf.

Von Bergen disarmed the maid, who in any case was unconscious, possibly dead. He motioned to his men to guard her closely and to attend to the policeman who had been shot. He approached the figure on the bed.

'I have done all that you requested, your excellency,' said Von Bergen, the obsequiousness of his tone somewhat spoiled by the fact that he was panting heavily. 'Your excellency?'

Rudolf, who heard these words, felt a thrill of horror. What had the Arch-Duke arranged, what possible *bouleversement* of their already extraordinary plans could he have set in motion that would so endanger the lives of those closest to him?

Von Bergen was leaning over the prostrate figure in the berth.

'Fetch a lamp, somebody,' he said. 'I can hardly see a thing in here.'

When the lamp was brought, it illuminated more of the inner compartment than had before been seen. The ornate padded facings and hangings ingeniously disguised its limited shape, which was, after all, simply a slice of railway carriage. It was designed to look more like a Berber tent.

Von Bergen busied himself to remove the cloth over the face, the gag between the teeth, the ropes that bound feet, arms and hands. The shape on the bed stirred as if from drugged sleep. It opened one eye.

He was a man of advanced years, bulky, but not corpulent. His power slumbered in him, like iron beneath rust. His hair, cut *en brosse*, was grey, but his moustache was still black. The moustache was remarkable, full without either stiffness or drooping, swept copiously to each side of his lip like a pair of shoulders. His beard was by comparison nothing more than a texture of bristle, the carefully cropped growth of a man who has not shaved for two weeks. The opened eye was a limpid blue, the haunted colour of bluebells in a wood. He opened the other eye.

This was not the Arch-Duke. This was not the profile of coins. And Von Bergen did not expect it to be.

But was there some hesitation here on the part of a minion far from the familiar dark places where power issues its whispered commands? Did he require some sign?

The man sat up and swivelled round on the bed to face the provincial lackey who had released him. He spoke.

'You are Von Bergen?'

There was a quick nod in reply, and a look of expectation and uncertainty.

'Your excellency?'

The moustache lifted its shoulders and emitted a deep chuckle.

'You are right to be so cautious, Von Bergen, when so many on this train are not what they appear to be. Even if I were to pronounce to you the secret syllables of our operation you would not be fully satisfied, would you? A single name, a code-word committed to memory, held in trust like a precious key? The very first piece of information that would be divulged under the simplest form of persuasion such as the prising up with small pliers of a thumbnail! I shall not insult you by pronouncing the word.'

Von Bergen seemed mesmerised by the commanding access of speech evidenced by the risen prisoner.

'No indeed, your excellency.'

'So you naturally require the evidence that I am who you expect me to be? The evidence that your instructions told you to ask for, and that you are too delicate to ask for directly? I admire your tact. Here.'

The man appeared to adjust the fastening of the glove on his left hand, and then reached out with that hand towards the gun still held by Von Bergen. Von Bergen looked down in amazement as, with a click, the finger and thumb opened stiffly and then closed firmly on the gun. As the hand drew back, Von Bergen attempted for a moment to retain the gun, but soon found that he could not. Even that slight grip, as apparently fastidious as a valet removing a hair from a lapel, was in reality as tight as a vice. He held the weapon in the air. A second or two passed. There was a further click, and an indistinct whirr, as of a released cog. The finger and thumb sprang open and the gun dropped into the man's waiting right hand. The finger and thumb remained in their released posture, stiffly measuring a half-inch, like an elegant shop-window dummy. Von Bergen could see that the hand was not gloved at all, but was an ingenious simulacrum of rosy celluloid.

'Your excellency!' he breathed, with the faint smile of someone to whom an honour has been done.

No, it was not the Arch-Duke, any more than it was Cyprian Pyramur, or Johann Schmeck.

It was Korn.

16

The Slipping of the Silver Wig

WHAT KIND OF a man was Korn to allow himself to be kidnapped under such circumstances? Answer: he was the kind of man eager for a chance to turn the tables by being kidnapped under precisely those circumstances. His was the greater prize.

All that had been a matter of speculation about him in the train during that long evening had contained an element of truth, but there is a private destiny which the powerful know is theirs and which the public cannot guess. Korn's network of influence might in theory have been sufficient reason to seize the reins of government, given the military support from Zemlinsz that would have underwritten any putsch. Zemlinsz's response to the unrest in Gomsza would have inevitably been to throw in his lot with the strongest party, despite his loyalty to the Arch-Duke. The nearer the wild Minski came to the capital, the closer was that moment of unlikely alliance. The more anarchists there were in the streets, the greater credibility the Commissioner of Police had with the military establishment, since only he could control them.

And yet (and what a telling proviso this was) all Korn's power had to be exercised in the name of the Arch-Duke. The commands were his, but the authority, as Beatricz had so rightly said, was the Arch-Duke's. When Korn broke the strikes in Mittgarten, he was able to make a deal with the miners. The rights of the coal-owners were severely limited. The same sort of thing happened at the

Morsken saltworks. But because these changes carried the ducal seal, the authority to put them into effect was the Arch-Duke's. It was no wonder that the Arch-Duke thought himself popular for a time.

But he was not popular with the local magnates, most of whom were German in any case. Their allegiance lay elsewhere. And in reality Korn could command a following wider by far than could be summoned into existence by secret plots and small pairs of pliers.

But he was not sure of it. That was the crucial thing.

And when his network of informers came up with the news that the Arch-Duke wanted him out of the way, he was delighted. From all crannies of the Court they came to him, ambitious equerries, disaffected private secretaries, even an old majordomo with a grudge about a missing bottle of tokay: something was afoot. Korn was to disappear.

'It is a ridiculous mistake,' he explained to his cronies, shrugging his shoulders behind his enormous desk in a room full of pipe smoke. 'He claims I am a source of corruption. Does he think this is really the time for some kind of holy crusade? He is like a man sawing off the branch of a tree, thinking to save the tree, while he himself is sitting on it. He should know that only I can prevent his downfall in the long run. And in the short run too, for that matter.'

Piece by piece he assembled the fretted enigma of the plot to remove him bodily from the political scene. It was never clear in all its details, but its point was plain enough.

'Do they think that things will change if I am made to disappear?' Korn asked in exasperation, pacing his room with his meerschaum tugging at his fleshy lower lip like a butcher's hook. 'And do they really think that packing me off to the German-speaking provinces is the right way to go about it? Does the Arch-Duke possibly believe that he still has any influence in Morsken? And Morsken of all places! The cool cheek of it! Well, now, you have to admire that particular stroke. That does have a touch of political imagination about it.'

And he had fallen silent in the middle of his room, directly beneath the chandelier, so that the light shone directly all round him in his smoke like a demon in the theatre. He chuckled. He was laying his own plans. For the operation was of such delicacy and moment that the Arch-Duke would only entrust it to someone who was very close to him. If he was to be hoist with his own petard, this was the ideal way to do it. Korn would play him out, as on a fishing line, before hauling him savagely in. And his kidnapper would be the ideal bait.

Korn had rubbed his hands with glee, or would have done so if he had two hands to rub. The gesture was limited to a cradling of his left arm, a massage of his left elbow, and a little hopping dance like a child eager for a turn at a game.

In the railway carriage, when his ordeal was over and he was with much greater point massaging parts of his body that ached from having been tied up, he very nearly performed the little dance again. But there wasn't very much room in the compartment.

To Rudolf, Radim and Romuald the whole business had begun to seem like a masquerade designed to keep them totally confused. They had been allowed to see so little of the bizarre figure confined in the schlafzimmer that he had taken on the enticement of the promised treat, even of an eventual revelation that might lend a purpose to their communal journey beyond the variously expedient circumstances of their individual escapes from Gomsza. In their sleeplessness they were ready to confuse the already confusing. Their strange companion's stories blurred in their minds the one with the other, until seducer and victim, parent and lover, tyrant and fugitive, were as one.

Her latest story, by being third in series, convention might have claimed on behalf of truth. But even this suddenly seemed to evaporate. For there turned out to be no Arch-Duke, only this darker figure of government, agent of terror standing not at the Arch-Duke's right but at his left hand, a man who was reputed to drink his vodka piping hot, a man who could command plays to be rewritten, a man of the little pliers. And what is more, as all were agreed, he was the man of the moment, the one man who had no need to leave Gomsza, the man whom the future addressed in terms of flattering endearment.

And now he had made them all prisoner. They were left in the abrupted remains of the Paris Express which were shunted beyond the station into a kind of enormous shed, open to the sky but partly surmounted by a framework of girders and gantries. The bandit who was ordered to do it grumbled a great deal, and perhaps because he felt put upon was induced to leave them a lamp and to tell them something of their fate. He was a lugubrious man who seemed to take great pleasure in pretending that their predicament was nothing to do with him at all.

'I expect you lot are going to be shot at dawn,' he said casually, with an air of comic exaggeration, as though they were schoolboys waiting to be seen by the headmaster. Since that was what very well might actually happen, reflected Rudolf, it was a singularly unhelpful remark to make.

'You'll not get out of here, either,' said the bandit, 'so don't think of it. His Excellency is going to be entertained tonight at the castle, but he'll be back.'

He peered at them closely through the carriage window, while making sure that all the doors were locked. Then he came up to their compartment again. Because there was no platform he seemed a very long way below them.

'Here!' he called up. 'Are you enemies of the state?'

'No,' said Rudolf emphatically. The others shook their heads.

'Funny,' said the bandit. 'His Excellency said you were.'

Then after a moment, he added:

'I am. So we're on opposite sides after all.'

He seemed to have had a moment of anxiety on this score, but now that he was satisfied he went away, whistling. They heard what sounded like great gates moving on rollers, clanging shut and being locked. Then all was silent.

'Where are we now?' asked Radim.

'It must be where they service the trains,' said Romuald.

'Actually,' said Rudolf, 'I believe we are in a device for changing the bogies. Look. The whole carriage can be lifted up off its wheels and then lowered again.'

'Why on earth?' asked Radim.

'Morsken is a frontier town near enough, isn't it?' said Rudolf. 'At one time they used a different gauge in Germany, so they'd have had to change the bogies. You'd have gone on to Berlin from here.'

'Before they built the through line?'

'Exactly.'

'So in theory,' put in Romuald, 'we could drive the train onwards and still get where we wanted to go?'

'Absolutely not,' said Rudolf. 'The old line can't exist any more. Or if any of it does, it wouldn't go very far. And we would have to change the bogies. Could you do that?'

'Of course not.'

'And in any case we are shut in,' continued Rudolf. 'With the place guarded by those policemen, I expect. They seem quite ready to use their weapons, don't they?'

'In other words, there's nothing at all we can do,' said Romuald.

'I think we should look to the ladies,' said Rudolf. 'That's what we should do.'

'Quite,' said Romuald. 'You can do that while Radim and I explore this yard we're in. Haven't you noticed? They locked all the carriage doors, but didn't realise that you can't lock the windows. Look, they still open normally. Easy enough to get out, I think.'

He began to climb out.

'Take care, won't you?' said Rudolf.

'Of course I will,' said Romuald, coming back into the compartment. He wiped his hands on a handkerchief. 'I think I'm going to have to squeeze out backwards.' He tried again.

'Yes,' he panted. 'This is better. Now I can stand on the door and then jump down.'

He did so.

'Hey,' Romuald called up softly. 'Be careful. It's much further to the ground than you think.'

Radim looked uncertainly at Rudolf.

'You don't have to go, you know,' said Rudolf. 'Stay here with us.'

'He'd better not go alone,' said Radim. 'Something might happen to him.' He started to ease his bulk through the window.

'Good luck,' said Rudolf.

Beatricz turned round from the other end of the compartment. She was kneeling on the floor, attending to Maddalejna.

'Where are they going?' she asked.

Rudolf came over to her. She stood up.

'They've gone to see what sort of a place we're in,' he said. 'To see if there's any way of escape.'

'Escape?' said Beatricz. 'They wouldn't have left any possibility of escape. Korn must intend to kill you.'

Rudolf gave a bitter laugh.

'I'm sure you're in a better position to fathom his intentions than I am,' he said.

She dropped her eyes from his. Even in the dim light from the bandit's oil lamp he saw the fullness of her eyelids, the sandy lashes.

'I'm sorry,' she said. 'We've got you into a lot of trouble, haven't we?'

'You could say so,' said Rudolf, coming to take her arm. She half turned at that moment, as if to avoid an embrace. He therefore simply touched her elbow, as if positioning a vase.

'You did insist on staying in the compartment,' she said. 'We were intended to have it to ourselves.'

'There you are,' laughed Rudolf, more out of embarrassment at his own posture, his fingers till stuck hopefully to the tip of her linen elbow, than because there was anything at all to laugh at. 'Intentions again. It shows that they can be thwarted. And by the simplest of unseen circumstances. You feared spies and pursuers, but were carrying your enemy with you all the time.'

'That is true of all life, isn't it?' she said. 'Even of the lowest. Luck in evading the predator is only a freedom to embrace the death that is waiting in one's own body. That, in the end, you can't escape.'

She turned towards Maddalejna.

'Some are content for it to be sooner rather than later,' she said. 'Providing there is reason for it.'

'How is she?' asked Rudolf.

'She?' answered Beatricz.

Rudolf looked more closely at the figure lying on the seat of the compartment. The face, seen clearly in its rigor of pain, the lips drawn back in something between a wince and a snarl, the eyes fixed at a point just a little beyond their credible focus, was a fine-skinned face with a delicate line of nose and jaw, but it was not the face of a woman. Where the head had been roughly laid against the armrest, the coiffeured silver wig had been slightly dislodged, revealing a line of paler hair beneath. The hands, curled at the chest as though fending off an invisible iron bar, were undisguisably masculine.

Rudolf let out a low whistle of surprise.

'Well, I'll be damned,' he said. 'You're none of you what you seem to be, are you?'

'It's sometimes quite easy to forget exactly who one is,' she said. Especially when it's become necessary to be other people. You can just as well *be* those other people. It doesn't really seem to matter any more.'

Rudolf saw that the maid who was not a maid had not moved. The face had withdrawn into a permanent image of the emotions it had at one instant been imperfectly controlling, like a photograph, and that instant was the instant of its death. When the face dies there is no need to look for other signs.

'Who was he?' Rudolf asked, gently. 'And who are you? If this was not your maid Maddalejna, then I guess you are not the Arch-Duke's youngest daughter Beatricz.'

'Perhaps, no almost certainly, I should be happier if I were,' she said.

Tears came into her eyes, but she ignored them. She sat down by the body, stroking its ankles as one might comfort someone sleeping. Rudolf sat down opposite her.

It was like a fresh beginning, in a way. The linen suit, with its absurd memories of moustache; the slipped wig; these two were now like actors when the play is done, exhausted in the green room.

'The truth when you reach it, if you ever do reach it at last,' she said, 'is not very different from the fictions. And that is because fiction is only a sort of version of the truth, or of its most significant elements. You already know a great deal about me, even though you may have discounted much of it. Because, after all, how could my successive stories have departed totally from the reality? Why should they have needed to? At the heart of every story is a relationship. Perhaps that is only what stories are, anyway: a defining of relationships. Really the only thing that misled you about my fictions was the omission from all of them of the one significant relationship of my life. Most of everything else was there in its essence, however changed in its detail, however contradictory in its successive appearances. But the most important relationship put in no appearance at all.'

'And this was with . . . ?' asked Rudolf, indicating with a gesture of his head.

'With Johann?' she said. 'Oh no, there was hardly anything like that with him.'

She had her arm crooked round the feet of the body, and now turned her head to look fondly at the dead young man. She leaned her head back.

'I think he might have liked it,' she said, as though the thought had never occurred to her before. 'I think he might have liked us to have had a relationship like that, dear Johann, but it never materialised. No, it was not with him. It was with someone else.'

'Are you going to tell the truth now?' asked Rudolf.

She made a grimace, a stoical sort of shrug with the mouth alone.

'You sound like a kindly papa whose patience is at the end of its tether,' she said.

'Kindly,' said Rudolf, 'but not impatient. And not a papa.'

'No,' she said. 'Of course not. You are the spiritual brother. A knightly protector. And so was Johann. Could he all the time, I wonder, have felt for me as you felt for your Delecta? How sad. I thought your story was so sad.'

'It's a chapter in my life that I now consider closed,' said Rudolf. 'Our stories were to explain why we were leaving Gomsza for the last time, if you remember.'

'It's ironical,' she said, 'that now you will never leave Gomsza at all, for Korn will certainly return to kill you. You want to be my knightly protector, and I turn out to be your death.'

At that moment a shot was fired outside. They went to the window, but could see nothing at first. Then they saw Radim and Romuald making their way towards the train.

'What happened?' they whispered down to the pair as they approached, stumbling over track and loose metal.

'The place is heavily guarded, all right,' said Romuald. 'We managed to find a little window at the end, rather high up, but I got on Radim's shoulders. They fired at me as soon as I stuck my head out. Can we come back in?'

They did so, with difficulty.

'They're all round the place,' said Romuald. 'All those raw lads kept up all night to stop us getting away.'

'If you think he's simply going to kill us,' said Rudolf, 'why doesn't he do it now and get it over with?'

'I said he was going to kill you, not me,' she replied, with undiplomatic frankness. 'Well, he may eventually kill me, I dare say, but not immediately. Perhaps he hasn't killed you yet because he hardly noticed you. Or maybe he gives a higher priority to a bath and a plate of goulash and dumplings. I'm sure he'll be back. And I don't think things will be very nice when he does come back.'

'I hadn't expected to die quite yet,' said Rudolf, 'so I would rather like to know as much about the circumstances of it as possible.'

He pointed out to the others the real nature of the dead Maddalejna. Radim removed the whole wig, uncovering cropped blond hair lying damply on the head like a cornfield after a storm. This dead young skull looked vulnerable, like a hatched bird. It seemed a desecration, but Radim was oblivious to such finer feelings. He turned the wig inside out, admiring its workmanship, and read out the label, which was that of a theatrical costumier on Ferencz Dovar Street.

'What sort of a charade is all this?' he asked.

'Yes,' said Romuald. 'I think you owe us a proper explanation.'

'I was about to do so . . .' said the woman who was not Beatricz.

'. . . to Rudolf here . . .' said the woman who was not Hilda.

'. . . just before you returned,' said the woman who was not Józef.

'We shall listen eagerly,' they said.

'If you don't fall asleep first,' she replied.

17

The Adventure of the Amorous Actress

YES, I MIGHT have been happier if I had been Beatricz (she said) since the relationship so far missing from my stories was with her father. I date the era of my active life (I was going to say, of my happiness, but I don't think that I have ever on reflection been truly happy) from my first meeting with the Arch-Duke. It would have been quite different, of course, to have grown up in his shadow, to have tested, as every daughter does, his own imperfect certainties against my own perfected uncertainties. If my relationship, such as it is, is daughterly, it is so without those frustrations of the unaccommodated will. He has no responsibility for my illusions: I have no shame for his frailties. In fact, I see none in him, and he, I suppose, is at the very least flattered by this fresh view, that in him the role and the person are suitably matched. In such a sense of flattery he would know himself to be as fooled as any dizzy girl would be by a striking profile beneath a crown, while I, as the current example of the said dizzy girl, should be able to realise that adoration is a fatal drug to the middle-aged. So there you have it. That is our conspiracy. I am allowed to make a dream of him in return for being fully acceptable as what I clearly am *not*: uniquely beautiful, uniquely available, uniquely bestowed.

How does such a situation occur? He has often said to me, in an attempt to dismiss it as dangerous, factitious or merely improper, that it is a mechanical arrangement bred of boredom, absence, family play-acting, or whatever. But that is his male way with emotion. As an actress I know all about play-acting. I can make myself cry. I could play Medea and Rosalind in one evening. How can real emotion become an arrangement? It doesn't exist for others to contemplate. It belongs only to itself. It isn't a shadow thrown on to the flat scenery of the theatre. It only throws shadows into the soul. But I sometimes think that men are so amazed to find that they have any emotions at all that they do indeed begin to admire them, just as an audience admires a play. Admiring your own emotions must be the beginning of the death of the soul, catching yourself in the mirror, hands raised to applaud your own besotted suffering, your own hoarded excitements. What is it that Rupert says at the end of Act I of *Haunted by the Future*? "You see before you a broken man, Anna, a man who has mislaid his own life. What grotesque carelessness!" And Anna, you remember, at that point still too cautious and uncertain, still worried about the stolen letter, only murmurs in an aside: "Ah Rupert, not mislaid! You gaze at it contentedly every day where it hangs in your favourite alcove of the future!" Curtain. A wonderful first act. I used to adore that play. I used to think that Melisjek was the greatest playwright in the world, because he understood those essential differences between men and women. Of course, I hadn't read Ibsen then. It must be national pride that makes us neglect Ibsen, mustn't it? We would like to think that Melisjek did it all on his own without any help from anyone. Whereas he couldn't have existed without Ibsen.

And when I eventually met Melisjek, at one of the Countess Copchka's soirées, I wondered that he could bear to exist at all. I had had some idea that a writer of understanding must be equally noble in his person, calm and god-like in his bearing, whereas our great Gomszan dramatist turned out to be a squat fussy little man, more concerned about getting his share of almond cakes than about imparting wisdom. And he stared at me over the tops of his spectacles quite greedily, as though I were some sort of cake, too, instead of quite a promising actress who had recently played one of his roles to general acclaim. At least, he looked as though he might be prepared to eat me if I were to lie on a plate with a sugary invitation. His knowing twinkle had quite that sort of implication. It wasn't serious, but if the plate happened to circulate in his direction he might just idly reach out his hand to it. Really, it was all up to me. It was fun. It hardly mattered. I was not supposed to have any feelings of my own.

Nearly all men are like that. Most of the men at Court are like that, anyway. Older men. Men of power.

Korn was like that with a tyrannical finesse. He maintained the pretence of indifference, of barely including any woman within his terms of reference. One would have thought that they were all of them, hostess, military wife, debutante, whatever, just so many articles of furniture to him, no more to be addressed in conversation than a footstool or a curtain drawn back from a terrace window with a brocaded sash. Most of the women, too, I'm forced to admit, were little more than sash-waisted curtains, drawn aside from the circles they graced so as not to impede, yet still framing, the view. But even so they were used to being flirted with. Korn's methods were sly. He relied on social neglect just short of rudeness, combined with pure self-conscious animal magnetism. You could not simply turn and leave any group he dominated, however much he snubbed you. Some invisible mastery kept you there, cravenly waiting for recognition. And doubtless some women, many women, were recognised. And called.

Everything about him craved attention, from the click of his heels to the way he drew his forefinger along the undersides of his moustache. The mere slope of his medalled chest drew the eye. But it was the business with his hand that acted as the hook which first caught you, and kept you in play. It came early in any encounter, perhaps at the moment when a flute of champagne was offered. He would touch the control at his wrist, as though buttoning a glove, and then reach out towards the footman's extended tray. The timing was perfect, the sound of the mechanism barely audible. Finger and thumb would part to admit the stem, then close to grasp it. The champagne would reach his lips without interrupting the flow of his sentence, and no one would have time to wonder why he should choose to drink with his left hand.

As an actress I suppose I should have expected more proposals and knowing gallantry than I in fact experienced. Or more disapproval. For I sensed that it was only the Arch-Duke's unusual cultural interests that allowed members of the theatrical profession openly into Court circles. Really, everyone was unusually relaxed about it, and I was rarely made to feel an intruder. If some idiot private secretary or ramrod colonel chose to make a joke or a fuss it wasn't long before he saw that he had better shut up or he would find himself out of favour. This was particularly true of the theatre, for the theatre was the Arch-Duke's passion, and he took it seriously.

Why wasn't the Arch-Duke like these other men? And why did he nonetheless exert a total fascination?

I was first presented to him after a performance of *Raczi Nowacks* at the Winter Gardens. I had played Grete, my first big part. I was quite unknown.

You know the scene when Raczi comes back from the war and hides in the barrel? And Raczi's mother and Grete are talking about him without knowing that he's there? I had this idea of playing Grete's little prayers not with a rosary as it's usually done, but with the peas that she's shelling for Mrs Nowacks. The director didn't think much of it, but I persisted.

The Arch-Duke passed along the line in a perfectly friendly way, nodding and smiling at the cast. He seemed slightly smaller than I had imagined him to be, more soft, more highly coloured. Well, you get used to the idea of the ceremonial, the monumental. In reality it was a surprise to find him ordinarily human. He was moving quite quickly, as though he had somewhere else more interesting to get to. No doubt he had.

But he stopped by me, and said he had liked the scene with the pea-pods. Everyone heard him. My place in the company was from that moment assured, and I should have realised it. But I could only see the Arch-Duke's warm smile as he spoke, and the creases at his eyes when he paused and his glance beamed upon me. He said he had grown up with the stories of Raczi Nowacks, and that whenever he was required to imagine what an ordinary Gomszan felt about anything, he thought of Raczi and was comforted.

"He's wily, isn't he?" he said, "and you think you can't quite trust him? But in the end he's got Grete to remind him where his duty lies. That's the best of the Gomszan attitude. Sceptical, but honest."

"And with ideals, too," I replied eagerly, thinking of Grete's vision of the cows. I don't think I was expected to reply on an occasion of this sort, and I could see one of the aides at the Arch-Duke's shoulder frowning at me above the handkerchief which he held at his mouth in what was intended as a gesture of delicacy but which made him simply look dyspeptic.

"You brought that across beautifully," said the Arch-Duke. "Utterly simple, but with a fiery intensity. You *were* Grete."

He was compelled by protocol to move on, but I was quite changed by the encounter. My whole body felt light and airy as though someone had vigorously cleaned me out like an attic with a broom, clattering at the wainscot, flinging open windows. My heart raced. I knew that something strange had happened to me. Or was it something that was going to happen to me? I never had nerves before going on stage, but I did now, even though I had just finished a performance. I had stage fright. It was like stage fright at my own life. As though my own life had become a part I had to play.

And indeed I always was Grete to the Arch-Duke. I think it pleased him to imagine that there really was something of the sturdy peasant in my background, something of the rude defiance that could touch a good king's heart in a fairy-tale. Whatever else I was, or whatever else he made me, that first illusion remained, and he insisted on calling me Grete. It was also a code of a kind, a cover for assignations. It was the unique name that a lover requires. And it was this beautiful myth of the king and his honest subject. I'm sure it lent an erotic thrill that my real social position, such as it was, could never have supplied.

I sometimes felt that I had no real identity. When I became part of the regular company at the Winter Gardens I lodged with the Pyramurs. You know something of the intense atmosphere of that household, because I plundered it for my stories. Needless to say, the incidents were not true, or not particularly true. That is to say,

Cyprian is neither a pathetic cuckold nor a sadistic tyrant, and Józef and Hilda have a perfectly normal relationship with him. Since my own father died when I was five I can only guess, of course, at what such a normal relationship is like. But the Pyramurs came to provide it for me.

And what about the Arch Duke's own daughters, you may ask? Was their relationship with their father normal? It seemed not, or not especially, but I did not know if this was because I was never to glimpse them together at the breakfast table, or because of my own guilt at appropriating their father to myself. Anna, the eldest, was already in demand for opening trade fairs. Although not yet married, she did not seem to be part of the household. Nor did Christina, who retained her own priests and also travelled, though not to centres of secular power. Curiously enough I saw possibly more of Christina than the others because she was the one who bothered to attend the theatre. Religion is a form of theatre, anyway, so I shouldn't have been surprised. Beatricz, the youngest and therefore the closest to me in age, was decidedly not interested in the theatre or in any of the arts. She shared with her mother a love of horses, and a tendency to plumpness.

How *can* you have agreed to believe that I was Beatricz!

Though, as I say, she has his love by right, and by nature. I have seen them riding in the park, wrapped up in furs against the slightest of November breezes. They might have been holding hands under the rug, except that hands were being vigorously waved at passers-by. I mean, you have to concentrate on that, don't you? Acknowledging the pairs of old ladies, the attentive soldiers, the patriotic old man munching an onion? And perhaps they were, after all, vaguely quarrelling, as I have heard Cyprian and Hilda quarrel about nothing very much, such as the indiscretions in the drawing-room of a small dog. And even if they were not, and their lives could not for their great wealth collide in such domestic trivialities, and under the fixed gaze of an attendant hussar for that matter, what was it to me? I knew it was just that I wanted that privilege for myself. Not the privilege of intimacy itself, mind you, but the privilege of subsuming it within a casual public appearance. I can understand men adopting nieces, god-daughters, and other official occasions of innocent paddling fingers, smacking cheek-kisses, playful admonitions about ice-creams and bed-times, and what not. I have known it done with daughters-in-law in terms of grave consultations about grand-children. These are the erotic economies of a hypocritical *monde*, licensed mislabelling. But when have you ever encountered the adopted *uncle*? Where are the privileges and indulgences of young women? It sometimes made me wonder about Christina's priests.

No, I wasn't actually jealous of the Arch-Duke's daughters. Nor did I think I was simply searching for a missing father. I wasn't interested in fathers. Or men of fifty. I was interested in the customary range of eligible males, encountered in my daily life and handled without embarrassment. I was perfectly normal. There was nothing to worry about.

I was simply in love with the Arch-Duke, and that was all there was to it. It was entirely more real to me than any of the relationships of my friends could have been to them, I felt, but I didn't despise their choices. I saw them equally as victims of circumstances, and though I could see where they had gone wrong, could imagine more suitable partners for them, and sometimes spoke up on the subject, I was not prepared to be so advised myself. Indeed, I took as much care as possible to let no one know of my affair with the Arch-Duke. Not even Hilda knew, though we spent long hours during which I tried to argue her out of her crush on the louche Grigory and to urge her in the more more interesting direction of Johann Schmeck, all to no avail. She would look at me very curiously during these conversations, not I think because she resented my intruding on her privacy (she was flattered by the attention) but because she was convinced that I had designs on Johann Schmeck myself. And I had no sooner convinced her that I hadn't, than she wondered *why* I hadn't, and whether I was not after all a passionless creature who put all her energies into her art and perhaps really disliked men. Such a belief suited me well enough, though it attracted a shade of pity and suspicion from Hilda, and she became less likely to go into raptures about the various athletic features of the attendant Grigory, as though these were things I could not naturally appreciate.

I had designs on no one because the design of my own life was already self-sufficiently complete, like one of those love-knots without beginning or ending. However complex or bewildering to the eye, there was no pause or break. It would go on for ever.

But of course I knew that it couldn't. It had begun, so it could end. And the more fateful and destined I felt the affair to be in its unlikely inception, the more inevitable would its conclusion have to be. Only something purely accidental might possibly, simply through oversight, forget to end.

In this paradox, love is an image of the whole world, and of our hope of its purposefulness. Only a meaningless universe could go on for ever. Only the uncreated, the accidentally existent, could forget ever to achieve its intended ultimate state. If love is a serious choice and not simply a random continuity, then it must have the shape and structure of a purpose. Like the knot.

The Arch-Duke, as you might imagine, didn't have any illusions of this sort.

"You're forgetting biology, Grete," he would say. "Biology is purpose enough, and requires no god. Biology is a field with a bull in it on the one hand and a field full of cows on the other. Are we any different? Our choice is just as limited, just as indiscriminate."

This sort of talk would make me eventually burst into tears. I would sit on the bed in our apartment, never having quite bothered to get dressed all day, and laugh and weep all at once while the Arch-Duke looked at me in quizzical amusement from an armchair, puffing away at a small cigar. And when my uncertain smiles at his methods of argument were quite conquered by my tears at the substance of it, he would produce some agreeable compromise.

"The living cell is mysterious enough for me," he would say, "and certainly more complex than any love-knot yet invented."

"Do you worship biology then, after all?" I prompted.

"I only worship you," was the expected reply.

One doesn't in sober moments quite accept the idea of being worshipped, but love is always slightly tipsy, slightly manic. I found it odd conducting philosophical arguments in my underclothes with a man, or indeed with anyone. I had no brothers or sisters, and hadn't been to boarding-school. Would I have been less forward if I had, I wondered? More worldly-wise? More cynical? My instinct is to take life as it comes, unlabelled. I hate sorting things out into their predictable roles. That's something quite secondary, often second-rate, frequently reductive. It is something that critics and (forgive me, Romuald) journalists have to do. When I played a great role with any sort of success I knew I was the agent of an unfathomable creativity, an embodiment of an alternative life as mysterious in its complexities as any real life. The playwright knows that, too, when he writes the role. Both transcend the reality. The mundane greedy Melisjek has to become the virtuous Anna before I can become her, and when I become her I leave behind all my own inadequacies, too. But the critic can do nothing but prod and sniff and grumble at this sublime process. He knows that when the process has worked he is superfluous. His only method is to dissect, to label. His set of labels tells him that Anna is a temptress. But he will also find the label "saint". What is he to make of that? Or of her sharp tongue? The truth is that the only reliable label is critically useless. Anna is a woman. Anna is simply Anna. Melisjek has transcended the roles that audiences have grown used to expecting. The modern drama no longer requires them, just as modern life no longer requires them.

I'm sure that if an invisible critic had seen me chattering in those tangled bedclothes, showing more whalebone and lace than is customarily exposed to male view, he would have had a label and a role for me. Well, I had no need of either. Whatever anyone might have called it, my relationship with the Arch-Duke was real enough to me, and therefore unique. For once I was playing myself, and playing myself beautifully.

Was it part of my own role in life to kidnap the Commissioner of Police with the assistance of a tiny cell of idealistic students? Well, yes, it must have been. It belongs entirely to that surge of confident self-realisation that is the sense of playing oneself to perfection. Once the Arch-Duke saw that the thing had to be done, he equally clearly saw that he could trust no one to do it.

In the turbulent and ruthless world of Renaissance drama you find a similar abnegation of trust. The Machiavellian monarch indeed should trust no one, and for this reason the eager opportunist cannot trust his monarch in return. "Who will rid me of this thorn in my side?" is the most dangerous rhetorical question ever uttered, since the opportunist's silent response puts all parties at risk, the victim, the assassin, and not least the man who stands to gain most from the act, the monarch. The question must be seen to be rhetorical, implying that it is impossible to be rid of the thorn. Yet at the same time, in a world where every day the possible is put to the strictest test, its very utterance becomes the fatal seed of the deed's full flower. What the monarch may imagine can be credibly realised, given the political framework of opportunism. For the possible is only the credible, and politics is the art of the credible. To lose one's will in the cause is to surrender gladly one's innate tendency to disbelieve. It's analogous to falling in love in that respect, and thus falling in love is a perfected example of idealistic opportunism.

I don't think for a moment that the Arch-Duke would ever have asked me to do it, but to me it was as natural as leaping into a burning building to rescue my child. Love required it.

And the beauty of it all was that I was the one person who might credibly bring it off. What were the alternatives? The political crisis called for considerable delicacy. You might wonder why an assassination was not contemplated, but when a bomb is primed you don't aim a blow at the firing mechanism. Nor do you snatch it roughly away. It must be dismantled with a watchmaker's fingers. Murder was not in the Arch-Duke's character, in any case, and a political victim of that magnitude would only have aggravated the situation. If Korn's disappearance could be made to look like a defection, an eleventh-hour and not entirely unlikely hedging of his bets, an escape to the West with masses of ill-gotten wealth, then it was wonderfully worth arranging. It would throw the Korn machine sufficiently to avert the feared coup. The bomb, in other words, would be shown to be something of a dud.

And why was I the one person who might credibly bring if off? It was because I was the only woman within a mile of Court circles who had not fallen victim to Korn's charms. I exaggerate, naturally. But I knew he was besotted with me. Do I need to give you instances I have used already in other contexts? You may have ascribed their boldness to the freedom of invention. Put them down rather to the honesty of someone who has never been much impressed by these animal secrets between men and women. Appalled, on occasion. But never sufficiently admiring or intrigued to wish to perpetuate them as secrets. Men like to claim that women entirely expect such liberties, at every possible opportunity. You three in particular may be glad to hear that this is not always so. If one does not connive at such secrets, they cease to be secrets, and are exposed as the insults they decidedly are. If some women are guiltily fascinated by Korn's stump that is their own affair.

In my natural politeness, and out of tactful consideration of my delicate position at Court, I had not given Korn any outright rebuff. If I had done so I might have felt compelled to refer to the Arch-Duke's authority to endorse it. With vacuous old goats like Count Roszla or the merely wistful, like Melisjek, my non-availability could be credibly assigned to whim. With Korn it was quite different. A *noli me tangere* would have been tantamount to a ducal command.

Do I make it sound as though the Court is a seething sink of passion? Not so. These relationships, or rather the half- and quarter-news of them that constitutes gossip, are merely nuance and speculation. And because, as you know, gossip is as circular and never-ending as the knot of love, its subjects are able ultimately to evaluate the rumours that concern themselves, to speculate upon, even to direct, the course that their secret fame will take. I knew very well that my reputation was a shining currency that could outbid any intrigue. I laboured to make it more so. Without being guilty of the slightest impropriety I nurtured Korn's fascination with me until he would have opened prisons at my bidding.

The larger mechanics of the operation were arranged by Count Ovir, an older cousin of the Arch-Duke's who had spent his life at a desk. His information must have been months out of date, or perhaps Korn already knew of our plans. Either way it seems fatal to trust a bureaucrat. There was probably a memorandum circulating. What fools we were! In an enterprise of this sort you can trust no one at all.

Could I even have trusted myself? I've hardly dared to face my reasons for doing it in the first place. Why did I offer? Why did I insist? What sort of a challenge was I issuing to myself?

Its great danger meant, of course, that I might never see the Arch-Duke again. I knew that, and perhaps consciously exploited it in order to put him on the spot. He might (I argued to myself) have decided at the last moment simply to come away with me himself, to accept the abdicated life that would surely be possible for him if he wished it. Or did the approach to Korn and the partnership with Johann symbolise my asserted independence of him as a man?

But he was never jealous, only amused at my anxieties. I knew it would seem coquettish to test him further. And always the country came first. His absolute loyalty to the integrity of Gomsza was unquestioned, even by Johann, who was perhaps in other respects his severest critic, and a great cynic in any case. "The Tsar will be here in a fortnight," Johann used to say, "and no doubt he will find the Arch-Duke at the Opera, taking bows with the singers, holding bouquets and smiling charmingly through the national anthem." Yes, that was quite right. And what I have never fully faced is the fact that his family would probably be standing there with him at the end, as the Cossacks rattled their sabres through the streets. He was loyal to his family, too, and I had no illusions about ever replacing the Duchess in any of her public roles. To make him talk about abdication was a dual challenge, and he faced it with honesty.

"To escape with you, Grete," he said, "would be the perfect solution to all life's problems. Where would it be? I would feed you figs in Luxor, or drift with you down the peaceable waterways of Kashmir. We could co-habit in a cloister in Chamounix. You are so tall, you already graze the clouds. Put you on an alp or a himalaya and your eyes would outshine the night sky. I can hear your merry laugh shaking bats out of old ruins and startling the shepherd boys with their sleeping flocks. You see, I am an incorrigible dreamer."

And he would continue whatever act of bodily devotion he had interrupted to create such an implausible vision, as it might be running his tongue along my vertebrae, slowly, attentively, like a child learning a scale on the piano with heavy thumb and slow breathing. No familiarity between us seemed remotely familiar to him. They say that a new lover is uncharted territory, but even the sketching of rudimentary maps looked like a novelty to him. He was excited by the commonest feature that our gender shares, as though he had never seen such a thing before. I have noticed such enthusiasm from practised diners-out at quite frugal banquets, but I knew this was not politeness to please a hostess. His passion was as unlikely and as extensive as lightning in August, and I suppose I guessed that it might be as soon ended as it had quickly begun.

Johann had a grudge against Korn. Who didn't? But there were particular friends, particularly tortured. As you know, the Commissioner of Police has a greater fear of nationalist pride than of an anarchist's bomb. He still feels himself to be dispossessed, an outsider. He resents the noble rooted feelings of those who have belonged in one place for ever. The combination of aristocratic indifference and artistic ferocity in Johann Schmeck and his friends, poorer than he, but free souls, infuriated him extremely. It was a double condescension. Johann was much in favour at Court, not least because he could stir the heart with a circus march into which a wrong note or two had been carefully inserted, and used his research into Gomszan folk tunes to brilliant advantage: in the most baleful passages of his concertos, just when the evil clatter of the orchestra is closest to an absolute plenitude of noise, the fiddle will break out into some luminous peasant melody that tames both the orchestra and the audience completely. Such music was quite beyond the pale at Korn's sickly soirées, and yet it laid claim to a new patriotic sweep and fervour which Korn did not dare to rebuke. If Korn were to gain absolute power (and my long wished-for escape with the Arch-Duke would doubtless have that sorry effect) he would take delight in proscribing such music. Nothing that did not immediately delight a drunken salt-worker would survive at all.

Why Count Ovir suggested that we deliver Korn into the hands of the Morsken workers I can't now imagine. I can see that it is like throwing Br'er Rabbit into the briar patch. Perhaps the dull Count has been in Korn's pay all along. Perhaps the whole thing has been arranged by Korn. Perhaps it is a bargain between Korn and the Arch-Duke. Perhaps I myself am simply a gambit in a larger combination between them, something to buy time for the regime, a desperate sacrifice or a cynical trade-off. No, no, I don't think that at all. I think the whole business is simply a futile error. Now Johann is dead, and Korn will make every bit of capital that he can out of the incident. He will come back to execute us, or if he doesn't do that he will make some show of us. Now he will be able to point to us as evidence of the Arch-Duke's unreliability, even of the Arch-Duke's treason. He will emerge as the one stable element in the government, simply through having been under threat. It will make him seem invulnerable. It will make him indispensible.

There is really only one chance to save the country now, and that is to get back to the capital and tell the Arch-Duke what has happened. Once he knows that the plan has failed he will not be caught unprepared, and if you can help me to escape then Korn will be short of evidence that there ever was such a plan. Nobody will credit these absurd provincial officials who have spent their lives accepting bribes. The whole affair will lack any sort of credence. Who will know which Mayor of Morsken to believe? It will seem like a frenzied dream invented by Korn as a cover for his own private adventure, for there is one fact that I have not yet told you which was of some significance in our plan. It was the one thing above all which contributed the most deadly risk. Not my assignation with Korn at the Hotel Ochs, not the elaborate seduction of his bodyguards by Ilena and Nina, not the concealment of the chloroform, none of these, but the fact that the Castle at Morsken is unique among the minor architectural splendours of Gomsza gave us most unease.

The castle belongs to Korn himself.

It was the greatest risk, and also the greatest beauty of the enterprise. For if anything were to go wrong (which it has) then Korn would be deeply embarrassed to be found in his own stronghold, like a marcher lord plotting a rebellion. Who would not be prepared to believe that he was himself planning to leave Gomsza? Or even that he had abducted the Arch-Duke's mistress as a hostage? The scenario seemed to us to have infinite possibilities. And Rudolf, dear, since you yourself have so beautifully explained it, you will have to agree that the principle of the purloined sphinx applies here. It must be a classic case, for who would ever dream of looking for a kidnapped monster in his own castle?

He has discovered our plan; knew it, alas, all along. He has hastened with his lackeys to the castle to prepare the next stages of his counter-plan, or to allay suspicion there by pretending to be on an ordinary visit about some trivial business. I do not know which. But I do know that he will be back, and that if we are to do anything, we must do it with all speed.

18

The Unfolding of the Flying Globe

'AN AMAZING STORY,' said Rudolf.

'I can believe it almost as much as I believed all the others,' said Romuald.

'You will have to believe it more than the others,' said Grete, 'because it is true.'

'Of course we must do whatever we can,' said Rudolf. 'And yes, we must do it immediately. Radim, you're asleep.'

The big man opened his eyes.

'No, I'm not,' he said. 'I was listening to every word. Asleep? How could I have been asleep? Sleep has been abolished, hasn't it?'

He shut his eyes again.

Rudolf felt his own eyelids drooping, and suppressed a yawn. It did seem that the night was to pass without slumber, for even if they did nothing at all, finding that there was indeed nothing to be done, they could hardly await the return of Korn and his extemporised Morsken brigade in a state of unconsciousness, however physically delicious that might be. Perhaps they had had some sleep already without quite knowing it? Rudolf wasn't sure that he had heard every word of Grete's story. He had missed the point about the whistled password, for instance, because the melody of it, from one of Beethoven's late quartets, had made him think instead of 'Oranges and Lemons' and he had imagined he was in the attic bedroom at Mavrinka, with Aunt Zizzie singing him to sleep. Grete's voice had a comforting, pointed insistence that sent her narrative along without any effort from the listener. She seemed to be telling it to herself.

But now she had delivered her story, and was looking at them for their response. Romuald shrugged.

'We're in a train,' he said. 'The boiler will still be hot. We could drive it back to the main line and return to Gomsza in comfort. The only trouble is, we're locked into a servicing shed which is surrounded by armed soldiers.'

'Hardly soldiers,' said Grete. 'Didn't you see them? All the soldiers are fighting on the Eastern Front in any case. This was some sort of militia, thrown together on the spur of the moment. They're probably asleep by now.'

'They weren't asleep when they fired at me not so long ago,' said Romuald. 'Would you like to try sticking your own head through that window?'

Grete ignored this.

'Couldn't we just drive the train at the wall and knock it down?' she asked.

'I doubt it,' said Romuald. 'We'd need to get up speed. It can't be done from a stationary position, and in any case we'd have to clear the debris off the line. They'd pick us off as easily as treading on ants.'

'Isn't it worth a try?' asked Rudolf.

Romuald looked at him wearily.

'I'll go and feed the boiler,' he said. 'Can I have the lamp?' He left the compartment, but returned in a moment. 'I can't get through from the fourgon, of course. I forgot. I shall have to climb out again.'

He swung through the carriage window as though he'd been doing it all his life, and disappeared.

Rudolf rubbed his hands together with satisfaction. Now at least they were active. How lucky it was that Romuald knew something about trains.

Radim opened his eyes again.

'You're an illusionist,' he said. 'Can't you make them disappear?'

'Go back to sleep,' said Rudolf.

'I told you,' said Radim. 'I'm not asleep. I'm thinking.'

'I wish you'd think to some purpose,' said Rudolf.

'I can see that you can't make *them* disappear,' said Radim. 'But perhaps you could make *us* disappear.'

'Oh Lord,' said Rudolf in exasperation.

'No, I see what he means,' said Grete. 'Suppose when they come for us they are led to believe by some means or other that we are no longer here. They would believe that we had escaped.'

'But we wouldn't have escaped,' said Rudolf.

'No,' said Grete. 'But it would give us time.'

'They would find us in the end,' said Rudolf.

'Perhaps,' said Grete. 'Who knows? They might really think we were gone. You yourself said that your Delecta seemed to believe so, when you disappeared before her eyes.'

'I see,' said Rudolf. 'When they come back here, bristling with rifles, you want me to put on a stage show?'

'Perhaps you could hypnotise them,' suggested Radim.

'I've tried hypnotism,' said Rudolf. 'I can't do it.'

There was a pause. In the darkness Rudolf felt Grete's hand reach for his, slim fingers and stroking thumb. The surprise made him completely alert, senses on duty, the mind speculating. The gesture was not unambiguous, part-contact, part-communication. As Rudolf's own hands received it, cool to his touch, he did not know whether it felt more like an important envelope or a small friendly animal.

'Don't be angry,' she whispered. 'We must think of everything.'

'Of course,' he replied. 'And I'm not angry. I just don't feel very resourceful. I don't feel I can make a worthy response to the situation.'

'You are worthy,' she said. 'You are all of you worthy. Don't you feel that this moment has come at last to test us all in our dealings with the world and what it requires of us?'

'What it requires of us?' repeated Rudolf. 'That has always seemed to me so fortuitous, so changeable. Today's challenges are not yesterday's challenges, and will never be tomorrow's.'

'If there is to be a tomorrow at all,' said Grete.

'Quite,' said Rudolf. 'And in that case the world's final challenge is merely arbitrary, the one last problem tossed your way before oblivion. For many people it is probably something quite ridiculous and terrifying, like trying to turn over in bed and not being able to.'

'Would you rather it were something like that?' she asked.

'Not at all,' replied Rudolf. 'Anyway it's not in the nature of these things to be interchangeable. One's trial is one's own trial, a personal affair.'

'With your name written on the charge sheet?' she asked. 'Rudolf, are you a fatalist?'

'What will be will be, as they say,' he responded.

'The one saying in the world that actually says nothing,' she said.

'It's only saying that the future is inevitable,' said Rudolf. 'Which is true.'

'Only if you play that very human trick with the tense,' said Grete. 'There is only one thing that we really know about the future, and that is that it hasn't happened yet, so it must be possible to avoid it. If someone throws a stone, you duck.'

'And it misses,' said Rudolf.

'Yes,' said Grete.

'Well, there you are,' replied Rudolf. 'You miss. You don't get a second chance. And what's more, it was always going to miss, wasn't it? Before you threw it, even? I mean, if it *did* miss it must have been *going* to miss. Suppose we were able to remember the future. It would seem just as ordered and matter-of-fact as the past does, wouldn't it? It might be the past that was mysteriously unknown.'

'I wasn't thinking of *you* throwing the stone,' said Grete wearily. 'I was thinking of it being thrown *at* you.'

'I don't see that it makes any difference,' said Rudolf.

'I'll tell you one thing,' said Radim's voice in the darkness. 'If we sit here all night making debating points, there'll be more than stones coming at us and I don't expect they'll miss.'

'I thought you'd gone to sleep again,' said Rudolf.

'I wish you wouldn't keep on accusing me of sleeping,' said

Radim. 'I don't see how anybody could sleep at a time like this. I'm thinking. I suppose you would say I'm thinking furiously. I've always wondered what thinking furiously could be like, because thinking has always seemed a very calm process to me, but now I know.'

'And have you come to any conclusions?' asked Rudolf.

'I think perhaps I have,' said Radim. 'It came to me suddenly as I was watching the moon scudding through the clouds. Can you see it from your side? It's beautiful. One of those five-eighths moons, shiny as a worn grain-scoop.'

They peered upward through their window.

'Can't see it,' said Rudolf.

When they had moved to Radim's side of the carriage and looked at the moon and agreed that it was a fine one, they wanted to know what it had to do with a possible means of escape.

'Two things occurred to me while I was admiring it,' said Radim. 'Two perfectly obvious things, but I needed to put them together to come up with the answer.'

'Go on,' said Grete.

'And when the answer came,' said Radim, 'it was not a welcome one to me.'

'Tell us, tell us!' exclaimed Rudolf.

'The appearance of the flying moon,' said Radim, 'means that there is a wind. The effect of movement is due to the clouds, which are moved by wind. There is a wind, isn't there? Listen, I can hear a regular creaking in the yard. It must be a loose piece of metal, a sign perhaps. The wind is making it creak. Can we tell what direction it's in?'

'No idea,' said Rudolf. 'And what has the wind got to do with it?'

'The wind is crucial,' said Radim. 'But most important of all is the fact that we can see the moon at all. What does that suggest to you?'

'It's beginning to suggest to me that you might be afflicted by mild lunacy,' said Rudolf.

'It's perfectly simple,' said Radim. 'There is no roof.'

'We already know that there isn't any roof,' said Rudolf. 'The machinery for changing the carriages was obviously too tall for them to have bothered building a roof. But the walls are enormous. They must be over twelve metres high.'

'Absolutely,' said Radim. 'But you see, they've shut us in here and don't expect us to be able to get out. The walls are too high, and despite Romuald's present efforts, probably too strong. We're not going to tunnel out, so that leaves the one direction that they haven't bothered about, but which is actually unimpeded. Upwards.'

'I'm not surprised that they haven't bothered about it,' said Rudolf. 'They wouldn't expect us to fly out of here.'

'No, indeed they wouldn't,' said Radim. 'But why shouldn't we?'

They could see no more of him than a dim silhouette against the pane of the carriage window. He was speaking quietly and reasonably enough, but now they thought he was completely mad.

'Don't understand you, old fellow,' said Rudolf.

Radim was unperturbed.

'We might,' he said, 'fly in my panorama.'

Silence.

'We might fly,' he said, 'in my panorama.'

Rudolf and Grete looked at each other, though they could see little more than the bodily proximity they already felt so strongly.

'We might fly in my panorama,' said Radim.

'You're serious, aren't you?' asked Grete. 'You're actually being serious, you lovely man. You really think we can?'

'I don't see why not,' said Radim. 'We'd need ropes.'

'Just a moment,' said Rudolf, as the significance dawned on him. 'You're suggesting that we turn your panorama into a . . .'

'. . . into a balloon,' agreed Radim. 'It is one already, virtually, when you think about it. It's a silk globe, something like fifteen or sixteen metres in diameter.'

'That's enormous,' said Grete.

'No, no,' said Rudolf, getting excited. 'It would have to be at least that big to carry us.'

'Do you know anything about balloons?' asked Grete.

'I once did an illusion while hanging from one high above the

Prater in Vienna,' said Rudolf. 'Though I'm not really an escapologist. It was tethered, and I went up in a basket.'

'Well, you see,' said Radim, 'the whole thing is folded in a basket already. You saw it when we boarded the train. But we'd need to attach it to the basket, wouldn't we?'

'I've got just the thing,' said Rudolf, attacking his sidewhiskers with enthusiasm. 'Yes! This is wonderful. In one of my acts I suspend a horse above the stage and make it disappear. The horse is in a large net. I have the net with me.'

'So it could go over the whole globe,' exclaimed Grete.

'Are all our things still safely in the fourgon, do you think?' asked Radim.

'Surely,' said Rudolf.

'How will we get them out?' asked Radim.

'That's a different matter,' said Rudolf. 'That could pose quite a problem.'

'Not the worst problem, either,' said Grete. 'Don't you have to fill a balloon with gas?'

They were silent again. The idea of a makeshift balloon had fired them to a pitch of frustration at the thought that they might actually be able to assemble such a thing relatively quickly and yet not be able to get it out into the yard, or inflate it. It needed the return of Romuald to renew their hectic planning, for he brought the news not only that he had stoked the boiler, but that a balloon could be powered by hot air as well as gas, and that heat was what they now had in plenty. What also emerged was that Romuald knew quite a bit about balloons as well as trains, because a few years earlier he had covered a ballooning story for the *Inquisitor*.

'Not a political story, of course,' he said. 'But I was interested in the military angle. And it had immense local interest. At the Universal Exposition the French were encouraging ballooning exploits of all kinds by setting up competitions, trials of endurance, of altitude, of horizontal distance, landing at the least distance from a fixed point, and so on. All the experts were vying with each other throughout the summer, and some records were broken. The most important contest was on 9 October. It was a contest of endurance and distance at the same time, with several of the most celebrated balloons vying with each other: Jacques Fauré's *Aeroclub* and Messieurs Balsan and Godard's *St Louis*, for example. They all set off from Vincennes aerodrome at five o'clock in the evening, and passed the French frontier at midnight. The Comte de Mont-Michel breakfasted over Breslau in his *Dedalus*, cooking himself an omelette aux champignons. You realise that much of the flight was undertaken at four thousand metres or more. You have to carry sand as ballast, and throw it out to gain altitude. You need oxygen. When the Comte's sand and oxygen ran out that evening he loosed his guide-rope over the roofs of Gomsza, then the anchor was thrown out into the fork of a tree, while the Comte loosened the gas valve. People flocked from round about to see the spectacle, and the Comte was conducted to the police bureau. I interviewed him there, where he was making a great joke about crossing frontiers without any of the unpleasantness of the custom house. I thought him quite a silly fellow. I expected him to pursue this line about aeronauts being the first free citizens of Europe, but he really only wanted to talk about the pleasure of passing silently above snowy peaks gulping alternate mouthfuls of cognac and oxygen. He couldn't see the military implications at all, and was more worried about getting the necessary authority to return to France. It was given, of course, and it took him and his assistant three nights and two days to return by railway while the *Dedalus* had taken only twenty-six hours and seven minutes.'

'We can't do anything like that,' said Rudolf.

'Of course not,' said Romuald. 'But Radim is right about the wind. It might make launching difficult, but it's a south-west wind if I ever felt one, and should move a balloon in the right direction. We wouldn't get much height, but it's warm so we wouldn't lose that height through cooling nearly as much as we might. There would have to be some means of heating the air up as it did eventually cool.'

'How far might we get?' asked Grete.

'Who knows?' replied Romuald. 'Anything might happen. I did a fair bit of research for my article, you know. The first air travellers of all went up in 1783 in a balloon three-quarters the size of ours. It was inflated over a straw fire for eleven minutes, and there was no continued heating of the air. How far do you think they went?'

'No idea,' said Rudolf.

'They went two miles in eight minutes. Not bad, eh? And despite landing in a wood they were quite unharmed. At least, the duck and the sheep were. The cockerel had a minor injury to its right wing as a consequence of a kick from the sheep.'

'We might do better,' said Grete.

'I think so,' said Romuald. 'The first untethered flight with human beings and a portable brazier went five miles in twenty-five minutes, later in the same year. And that's a long time ago.'

'But so many things are likely to go wrong,' said Rudolf.

'Oh, yes, yes, yes,' said Grete, 'but if we can get any reasonable distance from here we shall have a chance, shan't we? We can commandeer horses at the next village.'

'Let's see if we can construct the thing at all,' said Romuald. 'The first job is to see if the basket can be got out of the fourgon.'

They discovered that although the doors of the fourgon were also locked it was possible to undo the bellows connection that joined it to their carriage, and Radim's basket could then just be squeezed out above the couplings. In the fourgon they also obtained rope from packing cases, and of course Rudolf's net. In a cupboard they also discovered a quantity of footwarmers, for use by passengers in winter months, and some lamps.

'At least we shall be able to see what we are doing,' said Rudolf.

'I think we should save the paraffin,' said Romuald. 'How are we going to keep the air heated? I don't think we can use the footwarmers. We could fill them with hot coals from the engine (I think that's how they're meant to work in any case) but they're heavy and dangerous for the basket. We'd need too many of them. Couldn't we make a number of torches, with paraffin-soaked rags? One of those, held up at the opening of the balloon for as long as it burns, should give some lift.'

'Excellent,' said Rudolf. 'I'll do that, while you sort out the panorama. There should be some suitable wood lying about.'

The panorama proved heavier to handle than they had imagined. They could not lift it from the basket, but had to turn the basket over and tug it away from its contents which then lay tightly coiled beside the track. The panorama had been laid over on its panels alternately, like a map, then rolled inwards from each end. It had to be compressed to fit into the basket, but the pigment had as far as possible to be protected from sharp folds.

They set to work unfolding the panorama and unpicking the bottom ends of each panel preparatory to knotting them to the ropes that would secure it to the basket.

'I hope you realise the sacrifice that I'm making,' said Radim. 'We're about to blow away my life's work.'

'Preferable to a confrontation with that trigger-happy mayor,' said Romuald. 'Better than having your life blown away.'

'You're right,' said Radim. 'We have left Gomsza and were prepared never to return. We have to accept whatever a new life has to offer.'

'Perhaps,' said Grete gently, 'the new life for you always had to involve a complete break, and you must finally yield up this painting. It had, for you, come to represent Gomsza, hadn't it? Perhaps you cannot leave Gomsza in truth until it is destroyed.'

'It is not only Gomsza,' said Radim. 'It is the whole world.'

Rudolf returned at that moment with his arms full.

'You said that yesterday, old fellow,' he remarked. 'And I don't know what you mean now, any more than I did then. Look, I've found these axe-handles. Perfect for torches.'

'Well done,' said Romuald. 'Can you lend a hand here?'

'I meant,' said Radim, 'that since I had put everything into it, I had had to remove myself from it. That was part of my theory, if you remember. But in the act of giving over the whole world to posterity, I have left myself with nothing. For the world is everything that is not me.'

'Then,' said Grete, 'you may now give up the whole world and regain your soul.'

'I can't regain Alma,' said Radim. 'Can I?'

'Who knows?' replied Grete.

'I half expected her to walk out of the panorama when we

opened it up just now,' he mused. 'I can imagine it quite vividly: a few words of over-emphatic praise, brushing the dust of the attic off her skirt, an offer of tea. What *is* my soul, anyway? When I try to imagine what it might be, when I try to feel it inside me, that elusive thing like a forgotten name, all I am aware of is a kind of unlocated burden. A sort of generally dispersed pain.'

'Guilt, old fellow,' said Rudolf. 'I know just what you mean. Don't you, Romuald?'

'Doesn't everyone?' said Romuald. 'We all get one chance in life, and to fail it is to leave the soul dry and withered. I thought I must preserve myself at all costs, and have discovered that what I preserved is actually worthless.'

'My chance will never come again, to be sure,' said Rudolf. 'Having pretended that I was not worthy, I now see that in reality I set too high a price upon myself.'

'Dear musketeers,' said Grete, tying an expert reef knot, 'is there any sense in continuing these recriminations about the past? Having heard all your stories I am in the best position to see that no single failure is either exclusive of other possibilities of failure or absolute in itself. When the test is over, whatever the outcome, there is only the next test. Let me tell you a little story. And I assure you that this story pretends to be nothing more than a story.'

As they stood round the basket, unpicking and splicing rope, measuring lengths, fitting the net, adjusting tension, tightening knots, as easily and harmoniously as if they had been doing it every morning of their lives, like fishermen, the first lightening of the sky in the east hastened their fingers as it told them both of their destination and of the little time left at their disposal.

19

The Tale of the Three Apprentices

IN A CERTAIN town (said Grete) between here and the western sea, though you will never find it, there lived three brothers called Hans. It was confusing for them all to be called Hans, so the eldest was called Big Hans, the middle one was called Hans, and the youngest was called Little Hans. For most of the time people remembered to make this distinction, but sometimes they would forget and shout: "Hans!" and Hans would come running and they would have to say "Oh, I really meant Big Hans" or "I'm sorry, it was Little Hans I wanted." But they didn't mean to hurt Hans's feelings, so very often they sent him on the errand instead, or gave him the nice apple, instead of his brothers. In this way Hans became inclined to think that he was the only one who was really Hans, and that the others were simply a bigger and a smaller version of himself, and that no one in fact took very much account of them. Big Hans resented this, because it made him seem less important, but Little Hans didn't mind at all. "After all," he would say, "I'm only Little Hans anyway."

All three were apprenticed to a hard master, a blacksmith whose standards were exacting and who kept the rules of the Guild to the letter. The blacksmith was a widower whose only daughter had been struck dumb on her sixteenth birthday. It was a great grief to him, for not only did she not speak but she kept to her room and saw no one. The neighbours said she was bewitched by a kobbold, but the blacksmith said it was a punishment for his failings as a husband, as a father and as a blacksmith, and he worked all the harder for it and made his apprentices work hard, too, although he was a fair man and did not beat them.

"How can she have been bewitched by a kobbold?" he said. "The Guild has taught us that there are no such things as kobbolds."

But the neighbours muttered among themselves.

"It's all very well to say that the Guild refuses to acknowledge the existence of kobbolds," they said. "The Guild believes that there is a rule for everything and that its craftsmen can control the world. But the world existed before the Guild, and the kobbolds existed before the world, and the craftsmen, for all their skills, are powerless against kobbolds."

Big Hans, Hans and Little Hans were curious to hear more of the story. If a kobbold had really cast a spell on the blacksmith's daughter then perhaps they could find the kobbold and break the spell. They had never seen more of her than her pale face at an upstairs window but each of them was in love with her mystery and absence and became desperate to free her from her bondage of silence.

"How can we find the kobbold?" they asked the neighbours. But the neighbours were terrified at such a question, and stood with open mouths, wiping their hands on floury aprons.

"You must be mad to think of looking for the kobbold," they said. "Don't you realise that there comes a day for everyone when the kobbold is out looking for *you*?"

But the apprentices were not satisfied with this answer, which seemed like no answer at all.

"The kobbold has bewitched our master's only daughter, and taken her voice," they said. "We must find the kobbold and make him return her voice, or how will she be able to answer us when we ask her to marry us?"

"You are ignorant and foolish apprentices," said the neighbours. "She cannot marry all three of you, and for all we know may have no intention of marrying any one of you, or anyone else for that matter."

And they shut their doors against the apprentices because they had their work to get on with, and because they did not like to think much about kobbolds.

The apprentices went away sadly. They were not at all discouraged from their desire to find and defeat the kobbold, for it seemed that not only had this monster stolen their beloved's voice, but it was also the terror of the whole neighbourhood, and to defeat it would turn them into public as well as private heroes. But they were sad because they realised that only one of them could finally succeed. The neighbours were right: no girl, however kind and generous, could marry three apprentices at once.

Nonetheless, they prepared themselves for their quest in every way they could think of. Big Hans, who was frightened of insects and small animals, forced himself to catch spiders in the attic where they slept and put them safely out of the window. Middle-sized Hans, who was always jumping to conclusions, forced himself to pause and think again before saying anything. Little Hans, who knew that he could do nothing that his brothers could not already do, sat in the corner with a length of looped string, trying to create patterns that no one had ever made before. All of them worked hard at the forge, and begged their master to let them make swords and bucklers, but the blacksmith laughed at them and said: "There is no demand for swords and bucklers these days when everyone has made peace with his enemies. You must go on making horseshoes and ploughshares as I have taught you."

Denied the opportunity to make weapons, the apprentices sought the kobbold in divination and in dreams. They stirred their porridge backwards, and threw salt into the fire. They peeled apples in one long strip, and observed the flight of magpies. Nothing happened. Then one day Big Hans found a handkerchief in the garden. It was a small white handkerchief with cherries embroidered at the edges. He was sure that it had been dropped by the blacksmith's daughter, and so that night he slept with it beneath his pillow.

In his dream Big Hans found himself following a path out of the village that he had never taken before, one that led through thickets and thornbushes and over boulders eroded into weeping faces until he came to a broken bridge as far from anywhere as he had ever been. He awoke, and knew at once that the bridge led to the kobbold's castle. He dressed quickly, and tiptoed downstairs. In the hearth, among the dying embers of the fire, was a small night creature that might have been a lizard or a mouse. "I can help you," it said, but Big Hans was frightened of small creatures and so hastened out of the house with nothing but a hammer in his belt.

By the light of the moon he found the path out of the village and very soon came to the broken bridge of his dream. He waded through the icy waters beneath it, and eventually arrived sneezing at the kobbold's castle. The kobbold's voice came as a great wind down the turret-stairs and battlements, and Big Hans shut his eyes in terror.

"Big Hans, Big Hans," whispered the kobbold. "I know that you have come for the voice of the blacksmith's daughter. I stole it for myself, but it does not fit me."

"Then perhaps you don't need it after all?" stammered Big Hans.

"If I cannot use it," said the kobbold, "I don't see why anyone else should. Besides, one day it might fit me, and when it does my power in the world will be infinite."

And his own voice was like the stirring of dried leaves in the thorn trees.

"However," continued the kobbold, "I am surprised that you have not asked for your one chance to win the voice, for surely you know that it is customary in these cases to be given such a chance and that I am bound to give it to you."

And he led Big Hans to the great hall of the castle where the voice of the blacksmith's daughter sang in its cage like the most beautiful bird that had ever suffered captivity and the radiance from the cage shone on Big Hans's eyelids so that he opened his eyes. The hall was in darkness save for the luminous presence of the voice, and the kobbold could be heard but not seen.

"Here are three caskets," said the kobbold. "One of them contains the means to release the voice, and if you choose correctly

I shall be compelled to let you leave with it in perfect safety. If, however, you do not choose correctly, I can do with you whatever I wish."

To Big Hans this was like another dream, since he had heard of such choices in tales. But when the three caskets were ranged before him they were not like treasure-chests as he might have expected, but were of practical design such as a blacksmith's apprentice might be acquainted with. The first, and largest, was made entirely of iron, with iron feet, iron bands, iron hasps and strengthened iron corners. On it was written FULL. The second and third caskets were much less impressive. On the second was written SOME, and on the third LESS.

"Choose!" commanded the kobbold.

Big Hans pondered, but his choice did not take long. Whatever the second casket offered, it could not contain as much as the first, while the third was self-confessedly inferior to the second. As the eldest of the three brothers he was tired of not receiving his due. This resentment, for too long concealed by diffidence and timidity, broke out at last and he reached out his hand to point to the casket named FULL with all the boldness he had learned by reaching out to pick up spiders.

But the casket named FULL was empty, and when Big Hans raised his hammer at it in anger his hammer turned into a lizard which ate the arm that held it. Big Hans looked in outrage at what had been his right arm: where his hand should have been was the tail of the lizard, and the jaws of the lizard were in the very act of swallowing his shoulder. In a few moments Big Hans had been eaten up entirely.

Now Middle-sized Hans had seen Big Hans hide the handkerchief with the border of cherries beneath his pillow, and when his brother did not return the following day he guessed what had happened and so that night he too slept with the handkerchief under his pillow and he had the dream of finding the kobbold's castle as Big Hans had done. Early next morning he tip-toed downstairs, careful not to wake anyone up. The creature in the hearth popped its head out of the ashes. "I can help you," it said. But Middle-sized Hans laughed. "I don't see how you possibly could," he said, and he rushed out of the house without bothering to take anything with him at all.

By the light of the first blush of dawn he found the path out of the village and very soon came to the broken bridge of the dream. He leaped across it in one bound, and arrived at the kobbold's castle. Hammering at the door, he shouted out:

"Kobbold, kobbold, I have come for the voice of the blacksmith's daughter."

And the kobbold's voice came out of the darkness like the scuttling of claws across a dry cellar.

"You, too!" it said. "Well, you will have to make your choice."

The kobbold led Middle-sized Hans to the great hall of the castle, and presented him with the caskets. Surrounded by the glorious light of the voice of the blacksmith's daughter singing in its cage, he felt inspired in his choice. The first casket, called FULL, did not attract him at all. It might after all, he pondered, be full of anything. The third casket was a poor thing, but the second, of beaten brass with a long brass bolt to fasten it, was trim enough. "I need no more than will do the trick," said Middle-sized Hans to himself. "Some is quite sufficient."

In the casket named SOME was a key, which he immediately laid hold of, thinking to open the cage with it. But the key was white hot and burned through both his hands, and the kobbold took him in his agony and gave him to the lizard to eat.

Little Hans had seen both his brothers disappear, and he had seen them sleep with the cherry handkerchief beneath their pillows.

"If they have failed in their quest," he said, "how can I possibly succeed in their place? For Big Hans is strong, and Middle-sized Hans is quick, but I am well-known to be weak and clumsy and I can do nothing special except make cats' cradles."

However, he slept with the handkerchief, and had the dream, and crept downstairs the following morning, as his brothers had done before him. When the hearth-creature piped up: "I can help you", however, Little Hans did not ignore it, but went over and knelt by the ashes of the fire.

"Can you really?" he asked. "I certainly need all the help I can get."

So the creature presented him with a pair of gloves, and Little Hans couldn't tell whether they were made of fur or lizard-skin, so strange and fine they were.

"Wear these all the time," said the hearth-creature, "and you will not come to harm."

Little Hans thanked it, and put on the gloves, and set out across the landscape of the dream until he arrived at the kobbold's castle. Like his brothers he was presented with the choice of the caskets, and like his brothers he made an appropriate choice.

"The first two caskets are splendid-looking," he said to himself, "and their workmanship would satisfy even our master. The third, called LESS, is only made of pewter. It's very thin, and it is cracked at the corners. However, that doesn't mean that it cannot contain what I need to open the cage and release the stolen voice. After all, I am only Little Hans anyway, and I have always had to make do with less than the others."

The casket called LESS contained a length of wire, which like the key before it was white-hot, but when Little Hans took it up it did not burn him because he was wearing his gloves. To a good blacksmith's apprentice, who knows all about locks, a length of wire is as good as a key. Little Hans bent it into a shape more beautiful than any of his cats' cradles and unlocked the door of the cage. When the voice flew out, he caught it and put it in his shirt.

The kobbold was furious, and his shouting echoed in the stone passages of the castle like claps of thunder. He set the lizard on to Little Hans, but when it approached with open jaws and sharp teeth, stiffly snapping like a pair of wet green scissors, Little Hans simply bent and stroked it. The skin of the gloves melted into the skin of the creature, and then both melted away to reveal human skin and both his brothers were standing before him. Together they escaped from the kobbold and returned to their village where they gave the blacksmith's daughter back her voice.

When the neighbours heard it, they marvelled, for not only could she now speak, but she could sing. And the blacksmith, who was the most delighted of all, promised them anything in the world.

But the neighbours had been perfectly right when they said she couldn't marry all three of them. It was quite impossible. And Little Hans didn't think of pressing his own particular claim as the one who had actually succeeded in rescuing the voice.

"After all," he said, "I am only Little Hans anyway."

20

Arrivals and Departures

'YOU INVENTED THAT story expressly to remind me of my humiliation, didn't you?' said Romuald. 'The red-hot key?'

'Hardly, I think,' said Rudolf. 'The failure to claim what is rightly one's own is the true moral of the story, and it is I who am guilty of that.'

'What then,' added Radim, 'about the essential emptiness of plenitude? The hollow world? That surely alludes to me?'

Grete laughed.

'You have all managed to identify yourselves with the wrong brother, I'm afraid,' she said. 'You might just as easily have applied it in relation to your physical size, and you would still have been wrong.'

'What is the right interpretation, then?' asked Rudolf. 'Or is there none at all?'

The panorama was now clearly a balloon rather than a panorama, and lay beneath them like a beached whale, its collapsed folds ready to lift at a breath. Grete was strengthening the ring of its opening at the points where the panels were joined, having luckily found the needle and thread with which she had made adjustments to her suit such as the black arm-band. She looked from one to the other.

'I did say, didn't I, that the story was nothing more than a story?' she said. 'But you are right, of course, to seek interpretation, for why would I have told you that story in preference to any other?'

'Because,' said Rudolf, 'it is for some reason particularly our story. But in what way?'

'What is the most significant thing about such a story?' asked Grete.

'It seems to me,' said Radim, 'to show the necessity of decisiveness, and of recognising one's limitations.'

'Surely,' said Romuald, 'the point is rather one of persistence, the loyalty to an idea.'

'I would have thought,' said Rudolf, 'that it underlined the need for innocent faith, a belief in what one really is.'

'No,' said Grete. 'I didn't mean the moral of the story, although, as you have shown, that is for everyone to find for himself. I mean, what is the function of stories like these? It's to make us believe in the possibility of our success, whatever the crucial human quality we lack. The significant thing is that we each believe we can be Little Hans.'

'I see,' said Rudolf. 'But isn't there for each of us a single quality that we must attain in order to bring about that success?'

'There is the absence of such qualities,' said Grete, 'in all of us, and perhaps as many absences as there are potential hearers of the story. But behind all of them is the need for us to recognise the enemy to life, which is fear. The name of the kobbold is fear. The caskets referred to FEAR. It is fear which silences the truth which must be restored to the world, and which ultimately must be heard. To be fearsome is no better than being fearful: one must be fearless.'

'Do we know what that truth is?' asked Rudolf.

'We know it when we find it,' said Grete. 'And then we have to do everything in our power to make it live.'

They were ready now for the inflation of the balloon, which was to be accomplished by piping the hot air from the funnel of the engine through a tube made from a variety of objects sewn together, a kind of narrative cannibalisation of antimacassars, petticoat, canvas water-pipe used for filling the boiler, and Radim's trousers. Grete stood before them now in woman's clothing for the first time, looking wild and elated, her eyes piercing through their dark circles of fatigue, her short hair standing away from her head as though electrically charged.

'Like an ikon of liberty,' thought Rudolf.

'We do not even now know her real name,' thought Romuald, 'for Grete is only one of her many roles.'

'She is a madwoman,' thought Radim. 'But her madness is of the kind that requires the final sacrifice.'

And each thought privately the chilling thought that had first presented itself when they had unwrapped the panorama: the basket had been big enough to create difficulties in getting it out of the fourgon, but was too small to carry all of them. Indeed, it was quite clear that there was room enough for only two.

Could a rational choice be made between them? In terms of their contributions to the means of escape, Radim was the one. He had given up his life's work, whereas Romuald had merely known something about trains and balloons, fortuitous expertise which was no loss to him. Rudolf had contributed very little.

And yet it seemed to be Rudolf that Grete was most fond of, and Rudolf certainly who was the most taken with her. Would tender feelings dictate the choice? Would it be, then, an irrational choice?

And what about the most irrational choice of all? The drawing of lots would restore to Romuald a chance equal to that of Radim and Rudolf, and who was to say that chance in this case was really irrational? It would, after all, be the fairest method.

At this moment of choice, Korn was stepping into the motor car which Von Bergen had driven up to the castle gates. His brown polished boots parted from the cobbles one after the other with a faint rasp of grit, and each left on the running board the momentary imprint of the sole damp with the morning dews in the courtyard. It was no more than a two-hour drive to the railway station, and the hour appointed for his collection was late enough to have allowed ample time for recuperation during what had remained of the night: a deep bath perfumed with citrus oils, a dish of smoked trout and radishes, accompanied by the best imported pflumli, and four hours of sleep in a bed with ironed linen sheets – quite enough to restore the decisive energy of a busy man of affairs. The castle, though an echoing gloomy place whose domestic arrangements recalled centuries of spartan living, had been transformed by Korn into a haven of *gemutlichkeit* where his authority and whims could be freely indulged. The old servants kept the place in readiness, and tactfully at intervals hired new young servants for more intimate duties. One of these, instructed to soap her master's legs while he reclined in his steaming bath with the first cigar after long deprivation, felt it her duty also to respond to his casual remarks and rhetorical questions, as though she had been hired as a real human companion and not as a corporeal slave.

'Now,' mused Korn, describing the possible scenarios with small movements of his cigar, 'shall I simply set the train on fire and let them perish? Or shall I bring the girl back here as hostage?'

'Perish, sir, perish,' murmured the girl blithely, as she squeezed the sponge over the hinge of a knee. The water flooded at once both calf and thigh, flattening their hairs into glistening parallel lines.

'The Arch-Duke will deny all knowledge of it, naturally,' he went on to himself. 'But there would be much satisfaction in observing her despair at being abandoned. In the end there would be no nobility in it, no nobility at all.'

He leaned forward to deposit ash, and the girl transferred her attentions to his shoulders.

'Let them perish,' repeated the girl, without the slightest idea of what he was talking about.

He caught her eye.

'You,' he exclaimed. 'What do you know about it, you rogue?'

He put his cigar down on the edge of the bath so that he could seize her wrist and pull her forward, her childish face just a few inches from his. The foam from the sponge darkened the front of her starched uniform.

'That's what you think, is it?' he went on. 'So that you can have me all to yourself?'

The girl smirked at him cheekily.

'You have to learn to share here,' he said. 'Didn't they tell you that? You'll have to learn to play your part.'

'Yes, sir,' she said, lowering her eyes.

Later that night she was found in the servants' kitchen weeping tortured puffy tears and strings of abject saliva into her handkerchief. No one could console her.

In the car next morning Korn was decided. He gave his orders to Von Bergen as abruptly and momentously as if he were announcing a long-awaited military invasion.

'Get the girl and bring her to the car,' he said. 'I don't care what happens to the passengers in the carriage. I don't want them. You can let them go if you like.'

'As you please, your excellency,' said Von Bergen with a ready smile.

'Well?' snapped Korn. 'What are you waiting for? Let's go.'

At the great gates of the servicing-shed a few of Von Bergen's militia still slept against a stack of oil drums. Even when the car approached only a few of them made any effort to spring to attention or even appear to be awake. One of them, the gloomy bandit who had closed the gates on the prisoners, shambled forward with a careless air of lightly held responsibility.

'All present and correct, sir,' he said, touching his forehead with one finger. 'The prisoners were a bit restless at first, as you might say. They tried climbing out through a window but we soon put a stop to that. Then, Lord help us, they started up the engine again. But there's nowhere they can get to, is there? So we haven't interfered. Seems to me they can fool around as much as they like.'

Von Bergen brushed him aside impatiently.

'Your men are all asleep, aren't they?' he said. 'I don't see how you can tell what they're doing in there.'

Korn was close behind him. He gestured with his celluloid hand.

'They're certainly up to something,' he said. 'Can't you see that?'

A rounded shape was peeping just above the high walls of the shed, like a bald giant, a roped and quilted egg, an absurd carnival shape moving from side to side like the dumb clapper of a bell. Of course, the bandit and the dozing militiamen hadn't seen it: they were too close to the building. But Korn had seen it from the car, and, unlikely contraption as it was, he had guessed its function.

'What on earth is it?' asked Von Bergen.

'It's a balloon, you idiot,' snapped Korn. 'Your men have been sleeping off their schnapps all night and letting them construct a balloon!'

With the utmost speed Korn and Von Bergen opened the gates and entered the shed, followed by the bandit and his men.

They were doubly surprised.

Having originally expected to pick up a group of tired and demoralised prisoners they were alerted by the sight of the balloon to the idea of a hasty escape. They were not prepared for the sight that actually greeted their eyes.

It seemed dark inside the shed, for the morning sun was not yet high enough in the sky to lend much light. But what they saw was illuminated by two flickering torches on either side of what seemed like nothing so much as an improvised stage. Immediately in front of them on a pile of sleepers lay the body of the dead maid. Far beyond was an upright coffin in which was lying the Arch-Duke's mistress still disguised in her man's white suit. They ran towards it, and Von Bergen again had his gun drawn.

'Don't shoot,' said Korn. 'They've no time to get away now. What is this foolery?'

But Von Bergen would not have fired. He was transfixed by the forbidding and upraised hand of a saturnine figure in pointed whiskers, a skull cap and large black cape: the Great Tartini!

Behind the coffin was the balloon, fully inflated now and straining on the single rope that tethered it. The basket beneath it, hardly bigger than a hamper, was lashed at a dangerous angle with bulging extemporised knots. It seemed to be empty, but as the Great Tartini untied the rope to release it there was a moment of doubt. Why build and release an empty balloon?

In these few seconds Korn and Von Bergen were as transfixed as any theatre audience. Behind them gawped Von Bergen's motley assembly of policemen and bandits, enjoying not only the spectacle itself but their chief's evident perplexity. The woman they wanted stood before them. Who might be in the balloon? Those other two interfering passengers?

Before they could work out whether it was worth shooting at the balloon or not, the Great Tartini had passed in front of the coffin with a whirl of his cape, and had closed the coffin lid. He raised his right hand and a phosphorescent flash momentarily blinded them. Immediately he opened the coffin lid. The girl had gone! The Great Tartini himself climbed into the coffin, and closed the lid upon himself. The balloon continued to rise, slowly, sideways, the net of rope scraping against the brickwork of the back wall of the shed, where it lodged for a moment.

There seemed almost no time for effective action. When Korn tore open the coffin lid he knew he would find nothing at all. Before he could investigate the trick, a shout from Von Bergen drew his attention back to the balloon. A figure had now appeared in it holding a flaming torch which she held aloft as if to light the way into a dragon's cave. Her hair glowed like sparks in the light reflected from the torch. Her expression was exalted and triumphant. The access of hot air from the torch gave the balloon some further lift.

Von Bergen was grappling with the rope that had been left trailing from the basket, but it was hopeless. For a moment he had a firm grasp on it, and began, as it pulled him upwards, to walk the wall, abseiling in reverse. The bandit, who thought the whole performance a hilarious recompense for the tedium of the previous night, raised his hat in a cheer, and the rest of the men crowded round in response. Korn himself fired at the balloon, and missed. He took a more careful aim, but was thrown off balance by Von Bergen who had fallen back among the onlookers from a height of five metres, breaking his back. Grete had untied the rope from which he had been clinging, and immediately the balloon rose even higher, free of the shed altogether, caught by the wind, and sailing surely in the direction of freedom. More shots were fired, but none found their target. And at that moment the engine's pistons began the slow elbowing motion that heralded movement. The wheels began to turn. There was an escape of steam, and the train started to leave the shed.

These moments of theatre had done the trick. Not so much to ensure the safe passage of the balloon, for that might have been released minutes earlier, but to allow for the escape of the other members of the party.

For just as the blacksmith's daughter had not possibly been able to marry all three of the Hanses, and yet had not been presented with the outright claim of any one of them, so Grete had in the end no obligation to make either a rational, irrational or sentimental choice between Rudolf, Radim and Romuald. There was indeed only room for two in the balloon, but Grete claimed the body of her colleague Johann Schmeck for reasons that none of her musketeers could deny.

Was there a moment of tears at the choice, a sense of finality and farewell? Perhaps. But Rudolf's proposed illusion offered a chance of escape for all. Johann's body was divested of its maid's disguise and put into the basket. Radim put on the dress and wig as best he could and lay, in his unlikely bulk, as Maddalejna. Romuald put on Grete's suit and moustache, and climbed as Józef into the coffin, while Rudolf found his Great Tartini costume in his luggage. As Rudolf was performing the coffin trick, Radim made his way into the cab of the engine, and while Von Bergen and Korn were preoccupied with the balloon, Romuald and Rudolf slipped into the train behind their backs. All these things took only a minute. The engine was primed, and soon gathered speed. There was time for the bandit and his confrères to have leapt on board, but the demise of Von Bergen both distracted them and released them from their temporary obligation to his service. Having been ready to applaud his performance in attempting to walk up to the balloon, they now felt tempted to applaud the performance of the prisoners in so ingeniously effecting their escape. To the bandit in particular it seemed much in the adventurous spirit of banditry: perhaps they were enemies of the state after all. At any rate, his readiness to watch and cheer was now diverted to the musketeers' theft of the train, and Korn was left quite isolated in his impotent fury. His whole counterplot was collapsing about him.

Rudolf's philosophy of life was fully justified by this turn of events. The world needs illusions. The illusion of all illusions is that there is a better world than this one; that we are trapped by mistake in an imperfect version of what, with a little effort, we can all beautifully imagine. A magical trick symbolises the transference from one to the other. It is a sign of that possible miracle. Our desperate attempts to fathom the trick are in fact the precise opposite: we need to assure ourselves that there is, after all, no explanation. We look twice, and we look hard. We need convincing that the miracle can indeed occur.

The train sped freely from Morsken back to the frontier. Would the musketeers go on from there into exile, or would they risk a return to defy their weaknesses and claim against all odds, outrageously, righteously, passionately, their Delecta, their Alma, their Vera, the Gomsza of their dreams? Where would the wind and cooling air take Grete and her dear friend? Could any possible dream restore Gomsza to her? To her Gomsza was the touch of a hand, the look of eyes in a face that had just turned towards her in surprised recognition, a second glance in intensity of attention, as though the rest of the world had ceased to exist.

But for the moment, while journeys were still to be made, all faces were mere idea. Only the cold eyelids of Johann Schmeck, shut forever against the busy world that had given him his strange music, were there to remind her of her story. The rest was equally strange silence: only the wind in the ropes to accompany the swift movement of the balloon, and the slight creaking of the basket as she shifted within it.

That was not quite true. There was something else with her in the balloon. The torch, bound with a bulk of paraffin-soaked rags, was still burning vigorously and giving her more and more height. She held it higher into the aperture as it gradually dwindled, even half climbing on to the sides of the basket to do so, to maximise the effect of the warm air. She had other torches for future use, but didn't want to waste this one. As she held it higher and higher it illuminated more and more of the interior of the balloon, and she was given the sudden shock of seeing for the first time what Radim had described and what she in theory well knew it contained: the bird's-eye panorama of Gomsza!

It was all there: Peranski Street with its arcades and rows of green shuttered windows and little ironwork baskets of geraniums, the shallow cupola of the Town Hall in ridges of dull copper, the more robust golden dome of St Nepomuk's, the stone tower of the Institute like a fragment of fairy chateau with red turret and slit windows, the glass shed of the railway station with its baroque filigree façade, the miscellaneous roofs opposite, the small hotels and bistros of the commercial district, the flagpoles above the market with all the history of the Duchy contained in their gaudy heraldic array, the Arch-Duke's palace just visible beyond and to the left of the long bent thoroughfare of August 5th Street with its new tram-cables and old plane trees, and beyond that, the Penal Institution, the cotton mill and the old disused docks by the east turn of the river, the grey-roofed slums, and beyond that, beyond that, beyond everything the rolling violet and umber haze of the Wallenmar Mountains. It was all there above and around her! It was like a lucky sign, a promise of transportation, an instantaneous illusion, a piece of sympathetic magic – for how could it not be that the balloon (precarious as it was and far from its place of origin, not indeed itself, as not intended in the first place to be a balloon at all, not perhaps ever likely again to attain its original function) would mysteriously restore her to the place it contained and represented? As she hung there she felt a surge of absurd confidence in such a restoration, as though when the earth itself were created a moment was pre-ordained when the two views of Gomsza, the actual and the artificial, should be matched, and the linen would hover like a homing bird lovingly above the location it perfectly represented.